DEADLY RECALL

A JESSIE COLE
THRILLER

T.R. RAGAN

 THOMAS & MERCER

This is a work of fiction. Names, characters, organizations, places, events, and incidents are either products of the author's imagination or are used fictitiously. Any resemblance to actual persons, living or dead, or actual events is purely coincidental.

Text copyright © 2018 by Theresa Ragan
All rights reserved.

Published by Thomas & Mercer, Seattle

www.apub.com

Amazon, the Amazon logo, and Thomas & Mercer are trademarks of Amazon.com, Inc., or its affiliates.

ISBN-13: 9781503949232
ISBN-10: 1503949230

Cover design by Damon Freeman

Printed in the United States of America

PRAISE FOR T.R. RAGAN

Her Last Day

"Intricately plotted . . . The tense plot builds to a startling and satisfying resolution."

—*Publishers Weekly* (starred review)

"Ragan's newest novel is exciting and intriguing from the very beginning . . . Readers will race to finish the book, wanting to know the outcome and see justice served."

—*RT Book Reviews*

"Readers will obsess over T.R. Ragan's new tenacious heroine. I can't wait for the next in the series!"

—Kendra Elliot, author of *Wall Street Journal* bestsellers *Spiraled* and *Targeted*

"With action-packed twists and turns and a pace that doesn't let up until the thrilling conclusion, *Her Last Day* is a brilliant start to a gripping new series from T.R. Ragan."

—Robert Bryndza, #1 international bestselling author of *The Girl in the Ice*

DEADLY RECALL

OTHER TITLES BY
T.R. RAGAN

JESSIE COLE SERIES

Her Last Day

FAITH MCMANN TRILOGY

Furious

Outrage

Wrath

LIZZY GARDNER SERIES

Abducted

Dead Weight

A Dark Mind

Obsessed

Almost Dead

Evil Never Dies

WRITING AS THERESA RAGAN

Return of the Rose

A Knight in Central Park

Taming Mad Max

Finding Kate Huntley

Having My Baby

An Offer He Can't Refuse

Here Comes the Bride

I Will Wait for You: A Novella

Dead Man Running

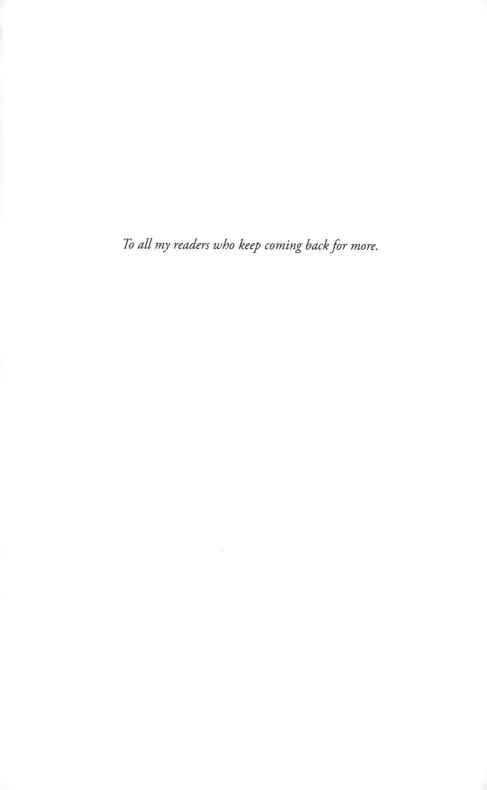

To all my readers who keep coming back for more.

PROLOGUE

"Dad?"

Stiff from hours of sitting beside his daughter's hospital bed, he lifted his head. Had he heard Hannah's voice? Or was he dreaming?

"You need to be strong, Dad."

He blinked to clear his vision. The curtains were drawn, leaving the hospital room drenched in gloomy shadows. His mind was muddled, weighed down by the emotional roller coaster of the past few weeks. He'd grown used to the smell of antiseptics and the faint beeping of machines, but he would never get used to the idea that his twenty-five-year-old daughter might be dying. Life without Hannah was unimaginable. She meant everything to him. Just as her mother had been, Hannah was filled with light and energy.

So much energy.

"Hannah," he said in a throaty whisper. "Are you okay? What can I get you?"

When was the last time he'd heard his daughter's voice? Two days ago? Maybe three?

"Hannah," he said again. "Are you thirsty? What is it?"

No answer.

It wasn't until he heard the drumming of what sounded like dozens of feet slapping against the tile floor outside the room that he realized the beeps from the machine had become one long, steady sound.

"Hannah!" he cried as the door opened and the lights were switched on, shedding clarity on the cold, hard reality of what his life had become—grief and sadness. So much sadness.

Hannah's eyes were closed, her skin the color of newly poured cement. Her hand was curled within his grasp. He could no longer see the rise and fall of her chest, no signs of movement or life. "Hannah," he whispered. "Don't leave me. Please don't leave me."

One of the nurses examined the machine while the doctor and another nurse worked around all the tubes and wires, checking vital signs.

Another alarm sounded, giving him a tinge of hope.

But nothing had changed. The oximeter was removed from Hannah's finger, and the machine was turned off.

A deafening silence followed.

The doctor wrote on Hannah's chart, then looked at him. Hollow words spilled out, one over the other, before he spoke to the closest nurse and then exited the room.

The door clicked shut, sending a wave of panic through his body. *Do something,* he thought as he watched one of the nurses remove the IV from Hannah's arm while the other simply gave him a sorrowful look.

He looked at Hannah, willing her eyes to open. *Please, don't go.*

A hand came to rest on his shoulder, and he broke down and sobbed.

ONE

PI Jessie Cole heard a faint knock right before the door to her office opened. Her ten o'clock appointment was on time. Jessie stood, introduced herself, and then asked Ashley Bale to have a seat in the chair in front of her desk.

"Should we wait for your husband?" Jessie asked.

"I'm afraid Nick won't be able to make it." Ashley fidgeted some before adding, "The truth is, he's not happy about my decision to go through with this."

Jessie could tell she had more to say, so she sat silently and waited for her to finish.

"As we discussed, Dakota, our newborn daughter, was abducted seven years ago. What I didn't mention to you on the phone is that since that time we've been lucky enough to have twin boys. They're lovely, and they keep me busy." She smiled. "That's an understatement."

"I can imagine," Jessie said.

"Don't get me wrong—my husband wants Dakota back as much as I do. Our hearts were broken when she was taken, but he believes if I never stop looking for her, I'll be taking something away from the boys."

Jessie's chest tightened. Her heart went out to the woman. But in cases like this it wasn't up to her to take sides or push her clients in one direction or another. "Maybe you and your husband should spend more time thinking about what's best for both of you. I'm happy to return your deposit, and we can—"

"No."

Just like that Ashley's expression changed from complacent to unwavering. Jessie lifted a questioning brow. "No?"

"No. I want to do this. I need to do this. That's why I'm here. I'm ready to move forward. I have to know what happened to my daughter." She pulled a binder from her bag and set it on Jessie's desk, turning it so they could both have a look at what was inside. She flipped the pages slowly, giving Jessie a glimpse into her world at the time Dakota was born. Pictures taken at the baby shower and then at the hospital, Ashley clearly overjoyed. There were photos of hospital visitors, too, and Ashley had taken the time to place a sticky note on every one, with names and relationship details such as cousin, aunt, mom, and so on. Every page was sealed within clear plastic.

Stashed within were ribbons and cards and scribbled notes with a long list of possible names for their baby girl. There were printed copies of posts taken from social media, people congratulating them on their new addition to the family, a colorful picture of the front yard complete with a sturdy wooden three-foot stork wearing a pink hat and bow tie announcing their new baby girl: Dakota Elizabeth, six pounds, twelve ounces, nineteen and a half inches, August 22, 2010.

They were halfway through the binder when Ashley stopped turning the pages and pushed it Jessie's way. "Everything else inside is what happened after Dakota was taken from us. Newspaper clippings, police reports, and, oh—" She reached into her bag again, pulled out two leather-bound journals, and handed them over. "My therapist at the time told me it was a good idea to put all my thoughts to paper, so that's what I did." She shrugged. "I can't say whether it helped me or not. I'm still here, so there is that, but I decided to give you everything. No reason to hold back."

Ashley Bale reminded Jessie of herself. Every fine line in her face told a story. It was the not knowing that did that to people, made them look weary and disillusioned by life.

"I'm hoping something here might be helpful in your search."

Jessie nodded. "I do have a couple of questions."

"Go ahead."

"In the paperwork you sent back, you mentioned that immediately after Dakota was taken, you looked at everyone differently. Friends, family, neighbors. They all appeared suspect. Looking back now, was there anyone in particular who stood out?"

Ashley cleared her throat. "I'm not saying it was fair of me to see everyone as suspect, but in certain cases, I had my reasons. For instance, Nick's cousin Wendy Battstel had just suffered a third miscarriage in a two-year period. She wasn't married, but she wanted a baby more than anything in the world. I always felt sorry for her."

"Did she live around here?"

"For a while, but she was having problems and moved away. She's sort of the black sheep of the family, and Nick doesn't like to talk about her." Ashley smiled nervously. "Of course, it would've been difficult for Wendy to pass Dakota off as hers, but still, the thought ran through my mind."

Ashley rubbed the back of her neck. "There was also a nurse. Her name was Sue. I remember her holding Dakota as if she didn't want to hand her over to me. She kept talking about wanting a baby of her own someday. Later, I asked about the nurse, but the hospital was adamant about there not being anyone on staff who went by that name."

"Did the police look into that?"

"Yes. In fact, they found her."

"Really?"

Ashley nodded. "Turned out she was a volunteer at the hospital, but the name on file was Kendra Foster. Her middle name was Sue. My husband doesn't know it, but after Dakota was taken, I kept a close eye on Kendra Sue."

"How so?"

"I spent hours watching her house. If she left, I followed her."

Jessie figured that was something she might have done herself under the circumstances. "And?"

"Nothing. For months I watched her leave for work, come home, go to the grocery store every once in a while, and then lights out by ten."

Jessie was about to comment, but Ashley lifted a finger to let Jessie know there was more.

"Before Dakota was born, I was a manager at a department store. At the time, a coworker had just found out that she couldn't have children. Her name was"—Ashley looked upward as if in thought—"Rose Helg. Yes. I guess her husband wasn't willing to adopt, so he asked for a divorce." She crossed one leg over the other. "It wasn't fair of me to judge these women and think the worst of them, but there you have it." She lifted her hands, palms up. "I'm a judgmental bitch."

"No. Sounds to me as if you were just a desperate mother."

Ashley met her gaze. "Thanks."

"It might be helpful if you could give me any information you have on these women and anyone else you can think of who drew your attention at the time. I'd like to talk to them."

"Okay," she said. "I'll e-mail you tonight. Does that work?"

"That'll be fine. I could also use pictures of you and your husband at the age of seven, the same age your daughter would be today."

Ashley thought about that for a second. "We've had two artist's renderings done of what Dakota would look like at the ages of one and four." She pointed toward Jessie's desk. "You'll see them inside the binder."

"Those will be helpful, too," Jessie assured her. "But I'd still like pictures of you and your husband, if possible. I know someone who uses age-progression software along with Photoshop and pictures of parents and relatives to create realistic images."

Ashley nodded. "I'll see what I can find. Is there anything else?"

Jessie opened the file. "I believe I have your cell phone number and your home phone."

"I'd prefer it if we corresponded through e-mail."

Jessie wondered if Nick Bale had any idea at all that his wife was going through with the investigation. The notion made her uncomfortable, but she liked Ashley, and she wanted to help if she could. "I'll shoot you an e-mail if anything comes up."

They stood and shook hands; then Jessie walked her to the door and saw her out.

Although statistics leaned heavily against Ashley learning the truth about what had happened to her daughter, Jessie knew from her own experience that the woman was surely plagued by continuous questions cycling through her mind. *Where is Dakota? What is she doing? Is she scared—is she safe? Is she alive?*

For ten years Jessie had asked those questions over and over—until three months ago, when the search for her missing sister had come to a tragic end. They'd found Sophie's brittle bones within a tattered and faded red dress, the same dress she'd been wearing the last time Jessie had seen her alive, protected beneath a blanket of thorn-covered vines.

Jessie was one of the lucky ones. She knew what had happened to her sister. There were no more questions, only sadness and regret and a Ferris wheel of if-onlys going round and round about what she could have possibly done to save her sister.

If only things had been different.

If only she'd stopped her from leaving the house that night.

If only . . .

Two

Ben Morrison, crime reporter for the *Sacramento Tribune*, was sitting at his desk opening mail when one particular letter gave him pause. After reading the first few sentences, his gaze swept to the signature at the bottom of the page:

> Sincerely,
> MAH

He checked the envelope and saw there was no return address. He went back to the beginning of the letter and started reading again.

> Dear Mr. Morrison,
> Greed killed my daughter. She was my angel and my life, and I refuse to let her go without letting the world know that greed is killing people every day. People need to know that their daughters or their sons could be next.
> My research has shown that you're an experienced journalist who appears to have no real agenda other than telling the story. And that's why I've come to you.

I need you to tell *my* story.

My wife and I met during college, married six months after we graduated, and had our first and only child two years after that. Once our daughter reached grammar school age, my wife returned to the workforce. We worked hard, earned decent money, went on vacation once a year, made some improvements to the house, and even managed to put a few dollars toward retirement. We lived in a small Victorian in a nice neighborhood, and other than the mortgage, we were debt-free when our daughter, at the age of twenty-one, was diagnosed with a disease that need not have killed her. For reasons that will become obvious, I will not be providing you with details.

My wife and I handled the situation as we had everything else—with purpose and resolve. With the right medications, treatment, and attitude, doctors assured us our daughter would recover. But an allergic reaction to the medication complicated matters.

I know you have children of your own. Have you ever had to watch your child suffer?

In the beginning, my daughter was angry with her body for deceiving her. Exhausted and in terrible pain, it wasn't long before her anger turned to fright, and she began to wonder if she would ever get better. She had no choice but to quit her internship at a large tech company. No more sports or morning runs through the park with her friends. Her joints were swollen. There were many days where the pain was so intense she lay in bed without speaking a word. She couldn't get to the bathroom without assistance. We all felt helpless. Once we found the right medication, our hope was renewed, and we were able to breathe again.

At least until she experienced her first seizure and reminded us things could always get worse, which they did. On my wife's way to see our daughter in the hospital, an uninsured driver hit her car head-on. She died instantly. They told me she didn't suffer.

My daughter was prescribed a new drug. She did everything she could to keep me from diving headfirst into a pit of despair after my wife's tragedy. And it was working, too, until I received a letter from Direct Health Inc. (DHI) stating their refusal to pay for the costly medication that was keeping my daughter from experiencing seizures. They said the drug was experimental. The doctors immediately stopped administering the medication.

To pay for the costly drugs, I sold my house, begged for money on social media, and worked long hours so I could keep my insurance since I still needed what little help it offered. Eventually the money ran out. The hospital, the doctors—everyone involved—watched my daughter's decline, and they did nothing.

Unlike my wife, my daughter didn't die instantly. She suffered for another year. Have you ever had to watch someone you love slowly deteriorate?

The lumps that appeared on her body were painful to the touch, but I couldn't help her to the bathroom without touching her. She couldn't walk without feeling as if there were dozens of needles sticking into the bottoms of her feet. The pain was excruciating. She couldn't move without crying. Her suffering did not continue for days or weeks, but for months.

If you talked to the people who know me best, they would say I am a calm and rational being.

But that was then, and this is now.

I'm mad as hell.

My daughter needlessly suffered and died too young because of greed.

Since I have been unable to get the insurance company's attention, I want you to contact DHI and see that I get an apology and reassurance that all experimental drugs will be covered for all patients henceforth. If, and this is a very important *if*, I do not see a photocopy of such letter on DHI's company letterhead signed by the president and chief executive officer, Owen Shepard, on the front page of the *Sacramento Tribune* on or before Wednesday, October 18, an innocent life will be taken.

Sincerely,

MAH

Something niggled, stopping Ben from tossing the letter in the trash. He thought about his accident. Even ten years ago the hospital bills had been astronomical. If not for the health benefits he received through his work, he would have been screwed. His wife was a nurse. She had told him many sad stories about patients who were turned away because they didn't have insurance. Even *with* insurance, two out of three people were unable to pay their hospital bills.

On the off chance someone's life could be in danger, Ben stood, scooped up the letter, walked across the fading parquet wood floor to his boss's office, and took a seat in one of two chairs facing Ian Savage's desk.

"Not now. I'm busy." Ian waved him away without bothering to look up from the pile of papers in front of him.

Ben slid the letter under Ian's bulbous nose, then waited a few seconds until watery gray eyes looked at him over wire-rimmed glasses. "What now?"

"Read the first paragraph, and then we'll talk."

Ian gave his attention to the letter. A full minute passed before he looked up again. "Just another crackpot."

"I don't know. I've been doing the crime beat for a while now." Ben pointed at the letter. "He's threatening to take an innocent life if his demands aren't met. What if he is serious, and we do nothing?"

Ian took off his glasses and rubbed the bridge of his nose. "So, what do you propose?"

"I'd like to give Owen Shepard at DHI a call. See what he has to say."

"Fine."

"And then I'm going to call the police."

"You really think that's necessary?"

"I do."

"Of course, if the person who wrote the letter had threatened a specific group or person, I might be concerned, but his threat is a little vague—don't you think?"

"I'd rather be safe than sorry."

"Okay, fine, fine. Get out of here and get it done."

Ben made a quick exit. After making copies of the letter and envelope, he returned to his desk and picked up the phone.

THREE

The next morning, running on the sidewalk along J Street with her niece's dog, Higgins, at her side, Jessie weaved a path around two women and a row of colorfully painted condos. She and the dog had taken up running after her sister's funeral. She'd needed something to keep her mind clear. The first couple of weeks had been grueling. Her muscles were always sore, and her lungs burned. Higgins had given up a couple of times, stopping in midrun and refusing to budge. She'd begun to doubt there was such a thing as a runner's high.

But after the four-week point, everything changed. She was less winded, and somewhere along the way her muscles adapted. Higgins was doing better, too, often challenging her to keep up.

It was October. The morning air was crisp. Temperatures would reach the high seventies by noon. Turning onto Nineteenth Street, she passed the old purple house she rented and headed straight for her office a block and a half away.

The building where she worked was two stories with narrow hallways and a maze of offices. Businesses included a marriage counselor, a home-cleaning service, Felix Newton Real Estate, a yoga studio, and an organic teashop on the rooftop.

She pushed through the front door, then held it open for Higgins. The pitter-patter of his paws against the wood floor was the only noise as she made her way down the hallway to the first office space on the right. Since she rarely locked the door when she left for her morning run, she didn't need a key. Pushing open the door, she was surprised to find someone waiting inside.

The dark-haired woman sitting in one of two chairs in front of her desk whipped around at the sound of the door opening.

Jessie recognized her at once. "Zee!"

Zee Gatley, a twenty-eight-year-old woman with schizophrenia, didn't bother to say hello or get up to greet her. Zee's father, Arlo, had hired Jessie when Zee went missing. Jessie had located her before she'd been physically harmed, but by then Zee had been held captive for days by a deranged serial killer.

Higgins went to Zee, sniffed, then stared up at her.

"Does he bite?" Zee asked.

"The only person I've seen him bite was the same man who kidnapped you."

"Oh, what a good dog," Zee said.

Higgins's stump of a tail wagged as she pet him. When she finished, Higgins walked over to his dog bed in the corner and plopped down.

Jessie took a seat behind her desk. "It's good to see you, Zee. How's your dad?"

"He's still dating Mrs. Dixon, the next-door neighbor. I think he's the happiest I've ever seen him." She frowned. "He thought it might be a good idea if I got a job."

"And what do you think?"

"Well, after mulling it over a bit, I thought it would be cool to become a private investigator."

Jessie lifted a brow. Her niece had also recently announced a new-found desire to become a PI.

"Dad said you told him you needed help, so that's why I'm here."

Jessie had talked to Arlo a few times. She couldn't recall telling him she needed help, but she had mentioned how busy she was on more than one occasion. "What exactly is it you'd like to do?"

"I want to work on cold cases, you know, look for missing people like you do."

"I thought you weren't allowed to drive." Jessie looked outside, thinking she might see Arlo waiting in the car. "How did you get here?"

Zee's eyes brightened. "My doctor said I had to be without symptoms before I would be eligible to drive again." Her chin jutted. "I've been taking my medication every day, and he signed off on the paperwork last week. I got my license yesterday."

"You're no longer hearing voices?"

"Nope," Zee said. "The voices are gone."

"I don't know, Zee. I wasn't looking to hire anyone right now and—"

Zee placed a clenched fist on the top of Jessie's desk. "I'm a hard worker and I'm dependable. And besides," she added, her words coming out fast, "Dad's new girlfriend comes over when he's at work. She's driving me crazy. You have to give me a chance."

Ah, Jessie thought. So that was the problem. She thought about everything the two of them had been through together. Zee was a good person. She was smart and strong-minded, and she deserved a chance.

"I'll do whatever you ask me to do," Zee said. "I won't fuck up—I mean mess up, I promise."

Jessie couldn't bear to turn her away. She reached for an envelope from her in-box and said, "When I first started my business, I handled mostly workers' compensation cases. Do you know what that is?"

Zee shook her head.

"If a person claims they were injured on the job, they can file a claim to collect workers' compensation, which is monies paid by the company they work for. If the company has reason to believe that the employee filed a fraudulent claim and they want to dispute the claim, the company will sometimes hire outside help to prove the employee is capable of doing their job."

"Weird. Do a lot of people lie about that stuff?"

"Most cases are legitimate, but statistics show that one to two percent are fraudulent."

"So you have to prove they're faking it?"

Jessie nodded. "We set up surveillance. It's not an exciting job, Zee. You basically sit in the car for hours at a time, watching and waiting. If you see the claimant lifting heavy items or walking without crutches, depending on the case, you have to take videos and pictures because the insurance company needs proof that they're not disabled."

"What if the person you're watching sees you?"

"I've had it occur a couple of times. When I was approached, I told them I was interested in buying a house in the area and was checking it out. Something like that."

"What if they never come out of their house at all?"

Jessie shrugged. "It happens. If they realize they're being watched, they'll figure out a way to sneak out the back, and you won't even know they're gone. Sometimes it's just a matter of outsmarting them."

Silence settled around them. Finally Zee blurted, "I'll do it."

"Maybe you should think about it for a day or two."

"No. I want the job. I already looked up the requirements to be an assistant to a PI. There are none."

Jessie said nothing.

"In case you were wondering, I have a high school diploma."

"That's fine."

"I've also taken some online courses."

"Very good."

"I can start work tomorrow."

Jessie clamped her lips together to stop herself from laughing. She'd already known there was no way she would turn Zee down, but she couldn't help but be amused by the girl's determination. "I'll give you some paperwork to fill out at home. Meet me here at eight o'clock tomorrow morning and we'll go over a few things."

"Okay."

"Five hours a day, five days a week. Minimum wage. Deal?"

"You bet."

As soon as Jessie handed her the paperwork, Zee jumped to her feet and headed for the exit. She got as far as the door before she turned back and said, "Thanks."

"You're welcome." Jessie watched her leave. When Jessie had been looking for Zee, she'd done some research on the mental disorder she suffered from. People with schizophrenia sometimes had a difficult time connecting with others. Many didn't like being touched or having others invade their personal space. Sometimes they withdrew from the world. Jessie didn't want to see that happen to Zee. If she could continue to get the right help and surround herself with supportive people, Zee could lead a satisfying life.

Four

"It's very important that he call me back," Ben told Owen Shepard's assistant at DHI. "This could be a matter of life and death."

The woman rambled on about Mr. Shepard being a busy man, and since he was in Arizona on business and wouldn't return until the next day, she wasn't sure whether her boss would be able to help Ben before then.

"You need to let him know what's going on. Tell him to call me at any time, no matter how late." Ben hung up the phone and rubbed a hand over his face. There wasn't enough time.

"Hey, Ben. Come see this."

Across the room his coworker Larry was leaning back in his chair, waving Ben over to his cubicle. Ben pushed himself to his feet, wincing as a sharp burning sensation shot through his right knee. A car accident ten years ago had left him with stiff joints and disfiguring scars on his left side. Ignoring the pain, he walked over to see what Larry wanted.

"Ring any bells?" Larry asked as he jabbed a finger at an eight-by-ten glossy of a man dressed in an expensive-looking suit.

Ben took a closer look. "What's his name?"

"Wow," Larry said. "You really don't remember."

People like Larry just couldn't wrap their brains around the idea that amnesia was a real and debilitating disorder. Ben had been working for the *Sacramento Tribune* for twenty years. The same car accident that had left him permanently disfigured had also left him with retrograde amnesia, and he didn't remember anything prior to the accident. Not friends. Not family. Nada.

"I've got work to do," Ben said. "No time for games."

Before he could walk away, Larry said, "This right here is good ol' DJ Stumm."

Ben's throat tightened. He didn't move, didn't say a word. *DJ Stumm.* Where had he heard that name before?

Larry pointed a finger at him and let out a guffaw. "I knew it! There it is. I see a flicker of recognition. I knew you would remember. Twelve years ago, you and I worked a crime scene together. It was one of the worst I had ever witnessed. A mother and her two young kids brutally murdered."

As Larry talked, something he did more often than not, Ben sifted through the pictures on Larry's desk. A naked woman hung from a rafter in a basement. A kid in the bathtub, another on the bed. Both children bludgeoned to death.

"I was a newbie around here," Larry was saying, "when all this went down. You happened to be the guy showing me the ropes. You taught me a lot that day—like how to become part of the crime scene without being noticed. Your mantra back then was 'look and listen.' You knew how to gather information without getting in any of the crime scene technicians' way." Larry reached for a picture. "This Christmas photo was taken weeks before the murder. The perfect family," he added under his breath.

Ben took it from him. Two kids, both under ten years of age. Their mother gazed fondly at her children while their father looked blankly at the camera. This time when Ben's gaze connected with the image of the man, a sharp pain sliced through his skull. "Did he kill them?" Ben asked.

"Yeah," Larry said, looking up at him. "All the evidence pointed to him. Bloody prints, empty bank accounts, etcetera. It didn't take long for investigators to learn from DJ's coworker that he'd fallen in love with a woman at his work. But get this . . . DJ didn't believe in divorce." Larry shook his head. "He slaughtered his kids and tortured his wife because divorce was out of the question. Fucker."

Ben agreed. "Still behind bars?"

The expression on Larry's face made it clear that it truly pained him to know that Ben couldn't remember the case.

"You allowed me to be your shadow for weeks," Larry said, his tone so sharp it made Ben think he was hoping to jog his memory. "I'll never forget the intensity and passion in your voice whenever you talked to me about that case. Bottom line: you wanted DJ Stumm caught."

Ben set the Christmas card photo back on Larry's desk.

"But they never found him," Larry went on. "Not until a few weeks ago, when they dug up a pile of bones in the city of Lincoln, not too far from the house where Stumm and his family lived before he killed them." Larry grabbed a manila envelope sitting on his desk, pulled out another eight-by-ten picture, and handed it to Ben.

It looked like a backyard. He could see a wood fence and a rosebush. Nearly half of the property had been dug up. At the bottom of a deep hole was a pile of human bones.

"Until this morning," Larry continued, "those bones were known as John Doe. Tests came back a few hours ago. John Doe is now officially DJ Stumm. He died twelve years ago, which means that all this time authorities have been looking for a dead man."

"How do they know he's been dead that long?"

"Get this," Larry said, straightening. "Stumm was buried under a patio beneath a water pipe that hasn't been disturbed. Water pipe was put in approximately four days after Stumm killed his family, which means Stumm was killed within that four-day window."

"Wouldn't someone have found the body when they installed the water pipe?"

Larry shook his head. "Pipe only went two feet under the ground. Another six to twelve inches and they might have seen the body."

"Interesting."

"Not just interesting. Downright incredible. You don't get too many cases like this, where time of death can be determined almost to the day. Somebody killed DJ Stumm within days of the brutal slaying. And whoever it was got him good. Was it his wife's parents? Her brothers? A cousin, uncle, lover? Too early to tell."

"Or maybe Stumm wasn't the one who killed his family," Ben offered.

"He was guilty, no doubt about it. All the evidence pointed to him: No signs of breaking and entering. Credit card charges for the rope used to hang his wife. DJ's fingerprints and his own blood was on everything, including the kids." He let out a breath. "Sad."

Ben examined the photo. There was machinery in the background. Past a stone retaining wall, he spotted a brick building. Between the graffiti and the broken windows, he figured the building had been long abandoned. Feeling dizzy, he pointed at a folder on Larry's desk. "Mind if I take the file back to my desk?"

"Sure." Larry frowned. "You okay?"

"Yeah, I'm fine."

Larry shoved the photos back into the file and handed it to him. "I'll need it back before the end of the day. Ian wants me to do a follow-up story on the case."

"No problem. Thanks."

As Ben headed back to his cubicle, he heard Larry say something, but he wasn't listening. He felt nauseous. Since the accident that took Ben's memories, doctors had said it was likely some or all of his memory would eventually return, but that hadn't happened until months ago, when he recognized a woman named Sophie Cole on *Cold Case TV*. Sophie turned out to be Sacramento PI Jessie Cole's younger sister, who had gone missing ten years ago. Hoping to find answers, he'd sought out Jessie, and together they had discovered that Sophie had been in the car with him when it crashed. She had been thrown from the car, and her skeletal remains were found down a steep ravine, buried beneath a thick tangle of brush. Although Ben still had more questions than answers as to why he'd been with Sophie that night, he couldn't deny that his memories were returning. Sophie had been real. She was not a figment of his imagination. Nor was she a part of a crime scene he had covered, which meant other images he saw in his mind's eye could also be bits and pieces of his past.

The images were appearing more often.

But the real problem, as far as Ben was concerned, was that his recollections were mostly bloody and disturbing images of dead people.

Were these gruesome images simply scenes from yet another grisly crime he'd once covered, or were they something else? His wife believed it was all just remnants of the work he'd been doing for so long, but he no longer shared her confidence. Not since he'd strangled a deranged serial killer with his bare hands. That was when everything had changed for the worse, and his visions became more vivid and frequent.

And now, just as when he'd recognized Sophie Cole, it was happening again. The name *DJ Stumm* lit up his neurons. That might be understandable, considering he'd worked the case, but it wasn't the pictures of the man or the crime scene that bothered him. It was the brick building behind the property where his remains were found.

Ben had been there before. He was sure of it.

And yet, how could that be? According to Larry, they'd only recently discovered DJ Stumm's bones.

By the time he reached his desk, his head was pounding. He took a seat and opened the file. The colorful graffiti scribbled across the brick building drew his attention again.

DJ Stumm. The name circled his brain like a runaway train sounding its horn, imploring him to look closer, dig deeper. Ten years ago, after his sister had made it clear she wanted nothing to do with him, he'd decided not to waste time worrying about his past. He'd had a beautiful family. He'd liked his job. He'd been happy.

But things were different now. He could feel himself changing, morphing into someone else altogether. It was as if he suddenly possessed an innate sense telling him something was wrong with him—that beneath his flesh and muscle and bone, a malevolent darkness lingered. If that was true, did this darkness involve his parents? His sister? An occurrence when he was a child?

He didn't know.

What he did know was that his past was trying to get his attention, incessantly tap, tap, tapping on his skull, letting him know it was time to find out who he really was.

FIVE

Jessie returned home after five. Olivia, her fifteen-year-old niece, was in her bedroom doing homework. "Hey there. How was school?"

"Fine." Olivia reached over to scratch the top of Higgins's head.

"I thought you were going to stop by the office after school and help me with the filing."

"Too much homework," Olivia said without looking at her. "Sorry."

Ever since her sister's funeral, Jessie had noticed a change in her niece. Olivia was only four when her mother had gone missing. Over the years, Olivia had been conflicted about Sophie's disappearance, never knowing if her mother had abandoned her or if something had happened to her. Now that they knew she'd been dead all along, Jessie thought Olivia might be feeling guilty for believing her mother had abandoned her. But so far, Jessie couldn't get her to open up. "Is there anything you want to talk about?" Jessie asked.

"No."

Jessie gave her a moment, but Olivia kept her attention on the schoolbook in her lap. "Okay, well, I'm going to make dinner. Spaghetti sound good?"

"Sure."

Higgins followed at her heels as Jessie headed toward the kitchen. Even the dog had grown tired of Olivia's somber mood and one-word replies.

Jessie's good friend Andriana was convinced that it was all part of being fifteen. Jessie wasn't so sure. Finding her sister had allowed Jessie to mourn and begin to find a way to move on. The hardest part of dealing with her sister's death was knowing that Sophie had been at the bottom of a ravine for all those years. Jessie and Sophie's mom had run off when they were in their teens, which was why the thought that Sophie might have done the same thing had crossed Jessie's mind more than once. And yet, she'd always known in her heart that her sister never would have left her only daughter behind.

After filling a pot with water, she added some olive oil and salt and then placed it on a burner while she made the sauce. Before she had a chance to ask Olivia to set the table, there was a knock on the door. The house was small—one long, narrow space made up the family room, dining room, and kitchen. She walked across the wood floor to the living room, peered out the window overlooking the street, and saw Colin standing there. She had met Colin Grayson, a homicide detective at the Sacramento Police Department, after Sophie went missing. Turning away from the window, she trotted down the stairs and opened the door.

Colin handed her a bouquet of daylilies.

"What are these for?"

"It's a bribe."

She lifted a curious brow. "A bribe?"

"I was hoping to convince you to be my date at a friend's wedding this Saturday."

She frowned. "This weekend?"

He chuckled. "You're doing it again."

"Doing what?"

"Answering my questions with a question."

25

"I am, aren't I?" she asked with a smirk.

He put a hand on the doorframe and leaned close. "Come to the wedding with me. There will be cake, and I know how much you like cake."

She had nothing to wear, and she was so behind at work. Besides, she wasn't a fan of weddings. Weddings made her question the bride and groom's reasoning for tying the knot. What was the point? Did they want to have kids? Was it a financial decision? Most important, how long would the marriage last? She knew it wasn't fair. Some people married for life, loving one another until death. It was just something she couldn't imagine finding for herself. A love so strong that you would be willing to make compromises every day for the rest of your life. A little self-analyzing would likely point to her parents' disastrous relationship as a reason she might have an aversion toward saying "I do." It also didn't help that most of her married friends had divorced within ten years. Even Colin was divorced with one daughter.

"Please," Colin said. "If I don't bring a date, I'll have all the bridesmaids and the matron of honor glomming on to me, and you know how I hate that."

She snorted. "A little full of yourself, wouldn't you say?"

"Just stating the facts, ma'am."

She rolled her eyes.

"Casual attire," he said as he straightened. "It's being held at a lodge close to Salmon Falls in Folsom. Nothing fancy."

"Shit! I forgot about the noodles on the stove."

"I'll take that as a yes."

"Yes," she said. "I'll be your date." Despite her aversion to weddings, she found herself looking forward to it. She needed to get out more.

"Perfect."

"Want to join us for dinner?" she asked.

"I wish I could, but it's my turn to take Piper to her dance lessons." He waved her away. "Go! Before you burn the house down."

"Okay," she said as she started up the stairs. "Say hi to Piper for me."

"Will do."

She heard the door shut as she reached the landing. Olivia was in the kitchen, stirring the sauce. Jessie went to the cupboard and grabbed two plates.

"My first high school dance is coming up soon," Olivia said.

"That's great! When is it?"

"Halloween night. Bella was wondering if I could spend the night. You know, after the dance."

Jessie looked at the calendar on her phone. "That's a Tuesday night."

"The dance ends at nine. And there's no school the next day since it's a teacher's conference day."

"That should be all right," Jessie said, "but I'll have to talk to Bella's mom."

"Why? You don't trust me?"

Jessie was taken aback. Olivia wasn't the type of kid who usually questioned her, and Jessie liked to think it was because she was fair-minded and logical when it came to parenting. "You know I trust you," she said as she grabbed two place mats from a drawer. "I just like to touch base, make sure we're all on the same page."

Jessie put the place mats and dishes on the table. "What's going on, Olivia? You've been unusually quiet lately."

Olivia continued stirring the sauce. "I guess you were right."

"About?"

"About Sophie. About people talking crap about her."

"What are they saying?"

"That my mom was a slut who'd been sleeping around since the eighth grade."

Jessie stopped what she was doing and looked at Olivia. Her stomach turned. "I'm sorry you've had to deal with this." Olivia shrugged, but Jessie could see that she was hurting. "Your mom was a good person. We all make mistakes."

"What about Grandma? Was she a good person?"

Grandma? Olivia had never talked about Jessie's mom before. "I was seventeen when my mom left," Jessie answered. "I really wouldn't know."

"Why not? You were practically an adult by that time."

"She was selfish—she only cared about herself."

"Have you ever thought about looking for Grandma?"

Jessie turned off the burner, then poured the noodles into a colander in the sink.

"Have you?" Olivia asked again.

"No. I have no interest in finding someone who obviously doesn't want to be found."

"How do you know? What if she's dead, like Sophie?"

Jessie said nothing.

"Maybe she always meant to come back," Olivia said, "but something happened along the way."

Jessie dumped the noodles into the saucepan on the stove, then brought the pan to the table and sat down. "Could you grab the Parmesan cheese?"

Olivia did as she asked and then sat down across from her. "So?"

"What?"

"So . . . what if something unexpectedly happened to Grandma along the way?"

"All these questions out of the blue . . . this isn't really about me and my mother, is it?"

Olivia scrunched up her nose as she sprinkled Parmesan on top of her spaghetti. "I was just questioning if you ever stopped to wonder if your mom was dead or alive."

"There's a big difference between what happened with your mom and what happened with my mom."

"How do you figure?"

"My mom didn't know how to be a mother. Parenting didn't come naturally, so when she got tired of squabbling kids, cooking, and laundry, she took off, plain and simple. Sophie, on the other hand, fell in love with you the minute you were born. I was there. I saw the love in her eyes every time she looked at you. My mother was selfish. Your mother was . . ."

"Also selfish. In the end, she thought partying was more important than staying home with her kid."

"She was young."

"She was your sister. I get that. But I'm tired of you trying to make Sophie out to be some amazing person who did no wrong."

"I never said she was perfect—"

"Give me a break." Olivia stood, bringing her plate of spaghetti to the sink. "She was a great singer, she baked goods for local charities, she loved me more than anything, blah, blah, blah. I've never heard you say anything about the fact that she got knocked up at fifteen and stole money from Grandpa's wallet."

"Stole money from Grandpa?"

"Every time I see Grandpa, he tells me stories about Sophie's wild ways and how she had a mind of her own and never listened to anyone."

Jessie tilted her head. "When was the last time you saw Grandpa?"

Olivia shrugged noncommittally. "I don't know. A month ago?"

Jessie didn't quite know what to say. They hardly ever visited Jessie's dad because Ethan Cole was a drunk. After her mother had abandoned them all—just got up and left one day—Dad had drowned his sorrows in booze.

Jessie's childhood had never been easy, but after Mom left, things had gone downhill fast. Dad had ended up in prison after driving while intoxicated, and Sophie had gotten knocked up. So much for going to college. Jessie had found a job as a cocktail waitress, rented a cheap place, and gotten her sister and niece out of Dad's house.

Jessie wanted to talk about Olivia's visit with her dad, but Olivia still had a lot to say about Jessie's sister.

"You and Sophie used to play with Barbie dolls and push each other on swings," Olivia was saying. "You probably shared a lot of laughs. Maybe you cried together, too, and argued most days, but I didn't do any of that with her. At least you knew Sophie well enough to feel her loss."

Jessie was about to chime in, but Olivia wasn't finished.

"You're lucky that you knew Grandma well enough to know you're glad she's gone. I never knew Sophie, and I don't want to spend the rest of my life feeling bad that she was dead all those days and nights when I was hating her for abandoning me."

"You didn't know. None of us did. You did nothing wrong."

Olivia dumped her spaghetti into Tupperware and put it in the fridge.

"You're not going to eat?"

"I lost my appetite, and I've still got homework to do." Olivia headed back for her room.

Jessie's shoulders fell as she wound noodles around her fork and took a bite. Raising a kid wasn't easy. When did you push them for answers and when did you leave them alone to sulk?

For now, Jessie decided, she would give Olivia some space. She needed to respect her niece's boundaries and yet make sure she didn't become too independent too soon. Sophie had been Olivia's age when she began sneaking off with her friends and getting involved with the wrong crowd. She'd partied too much, stayed out too late, and stolen cars.

Blindly, Jessie chewed and swallowed, wondering how in the world she was going to get through the next few years in one piece. Parenting was tougher than she'd ever imagined.

Six

The next day, after being briefed earlier that morning, Zee went to Lindsay Norton's house on Fourteenth Avenue in Sacramento. Lindsay Norton was a fifty-one-year-old widow with two grown kids who both lived more than sixty miles away. According to the workers' compensation form, Lindsay Norton claimed to have hurt her back while moving boxes at the grocery store where she worked. This was her third claim in eight years, which apparently was a red flag for the insurance company.

Zee couldn't believe she was working for Jessie Cole and already doing surveillance. Excitement coursed through her veins, heightening her senses. She'd been paranoid all through childhood. The world had been one big conspiracy. People were out to get her. She couldn't count the number of psychiatric nurses and quack doctors she'd seen over the years, but it was her father who had brought her some normalcy. No matter how bad things got, he never gave up on her.

Most days were like walking a tightrope. She did her best to stay balanced, but really, she never knew if or when she might teeter off the edge. But not today. Today was different. She felt normal. And happy.

She glanced at the equipment Jessie had loaned her and smiled. She was a real-life private eye.

It felt good to be useful.

Holding the Canon EOS 6D Jessie had loaned her, she adjusted the focus, and zoomed in on the front of Lindsay Norton's house. The curtains were open, but the glare on the window prevented her from seeing inside. Jessie had also loaned her a decent pair of binoculars. She put the camera down and fiddled around with the binoculars before looking through them. They were heavy duty. *Wow.* She could see right through the window: a leather couch, table, and large-screen TV. The mantel above the fireplace was lined with framed pictures. She could see fake hydrangeas in a white vase. The binoculars were awesome. No bounce at all and a clear view.

Something in her peripheral vision caught her attention. All the action was happening next door. Turning to her left, Zee continued to peer through the binoculars. A man and a woman were standing halfway outside a side door leading to the garage. Judging by the looks on their faces, they were arguing.

Zee opened the window, but they were too far away for her to hear what they were saying. She zoomed in for a better look and didn't like what she saw. The man had a good grip on the woman's forearm and was trying to pull her inside the garage, but she was fighting him. The woman was upset, and she was also unsteady on her feet, sort of wobbly.

Zee wondered if the woman had just woken from a nap or if she was drunk. Her dark-brown hair was a tangled mess. She looked young. Eighteen, maybe younger. Zee's heart rate quickened. She needed to do something, but what?

Twisting around, she set the binoculars on the passenger seat. By the time she reached for the door handle, the couple was gone. The door to the garage was closed.

She sat there for a moment, breathing, watching.

When her phone rang, she gasped, then took a breath to calm herself. Caller ID told her it was Dad. She picked up her phone and hit the "Talk" button. "Dad," she scolded. "I'm at work."

"I know, honey. I just wanted to see how everything was going."

"I really shouldn't be on the phone, but since you called, maybe you could help me out with something."

"What is it? What's wrong?"

"Nothing's wrong. Not really. I'm doing surveillance today, watching a woman who claims she injured herself on the job."

"Oh no. What happened? Did she see you?"

"No, Dad. She hasn't even come out of her house. Her neighbors made an appearance, though, and they were arguing. It looked like the man was getting a little rough, grabbing the woman and trying to pull her back inside. I didn't like it."

"Where are they now?"

"Right before you called they disappeared through a side door into the garage. What should I do?"

"Nothing," he said. "I think it's best to keep doing what you were hired to do."

"What if he's hurting her?"

"You didn't see him raise a hand to her, did you?"

"No, but—"

"I think the best thing you can do is leave it alone. Whatever you do, don't approach anyone, okay?"

She saw the front door to Lindsay Norton's house open. "I've got to go, Dad. I'll see you tonight." Without giving him a chance to say goodbye, she disconnected the call and then grabbed the camera, setting it to video. Lindsay Norton stood on the front step of her porch, looking around for a second or two before she made her way to the mailbox at the end of a short driveway.

Zee sank down low in her seat, hoping she'd parked far enough away to not be noticed. She videotaped Lindsay Norton as the woman walked, tall and erect, down the stone path. Lindsay Norton stopped and tilted her face toward the sun. By the time she got to the end of the driveway to collect her mail, she made a big show of wincing as she reached a hand to her lower back. She then struggled at a snail's pace to carry a few envelopes back into the house.

Feeling impatient, Zee glanced over at the neighbor's house. What she really wanted to do was walk up to the front door and knock. She could tell whoever answered that she was doing a survey and just had a few questions, maybe get a peek inside.

I wouldn't bother, a voice inside her head said. *She's probably dead.*

Oh, brother. You're such a drama queen. Don't listen to her, Zee. You're lucky to have this job. Don't do something stupid and mess it up on your first day.

"Shut up," Zee said. "Both of you." She needed to think, but the voices sometimes made that difficult. Although proud to have gotten the job, she didn't like knowing she'd lied to Jessie about no longer hearing voices. The truth was, even when she took her medication regularly, she heard them. Lucy, Marion, and Francis. They never stopped. They were her constant companions whether she liked it or not. She had lied to her doctor, too. How else was she supposed to get her license and a job?

Even at this moment the voices were bickering, although they had turned the volume down a notch. "If you don't stop it," Zee warned, "I'll quit this job and start taking Clozapine, which will make me sleep all day, and I'll never have to listen to any of you again."

Silence. Finally.

Jessie Cole was giving her a chance to gain on-the-job experience. Zee refused to let her down. This was her opportunity to prove she could help people in a meaningful way. But she also knew firsthand, after seeing Jessie go head-to-head with a notorious serial killer, that being a PI could be dangerous. She wondered if there would come a time where she would need some professional firearms training.

You're a crazy girl. They won't let you carry a—

She growled.

The voices stopped.

Of course she would need a weapon. What if she ever happened upon another madman? She'd never been a people person, but she'd really thought the young man who had befriended her months ago had been different. Sadly, after he'd proven to be a psycho killer, she no longer trusted her instincts, which was why she was going to take her father's advice and sit here and do her job.

Looking away from the neighbor's house, she picked up the binoculars and focused on Lindsay Norton's front window, just in time to see her shut the curtains tight.

Seven

Ben sat quietly as his therapist, Lori Mitchell, scribbled in her notebook. Lori was in her late forties. Tall and thin. Dark hair, wispy bangs. He had no idea what she might be writing down, since he hadn't said much in the twenty minutes he'd been sitting across from her.

The first time he'd met Lori was ten years ago, after the car accident. For the next three years, he'd met with her every month. Back then, the process had seemed like a waste of time since he'd had absolutely no memory of his life prior to the accident. What was he supposed to talk about?

His wife, whom he'd met at the hospital where he spent months recovering from first-degree burns and broken bones, had insisted it was important to his well-being that he talk about his experiences and "get it all out." She worried he might be frustrated that he couldn't remember his childhood—let alone friends or family.

It had been distressing at first to realize he'd lost his whole identity along with his memory, but in the end, he'd decided there was no point in looking back.

But that was then, and this was now.

He'd recently been experiencing what he sometimes thought of as out-of-body experiences. The first time it had happened, he'd seen himself raise a knife and plunge the blade into one of his coworkers. He'd seen the blood. Hell, he'd smelled it. And then, in the blink of an eye, it was over. No knife. No blood. Just his coworker with a smile on his face as he'd said goodbye and walked away.

Ben also saw flashes of people and places in his mind's eye. Eighty percent of the time the people he saw were dead. Gory images of a woman lying in a crumpled heap in the middle of a vast field; a man sitting behind the wheel of a black Mercedes, a cord wrapped around his neck; an elderly man in a bathtub, facedown in his own blood. A few months ago, when the images had first started, he'd figured it came with the job. He was a crime reporter. He had a police scanner. Sometimes he arrived at the location of a crime before the police did. He'd seen a lot of blood and gore throughout his career, so it all sort of made sense. Not too long ago he'd taken the time to examine some cases he'd once worked on. He read articles and sifted through files, hoping to find something that might be related to the images he was seeing.

Unfortunately he'd turned up nothing so far.

And then he'd ended up face-to-face with a crazed killer, and something had changed inside of him. Like a light switch flicked on. He needed to look into his past and find out who he once was. His sister might be the key to unlocking his past, but she'd made it clear she wanted nothing to do with him.

"Ben," Lori said, interrupting his thoughts. "Is everything okay?"

He zeroed in on the therapist, surprised to see her staring at him.

"Did you hear what I said?"

"No. Sorry."

"Everything you've told me today about the images you've been seeing . . . I get the feeling you're merely saying what you think I want to hear."

"I'm not sure what you mean."

"Well, when you talk about the dead bodies and the blood, at times it seems as if you're describing someone else's emotions. Not your own."

"Maybe I am describing someone else's emotions," he said thoughtfully. "But maybe that someone is actually my old self, you know, the person I used to be." He lifted his hands in question.

"Interesting," she said. "Have you had any episodes recently?"

"Not the sort I think of as film reels, whole scenes played out in my mind with me being a main character."

"What about the bloody images? When was the last time you saw an image you would describe as macabre?"

"This morning."

"Are they always the same?"

"Not always. But there are three dead people I see on a regular basis."

"The dead woman in the middle of the field?" she asked.

"Yes. And also the man in the black Mercedes and the old guy facedown in the bathtub."

Lori scribbled down notes. "And the others?"

"Too many to name. Glimpses here and there of random dead people. Strangled, stabbed, drowned. Nobody looks familiar."

"Hmm."

"There is something that happened at work yesterday," he went on.

Lori straightened in her chair.

"My coworker showed me pictures of a case we worked two years before my accident. One of the pictures he shared was of a man who authorities believe killed his wife and two kids. My coworker said it was one of the most horrific crime scenes he'd ever seen."

"And did you recognize the man?" she asked.

"No, I didn't, but his name sounded familiar. When I saw a picture of the site where his remains were found, though, I experienced the same sensation as when I first recognized the image of Sophie Cole on TV."

"Can you describe that sensation for me?"

"Uncanny, unnerving."

"When it happens, does it frighten you?"

"No. It's more of a surprise. Almost as if my brain is short-circuiting."

More scribbling on her notepad.

"There's something else," he said.

She looked up at him.

"I've been at war with myself over what happened with the Heartless Killer."

She nodded as if she understood, which nobody could unless they'd killed a man with their bare hands.

"You saved three lives that day," she said. "You're a hero."

"I killed a man."

"He was a cold-blooded killer."

"I should feel remorse."

"Isn't that what you're doing by warring with yourself over what happened?"

He shook his head. "Every time I'm brought back to that moment when I was nose to nose with him, it's amazingly clear to me that I knew exactly what I was doing."

"You were angry."

"Perhaps," he agreed. "And yet I was also fully aware of my surroundings. When my hands were wrapped around his throat, I could feel his pulse. I could have stopped choking him, knocked him out, and waited for the police."

"Did that thought go through your mind at the time?"

"Yes."

"But you didn't stop," she stated.

"No. All I could see was the girl he'd locked in the box and left to die. So I kept squeezing."

"And how did you feel in that moment?"

"Good," he said. He inhaled. "I felt really good."

All he had to do was close his eyes and imagine his hands wrapped around the man's throat to bring himself back to that moment. His pulse would race as he recalled an evil darkness settling over him like a good friend. His muscles would tense, his jaw would harden, and then, like the blossoming of a flower, he would slowly come alive.

EIGHT

At 6:30 a.m. on Wednesday he awoke in a sweat, his dream of holding Hannah in his arms as she struggled for each breath still vivid.

The shades were drawn, and the room was dark. It took him a few seconds to calm down before he remembered that this was do-or-die day.

He threw off the covers, put on his slippers and robe, and headed for the kitchen. After getting the coffee started, he walked to the end of the driveway to grab the paper. Five minutes later, with coffee in one hand and paper in the other, he took a seat on the sofa. As he read every headline on the front page, his insides knotted. He inhaled, then turned the page and read every article, column after column, before moving on to the next page.

He stopped halfway through one particular article about a woman in Elk Grove who'd hidden in a closet after hearing an intruder enter her house. She was quoted as saying, "The silence was deafening."

The silence was deafening.

He could relate. The silence was not only deafening but thickened the air and made it difficult to breathe. Everything had changed once he'd sent the letter to Ben Morrison.

He took another breath.

He was procrastinating.

He wasn't quite ready to see what was or was not inside today's paper. Although he'd said he wanted to see the letter on the front page, anywhere in the newspaper would do.

This was the boy's last chance for survival. He didn't want to kill him, but he had no choice. His mind was made up. He'd exhausted all other options—sent countless letters to DHI as his daughter battled for her life. In response, he'd received their standard form letter. Around that same time, he'd contacted the local media, but they had made it clear that his story was a dime a dozen. A drug not being covered by an insurance company wasn't news. It was life.

And then it had hit him.

If he wanted to draw attention to his cause, he would need to take drastic measures. Death and destruction were the only way to capture DHI's and the public's attention.

If he took an innocent life, the news media would be all over it. People killing people made headlines. It was too late to save his daughter, but her death would not be in vain. He wanted the world to know what was going on. And that it could happen to them.

Who better to spread the word than a man with nothing to live for and therefore absolutely nothing to lose?

The truth was he was angry it had come to this. This was DHI's fault. Not his. He was not a monster. If anything, he was numb. Nothing seemed real any longer. As far as he was concerned, the people who would lose their lives were not human beings. They were merely pawns in a game, and he was going to make the first move.

His gaze drifted around the living room and settled on an old-world map. He'd been renting the place for two weeks now, and yet this was the first time he'd noticed it. The map made him think of his wife and all the plans they'd made to travel abroad. Her life's dream had been to spend a month in New Zealand. He'd always thought that someday he would take her there.

He stretched his neck, feeling the pull on his muscles and tendons. And then he turned another page. Feeling a sense of urgency come over him, he read faster, still careful not to miss even one word. When he finished, he gulped down the rest of his coffee, which was now cold, and then made his way to his bedroom to get dressed.

It was time.

———

Jessie had just gotten to the office and taken a seat when Zee came barreling through the door to her office. Higgins jumped to his feet, ears perked, eyes bright.

"It's okay, Dog," Zee said as she approached Higgins and patted his head. "I'm not going to bite you."

Jessie laughed.

Zee walked to the chair in front of Jessie's desk and plopped down into it. "Since it's the end of the week, I thought I'd come here on my way to Lindsay Norton's house and give you an update."

Jessie glanced at the clock. It was 7:45 a.m. "It's early."

"Yeah, I couldn't sleep so I figured I might as well get the day started."

"How's it going so far?" Jessie asked.

"I'm afraid Lindsay Norton might be a dud."

"How so?"

"She's only exited her house twice. Both times she made a big show of cringing and putting a hand to her lower back as if getting the mail was too much effort. The first day I fell for it hook, line, and sinker. But the second day, I noticed a bit of a kick in her step, right up until she got to the driveway." Zee scratched her nose. "I think it's possible she knows she's being watched. I took pictures and videos. I guess we'll just have to wait and see what happens."

"Not much else you can do," Jessie agreed. "So the equipment is working well for you?"

"Yeah, it's all good."

Usually Zee was in a hurry to leave, but she didn't move. "Anything else?" Jessie asked.

"Well, since you insist on twisting my arm," she said. "I saw something the other day that troubled me."

Jessie waited.

"While I was watching Lindsay Norton's house, I witnessed something disturbing going on next door. I saw a man and a woman arguing. They were standing by a side door leading into the garage. The woman looked much younger than him, and she seemed scared. He had a tight grip on her arm and wouldn't let go.

"The only reason I saw everything so clearly was because of your binoculars. His fingers were digging into her arm. He was being aggressive, and we didn't—I mean, *I* didn't like it."

"Was she able to leave?"

Zee shook her head. "I turned away to put the binoculars on the passenger seat, and when I turned back they were gone. The door was closed."

"Listen, I've done a lot of surveillance over the years, and I can tell you you're going to see lots of people doing strange things out there. But if they're not breaking the law, and they are not violent, you need to look the other way. I don't mean to sound callous, but you have a job to do. Now, if you *do* see something violent, then that means it's a job for authorities. And you need to dial 9-1-1."

Jessie opened a drawer, grabbed a business card, and handed it to Zee. "Colin Grayson is with the police force. Call him if you ever feel as if someone's life might be in danger."

Zee stared at the card.

"Would you rather not watch Lindsay Norton? I understand if surveillance isn't something you're comfortable doing." Jessie glanced at the pile of papers in her in-box. "I'm sure I could find something else for you to do around here."

Zee's head snapped up. "Oh no. I know I've only been doing this for a couple of days, but I love it! I'm pumped about this job, and I appreciate you giving me this chance. I want to learn all I can. I even ordered some books online. They should arrive at my house in a few days."

"What sort of books?"

"Mostly how-to books—how to search public records, how to develop PI skills, everything I need to know about new and improved investigative techniques like GPS tracking systems." Her face became animated. "Did you know you could use drones to spy on people? They're only about two hundred bucks at a high-end toy store. All you have to do is keep them fifty to seventy-five feet high so nobody can hear anything."

"Drones are probably difficult to pilot."

Zee snorted. "All we'd have to do is visit a college campus and find some geek to help us out. Gamers love that stuff."

"Sounds like you're very serious about all this."

"I am," Zee said.

Before Jessie could say anything more, Zee was on her feet and heading for the door. "Thanks for the update," Jessie called after her, but she was gone.

Jessie looked over her shoulder at Higgins. "What have I gotten myself into?"

Higgins lifted his head and looked at her curiously.

"It's okay," she said. "Everything will be fine."

As long as Zee didn't approach the neighbors and kept her updated, what could possibly go wrong?

NINE

Friday morning Ben arrived at work an hour later than usual. He grabbed a cup of coffee from the lunchroom, and then made his way to his desk, where he promptly began sorting through his mail.

The envelope on top was thick and padded. He recognized the handwriting at once. His skin tingled with impending doom as he reached for the letter opener.

Damn. This didn't bode well. He'd never received a call back from Shepard, and when he'd notified the police, they had told him there was nothing they could do unless he had a name or proof that a crime had been committed. Ben had neither. He'd had no choice but to hope that MAH was nothing more than a practical joker.

Inside the envelope Ben could see a letter on white paper and a thumb drive. Droplets of red, like tiny freckles, dotted the paper.

Ben swiveled in his chair, opened his bottom desk drawer, and pulled a pair of thin latex gloves from a box. He was a crime reporter. He knew how this worked, and this time he wasn't taking any chances.

Mr. Morrison,
I'm wondering if I've asked the wrong person for help.
I thought you were a man of morals, someone who

cared about social injustices. I considered sending this letter to one of your competitors. Maybe then someone might take me seriously. But then I realized the fastest way to get your attention was to provide proof.

So, here it is . . . live and in full color.

When you're done talking to your superiors, and after you've called the authorities, I ask you once again to contact DHI and see that I get an apology, along with reassurance that all experimental drugs for all patients will be covered from here on out. I hate to be redundant, but I repeat: if I don't see a copy of said letter on DHI's company letterhead signed by the president and chief executive officer, Owen Shepard, on the front page of the *Sacramento Tribune* by Monday morning, another life will be taken.

Sincerely,

MAH

With gloved hands, Ben reached inside the padded envelope and pulled out the flash drive. Spotting another item at the bottom of the envelope, he gently shook the contents onto his desk. It was an ID card. TYLER McDONALD

DRY CREEK ROAD, RIO LINDA, CA

Heart racing, Ben picked up the flash drive and inserted it into his computer. His screen lit up in shades of gray. The grainy picture wobbled, as if the camera was being propped on an unstable surface. And then came a distorted voice: "Testing one, two, three. Testing one, two, three."

Ben turned up the volume.

The picture on the screen stilled and became clearer, revealing a cinder-block wall. No shelves or decorative items. *An empty warehouse?* Ben wondered.

"Testing one, two, three," the voice said again. A male voice. Slightly muffled. The camera lens shifted slowly to the left until Ben saw a young man sitting on the cement floor, his back straight against the cinder-block wall. The camera zoomed in on his face. Tyler McDonald. His reddish-brown hair had been cut since the picture on the ID was taken, shaved closed to his head around the ears, longer on the top. His green eyes were shaded with fatigue, his expression haunted.

"Tyler," the voice said. "Tell whoever is watching why you're here."

Both of Tyler's shoulders slumped as if he'd been asked the same question hundreds of times already. "I don't know," he said, trying to get free. His arms were behind him, out of sight, most likely bound with tape or rope.

In the background, Ben thought he heard the sound of a magazine being loaded into a pistol.

Sitting taller, eyes wide, the young man looked directly into the lens of the camera. "Why are you doing this?"

"You know why."

"I told you. I've only been working for DHI for a short time. I never met Owen Shepard. He wouldn't know me if we bumped into each other."

A long pause.

Ben hoped this wouldn't end badly, but instinct told him it couldn't end any other way.

"I had nothing to do with Han—"

A gunshot sounded. Tyler McDonald's skull exploded. A second later, the screen went from red to black.

Ben's stomach turned as he stood silently in front of the computer, waiting to see if there was more.

Nothing.

His insides twisted at the thought of the young man losing his life.

He grabbed the flash drive and the letter and made his way to Ian's office. His boss frowned at him as he came through the door. "Why do I have the feeling you don't have good news for me?"

Ben put the letter on Ian's desk in front of him. "Don't pick it up," Ben said. "Just read it."

Ian did as he asked. "Is that blood?" Ian looked at Ben and more specifically at the flash drive Ben had clasped between two gloved fingers. "Is that the proof he's referring to?"

"It is."

"Not good?"

"No. Shot him in the head at close range. Not pretty."

"Fuck."

"Yeah."

"Where's the first letter?" Ian asked.

"Filed away at my desk."

"Did you ever call this Owen Shepard at DHI?"

"I did. More than once. He never returned my calls. I also called the authorities, but there was nothing they could do unless I had a name or evidence that a crime had been committed."

"Okay. Good. I don't want to take any crap for this once the public finds out what happened."

"What about Shepard?" Ben asked. "Want me to give him another call?"

"No. I'll call the authorities and leave it to them to handle Shepard. You," Ian said, pointing a bony finger at him, "get to work on the story. It's ours."

"What about the victim's right to privacy?"

Ian waved both hands in the air in front of his chest. "Same as always. Don't mention any names until I negotiate a deal with the police."

Back at his desk, Ben tried not to think about what he'd seen on the screen, but it was no use. Scrambled bits of brain matter and skull splattered across the lens had triggered something within. He grabbed his coat and left the office. He needed to breathe. Minutes later he was in his van, driving down L Street.

He thought of his wife and how she had no idea how much worse everything had become. Long-forgotten memories were returning. He was sure of it. Until he knew what it all meant, though, there was no sense in worrying her.

If Melony could see him now, she'd have him hospitalized. He had no idea where he was going when he merged onto the highway. Thirty minutes later he took the Lincoln Boulevard exit off Highway 65. He made a left at the stoplight and then another left farther down the road. After what seemed like an endless route of stops and turns, he found himself on a quiet, tree-lined street. Finally, he pulled to the curb and shut off the engine.

For the next few minutes he did nothing but listen to the sound of his breath as he wondered where he was.

And then he saw it.

He climbed out of the van and walked down the sidewalk, kept walking until he was across the street from a two-story house on a level lot with a wide concrete driveway and two-car garage. His hands and forearms quivered. This house had once belonged to the Stumm family.

When he closed his eyes, he saw a small boy run out the front door. A young woman came running after him, grabbed him around the middle, and carried him back inside. The boy's laughter filled the air.

Ben opened his eyes and the vision disappeared. Nobody was there.

As he walked back toward his van, a searing pain grabbed hold of his chest and squeezed. He slid in behind the wheel and leaned over to open the glove box, where he found a bottle of pills his therapist had prescribed. Something to help him relax. He didn't like taking medication, but he unscrewed the lid and popped a pill into his mouth, then chased it down with water.

Leaning back against the headrest, he closed his eyes.

He turned the key and started off again. Six and a half minutes later, he did exactly the same thing as before. Pulled to the curb, turned off the engine, and climbed out of his van.

The pill was working. He was less anxious. His hands were steady. Good. Again he found himself in a residential area. These houses were newer.

"Ben!" he heard someone yell.

He turned toward the sound of the voice, saw Larry jogging across the street toward him. "I was hoping you would show up," Larry said when he caught up to him. "We're over this way."

It wasn't until that moment that Ben realized where he was. This was the place where they had found DJ Stumm's bones. Somehow he'd known where to go. He looked around, and in the distance he saw the brick building he'd recognized in the picture.

"Did they find anything else on the property?" Ben asked.

Larry shook his head as they walked. "Nothing so far. No more bones. No additional bodies. They're running tests on the soil where the bones were found. It'll be a while before they know whether they have any DNA belonging to a second party, someone other than DJ Stumm."

Larry lifted the yellow crime tape so Ben could duck under it. Forensics was all over the place, gathering samples and taking measurements and photographs. A woman in uniform closely examined the perimeter fence and took notes.

"A secondary review?" Ben asked.

"Quality control. They want to ensure a thorough search."

Twelve years, Ben thought. *What could they possibly find after all that time?*

Ten

Jessie sat at a table, sipping the last of her champagne as she admired the interior of the building. The wedding ceremony had been short and sweet, held inside a clubhouse close to Salmon Falls. The stone pillars and reclaimed-wood flooring in the main room gave the lodge a cozy touch. A dozen rustic wood tables had been set up with mason jars filled with daisies as the centerpieces.

Twenty minutes ago, Colin and three fellow police officers had been called away to have group pictures taken with the groom, leaving Jessie alone with Lisa, a retired police communications officer who liked to talk.

"Colin's ex-wife is beautiful, isn't she?" Lisa asked. "God, if that was my husband's ex-wife, I think I'd die from envy alone."

Jessie followed the direction she was looking. It was true. Kimberly Grayson was beautiful. She had short honey-blonde hair and curves in all the right places.

"My husband filled me in on everyone before we got here," Lisa said, flitting easily from one subject to another. "He told me who's who and what everyone does for a living—you know, stuff like that."

Jessie finished off her champagne.

"See that man over there—oh, never mind—don't look. It's Owen Shepard, CEO of DHI, one of the biggest health insurance companies in the United States."

Too late. Jessie glanced in the direction Lisa pointed. The man heading toward them was tall and broad-shouldered. She guessed him to be in his early sixties.

"Not only is he a zillionaire, he's divorced and single," Lisa said out of the corner of her mouth before he reached their table.

Lisa offered her hand as he approached. "Owen Shepard. I don't know if you remember me," she said as he took her hand in his. "I went to school with your sister. This," she went on, gesturing toward Jessie, "is Jessie Cole, the private investigator who helped take out the Heartless Killer and make our streets safe again."

Before Jessie could respond, he took Jessie's hand. "It's a small world and a pleasure to meet you."

Puzzled, Jessie wondered what he meant by that.

He needed no prompting to explain. "I called your office earlier today and left a message." He looked around. "I realize this isn't the best time or place to talk, but would it be possible to have a quick word with you?"

"Go ahead," Lisa said. "You two chat. I see a friend across the way I'd love to say hello to."

Jessie had no idea what the man wanted to talk to her about, but before she could stand, he slid into the empty seat next to her. "I hope you don't mind talking business. I'll be quick."

"I don't mind at all." She got a whiff of his cologne. He was certainly handsome, and she found herself intimidated by the intense way he looked into her eyes.

"The truth is, I could use your help."

Jessie raised a brow.

"After returning from a business trip," he went on, "I learned that a disgruntled client of my company, DHI, has threatened to take the lives of innocent people. He actually killed one of my employees."

Jessie was taken aback. "The police are involved?"

"Yes, of course." He raked a hand through his silver-tipped hair. For the first time since he'd sat down, she could see that he was upset.

"Maybe you should start from the beginning."

He nodded. "The disgruntled client sent a letter to Mr. Morrison at his work."

"Ben Morrison at the *Sacramento Tribune*?" she asked, surprised.

"Yes."

"Why wouldn't the client have contacted you directly?"

"Apparently he's written DHI in the past but never received a response. My staff is doing all they can to figure out who this person is. He signed the letter 'MAH,' and since we insure over five million people across the United States, it's going to take time."

"What did the letter say? Is there something this person wants from DHI?"

"He lost his daughter, and he's angry. He wanted me to write a public apology giving assurance that experimental medications for all patients in the future would be covered."

"Did you write the letter?"

Owen raked a hand through his hair again. "By the time I returned, it was too late. And even if I had written a response, I'm worried it would only be a matter of time before he realizes nothing has changed as far as coverage goes." He raised his hands. "It's not up to me to make those types of decisions. And even if it were, it doesn't happen overnight."

"Are you afraid he'll continue to kill?"

"Yes."

Jessie said nothing.

"If the public gets wind of what's happening, this man could ruin DHI's reputation." He paused. "That's where you come into the picture. If I hire a private investigator, especially one with your experience, I might be able to reassure employees and board members that DHI is doing all they can."

Ahhh. Owen Shepard, it seemed, was more worried about his company than about the possibility of more lives being lost. "You said one of your employees was killed. Did you know him or her?"

"No. I've since learned he was a new hire at the general office in Sacramento. We have somewhere around ten thousand employees."

"What is it exactly you would want me to do?"

He tugged at his tie. "I want you to find this lunatic."

"I work mostly on cold cases," she told him, put off by the man since he'd outright said that hiring her was merely a way for him to make his company look like it was doing all they could. "My specialty is searching for missing persons."

"Think of this as exactly that—you'll be searching for a missing person."

"A person with no name," she said.

He gave her an imploring look. "I need your help. I'm begging you."

He was doing nothing of the sort.

"My office Monday at three o'clock?" He pulled a business card from his pocket and handed it to her.

Clearly the man was not used to taking no for an answer. "Three o'clock sounds fine," she said, figuring it wouldn't hurt to meet with him, hear what he had to say, and find out if he had a plan.

He stood, thanked her, and then walked away to mingle with the crowd. Gone as quickly as he'd come. Jessie didn't know what to think about him. Self-assured one minute, cold and aloof the next.

"Would you like to dance?"

Colin had returned. He held out his hand for her to take. Jessie laughed as he helped her from her chair and quickly led her to the dance floor. "What's the hurry?"

"I saw that man hovering over you, and I knew it was time to show everyone that you were taken."

"I didn't know you were the jealous type."

"There are a lot of things you don't know about me," he said as he led her to the dance floor.

Jessie wanted to ask Colin about the case Owen Shepard had talked to her about, but she decided it could wait.

As they moved to the music, Jessie realized she'd never danced with Colin before. He appeared to be in his element. The song was off tempo and hard to dance to, so she basically stood in place and moved her arms as she watched him entertain the crowd.

There was so much she didn't know about Colin Grayson.

Their relationship was complicated. They had met ten years ago at the police station right after her sister had disappeared. Colin had been a great listener and a shoulder to lean on. Their relationship had escalated quickly. But then Kimberly Grayson had shown up at her doorstep to let Jessie and Colin know she was pregnant. Colin went back to his wife, and Jessie put all her energy into raising her niece and searching for Sophie.

Less than a year ago, she'd run into Colin. He was divorced, and so they went out for coffee and played catch-up. They had been close friends ever since.

The song ended, and Jessie started to walk off before Colin reached for her hand and pulled her back to him, smiling mischievously. It took a second for her to realize the song playing was "You Never Can Tell" by Chuck Berry. *Pulp Fiction* was the first movie she and Colin had watched together all those years ago.

"It's on," she said with her own mischievous grin, and for the next few minutes they locked gazes and did their own stylized version of the twist. When it was over, people clapped, making Jessie blush.

"One more dance," he said when the DJ played "Can't Help Falling in Love" by Elvis Presley. Before she could answer him one way or another, Colin pulled her close against his chest.

"I didn't know you could dance," she said, enjoying the feel of his arms wrapped around her waist.

"It's been so long," he said. "I wasn't sure if I still had any moves."

She couldn't remember the last time she'd had this much fun.

"I feel like I'm back at my high school prom," he told her.

"I never went."

He pulled away slightly, his expression one of astonishment. "Stay right here."

She stood in the middle of the dance floor and waited while people danced around her. Colin was back in under a minute with a daisy that he gently tucked behind her ear. "There. Your corsage."

She thought the gesture was sweet. "Thank you."

They finished the dance and then walked off hand in hand. "After the bride cuts the cake, what do you say we drive through the automatic car wash and make out?"

She laughed. "Is that a thing?"

"Are you kidding? For at least five glorious spot-rinsing minutes you'll be transported to another world."

The thought of making out with him made her insides flutter in a good way. Before she could respond, his phone buzzed.

She watched his expression change as he listened to the caller. Whatever it was, it couldn't be good.

"What is it?" she asked after he was finished.

"My father."

She had met his parents only once before. They were in their late seventies and lived on ten acres in Rio Linda, over twenty miles away. "Is he okay?"

"He's had a stroke. I've got to get to the hospital."

"I'm sorry."

"Me, too. I dragged you all this way and now—"

"Colin," she said, stopping him from finishing. "Don't worry about me. I can go to the hospital with you."

"Come on," he said, taking her hand in his. "I'll drop you off on the way."

Eleven

First thing Monday morning, he read the front page once, twice, and then again.

There was nothing there.

In disbelief, he skimmed the entire newspaper.

He stood, his hands shaking as he crumpled the paper in his fists and tossed it aside.

Owen Shepard had let Hannah die, but not before making her suffer hour after hour, day after day. Endless whimpering cries as she tried to get comfortable enough to sleep. When the pain became unbearable, his daughter had asked him to end her life. It was the only way she said would end the pain.

But he'd been weak.

Now, looking back, he wished with every part of his being that he'd done what she'd asked.

It was Owen Shepard's fault that Tyler McDonald was dead, too, and that another innocent life would be taken soon. The anger inside him was growing stronger, fed at first by the need to see that changes were made and that others like his daughter didn't needlessly suffer. But now it was becoming more about teaching Owen Shepard and everyone who worked for DHI a lesson.

As he made his way to the garage, his body vibrated with hatred. He would kill as many people as it took to get Owen Shepard's attention. Ten. Twenty. Thirty. It didn't matter. He glanced at the clock. It was early. He had plenty of time.

In a burst of energy, he went to his room and hurriedly dressed. He then grabbed the duffel bag he'd packed in the event Owen Shepard didn't cooperate. Inside the bag were his gloves, cuffs, rope, gun, video recorder, and Taser.

His movements were robotic as he grabbed his keys from the bowl on the kitchen counter and made his way to the garage, where he climbed behind the wheel and started the engine. As the garage door whirred open, he slipped on his gloves.

His next-door neighbor waved as he passed by.

Despite the rage flowing through his veins, he thought of his wife and how she would have liked the neighborhood. Hannah, on the other hand, had always talked about living in a big city. In an apartment with lots of windows, where she could see the skyline in the distance. He swallowed. His eyes watered. He kept his hands steady at ten and two o'clock, and he kept his eyes on the road.

It took him fourteen minutes to get to Jefferson Boulevard. He pulled into the parking lot, drove to the back lot where he knew Brad Elton, CFO of DHI, parked every day of the week.

He had done his research.

One thing he had that most people didn't was time. He had plenty of time to get it right. He'd chosen the CFO as his next victim for two reasons: because of where he parked—an area that lacked cameras—and because he arrived earlier than other DHI employees did.

He parked. Turned off the engine. Waited.

Despite the morning's chill, sweat formed in a light sheen on his forehead. He wiped it away with his sleeve.

Exactly sixteen minutes later, Brad Elton pulled his sleek black BMW into his allotted parking space.

He climbed out of the car when he saw the BMW pull into the lot. "Excuse me," he called when Brad exited his car.

The CFO turned around.

Waving a crumpled piece of paper through the air, he said, "You wouldn't happen to know where I could find a Victoria Hadley, would you?"

Brad gave him the once-over. "Mind telling me why you're looking for Victoria?"

A little research on the Internet had made it easy to learn that Brad had been dating Victoria for the past six months. "Just an Uber driver trying to do his job," he said cheerfully.

"Victoria doesn't work here."

"Well that's odd," he said with an exaggerated frown. "She called me less than fifteen minutes ago saying she needed a ride and specifically asked me to meet her in the back parking lot." He acted as if he was going to hand the note to Brad to read for himself and then purposely dropped it. The wad of paper rolled to the ground close to Brad's feet. When Brad bent down to pick up the note, he pulled out the Taser hidden under his coat and struck the CFO right between his neck and collarbone.

Brad dropped like a swatted fly, his arms and legs stiff, his body dancing from the electric charge.

Thankfully nobody was around.

He worked quickly, his heart racing as he opened the back door of his car, grabbed hold of Brad's upper body, and pushed him more than halfway into the back seat. He then rushed to the other side and dragged him all the way inside.

Doing his best to stay calm, he zapped Brad twice more, then made quick work of cuffing his wrists and tying his ankles. Moving fast, he closed the doors, picked up Brad's briefcase, then slipped behind the wheel and drove off.

Twelve

After going over the Dakota Bale abduction case for the umpteenth time—something Jessie did with every one of her investigations to get to know the case inside out before she got started—Jessie realized there was no great place to begin.

She tried not to pay too much attention to the conclusions the police came to in their reports because she didn't want to be swayed by deductions from the past. The only way to solve an old case was through analyzing the evidence and witness interviews. For that reason, she figured she would begin by reaching out to the women Ashley had mentioned when they had talked in person. Starting with Rose Helg.

Rose had been Ashley Bale's coworker when Ashley was pregnant with Dakota. After suffering a series of miscarriages and then divorcing her husband, Rose had registered with a sperm bank and finally been able to conceive. She and her three-year-old daughter lived in Rocklin.

On the drive there, Jessie went over the facts of the case: Dakota Bale had been born early on a Sunday morning at Mercy General. Hours after the last visitor left, Ashley Bale was given the choice of keeping the baby in her room overnight or having her newborn sleep in the nursery. After ten hours of labor and a long day of visiting friends and family, she was exhausted, and so she didn't hesitate to opt for the latter.

A decision she would regret every second of every day since.

In the wee hours of the night, Ashley had hit the button wrapped around the hospital bed railing and asked the nurse to bring her baby to her. But Dakota was nowhere to be found.

It was clear from reading her journals that Ashley blamed herself for Dakota's abduction. She also seemed certain everyone else, including her husband, blamed her, too.

Ashley Bale felt as if she was being judged.

And it was no wonder.

Jessie had cringed as she read the articles that were now yellowed and flattened within the scrapbook pages. Some of the articles were about new moms who opted to breastfeed in public, or not breastfeed at all. It seemed to Jessie that mothers were damned if they did and damned if they didn't. If you worked outside of the home, you should be ashamed; if you were a stay-at-a-home mom, you were lazy. New mothers couldn't win.

After receiving an e-mail from Ashley that included pictures of her and her husband at the age of seven, along with the names of and other pertinent information about visitors on the day Dakota was born, Jessie made her own list of suspects. She didn't care whether or not authorities had determined the people in question were innocent. She would start fresh. Just as Ben Morrison had done when he'd helped her search for her missing sister.

Ben Morrison.

A wave of guilt swept through her. She hadn't talked to Ben since Sophie's funeral. If not for Ben, she might never have discovered what happened to Sophie. If not for Ben, she would have likely been killed by a madman. She owed him her life, and yet she hadn't called him to say hello or find out how he was doing. She made a mental note to do just that.

It was nine o'clock when Jessie pulled up in front of Rose's house, a small one-story home on a quiet street. She grabbed her bag and headed across the walkway to the front door. Before she could knock a second time, Rose opened the door.

Jessie introduced herself, told Rose she was a detective working on a cold case concerning the abduction of Dakota Bale.

"You're in luck," Rose said. "I just made a pot of coffee. Would you like to come inside?"

"I would love to. I won't take too much of your time."

Rose's little girl was in the living room, sprawled out on the carpet, scribbling in a coloring book while *Beauty and the Beast* played on a big-screen TV.

"How is Ashley?" Rose asked as she poured them both a cup of coffee and gestured for her to have a seat at the kitchen table.

"She's busy with her twin boys but still struggles with not knowing what happened to her daughter."

"Understandable. And what about her husband?"

"I haven't met him," Jessie told her, "but I'm sure it isn't easy for either of them."

"Are they still married?"

Jessie nodded. "Were they having problems back then?"

"Ashley didn't mention anything to you?"

"No."

"Hmm. Interesting." She flicked a finger at Jessie's untouched mug. "Did you want cream or sugar? I forgot to ask."

"Black is fine." Jessie took a sip before she asked, "Did you know Nick?"

"No, not really, although he did show up at the department store every now and then. Based on what little I saw of him, I didn't like him."

"Why?"

"We all worked in the back office, and every once in a while Nick would come by unexpectedly. I'll never forget the time Ashley wasn't at her desk when he dropped by. He sat right down in front of her computer and checked her browsing history. After that, he sifted through her desk drawers as if he was looking for something."

"Did anyone ask him what he was doing?"

She shook her head. "No, when Ashley caught him snooping, they argued, something they often did when he called her at work." Rose exhaled. "Ashley was sweet. We all liked her. She didn't need to put up with that man."

"Any idea what Nick might have been looking for that day?" Jessie asked, trying not to come across as too pushy. Jessie had talked to many people over the years, women like Rose Helg, who were bored and eager to talk to someone, even a stranger.

Rose sighed. "Maybe it was only a rumor, but back then it seemed everyone in our department thought Ashley was seeing another man. I think her husband was also suspicious."

Jessie wondered if it was true. "Any guess as to who the man was rumored to be?"

She paused to think for a moment before shaking her head. "I don't recall. But I guess I bought into the rumors because Ashley often complained about Nick being overly possessive and controlling."

"Do you remember seeing Nick on the day you visited Ashley at the hospital?"

"Yes, of course. I'll never forget how incredibly unhappy he seemed."

Rose didn't have much to add after that, so after a bit, Jessie thanked her for her help and made her way back to her car.

Sitting quietly behind the wheel for a moment, she thought about Nick Bale. Possessive and controlling, and he didn't like the idea of Ashley searching for their daughter. It made no sense to Jessie that he wouldn't want to be involved in the search, even if it was seven years later.

She straightened as an idea came to her. Maybe Ben Morrison could help her. Using Bluetooth, she scanned her contact list, located Ben's number, and hit the "Call" button. He answered right away.

"Jessie," he said. "It's good to hear from you."

"I should have called sooner, just to say hello."

"No worries."

"I was wondering if I could come by your office. I realize it's short notice, but I need to talk to you about a missing person's case."

"I'd love to see you."

"Is now a good time?"

"If you don't mind chaos, come on over."

"Chaos is my middle name."

"Sounds as if nothing has changed for either of us."

As soon as Jessie disconnected her call with Ben, the phone rang. It was Olivia.

"Are you at the store?" Olivia asked without prelude. "We're out of milk."

Jessie shook her head. "Hello to you, too. My day has been busy, but fine overall. Thanks for asking." She swore she could hear her niece rolling her eyes.

"Sorry," Olivia said. "I wasn't sure if you remembered that I got out of school early today and we were going to go shopping."

Damn. She'd forgotten. "Something's come up. Do you mind if we go shopping this weekend?"

"Fine."

"I'll pick up milk on my way home, okay?"

"Sure."

Jessie pulled out of the parking lot and merged onto the main road. Olivia had recently turned fifteen. She was showing all the signs of being a teenager. Acting sullen, and answering questions with a yes or no. According to a parenting source on the Internet, one-word answers from teenagers were perfectly normal. She'd also read that good parents gave their teenager leeway, which Jessie had always done.

Parents were supposed to choose their battles wisely, talk about rules and discipline way in advance so nobody was caught off guard.

Jessie had made the rules she expected Olivia to follow very clear, hadn't she? She had talked to Olivia about drugs many times. She frowned as she realized they hadn't discussed sex. It just never seemed necessary. But now she wondered if she'd been naive.

Eyes on the road, Jessie tried to get a kink out of her neck. The thought of failing Olivia weighed heavily on her shoulders. She was doing the best she could, wasn't she? She'd made a point of keeping the lines of communication open. That was important. And she and Olivia had a plan for every possible scenario. For instance, if Olivia was at a friend's house and a parent had been drinking, Olivia was to call Jessie or Jessie's good friend Andriana for a ride. *Let it go,* she told herself as she pulled to a stop at the light.

It was noon by the time she walked inside the *Sacramento Tribune*'s office where Ben worked and signed in. Before she had a chance to take a seat in the lobby, Ben greeted her with an awkward bear hug, then gestured for her to follow him through a maze of cubicles.

It was good to see him.

Ben was a big guy. Tall and thick in the neck. His accident ten years ago had left him with multiple scars, mostly on his left side. Depending on the lighting and the clothing he wore, the scars sometimes stood out, running down the side of his face, neck, and arm like a river of valleys and ridges.

"Can I get you some coffee, water, anything?" he asked as she followed him across an open area where some of the staff were congregating outside a cafeteria, sipping coffee and chatting during their break.

"No, thanks."

Ben's cubicle was a large space partitioned off with tall metal walls. "Will this do or would you rather we talk somewhere more private?"

"This is fine." She took a seat in the chair in front of his desk. "Beautiful family," she said, gesturing to the pictures decorating his shelves.

He sort of perked up as he pointed everyone out. "That's my wife, Melony, and kids, Abigail and Sean."

"Your son is tall for his age."

"And I can't get him to play basketball. It's a shame." His head tilted to one side. "Enough about my family. What did you want to talk with me about?"

"Two things. I ran into Owen Shepard over the weekend." She glanced at her watch. "I'm meeting him at his office at three o'clock to discuss the letters you received from MAH."

"Interesting. He wants your help with the case?"

"Apparently." She lowered her voice. "I think he's more worried about DHI's reputation than he is about innocent people losing their lives."

"He hasn't bothered to return my calls, so I wouldn't know." Ben rubbed his chin. "The police are on the case now. I'm sure he realizes that."

She nodded. "I get the feeling he's hiring me to cover all bases—you know, show his board members that he's doing everything he can to find this guy."

"Well, this MAH guy means business. And if Owen Shepard doesn't take him seriously, more people will lose their lives."

"Once I know exactly what Shepard wants from me, I might need to pick your brain."

"I'm always happy to help. When I read this guy's letter, I thought he came across as genuine." Ben gave a halfhearted shrug. "I understood his frustration. I could relate with the fact that I would do anything to protect my kids."

"But his daughter is gone," Jessie said. "Killing people isn't going to bring her back."

After a short pause, Ben said resignedly, "The love we have for our kids can make us do crazy things."

Jessie found herself wondering if she should be worried about Ben. He'd lost some weight, and he seemed listless. "Are you all right?"

"Just a little tired. What else do you have going on?"

Jessie forced herself to let it go. "Seven years ago, at Mercy General, Ashley and Nick Bale gave birth to Dakota Elizabeth Bale, a healthy baby girl."

"Born August 22, 2010," Ben cut in. "Six pounds, twelve ounces. Taken within twenty-four hours of being born. Never to be seen again."

"Great memory."

"The irony," he said with a smirk. "Who hired you? I'm assuming it wasn't Nick Bale."

"It was his wife." She raised an eyebrow. "Why not Nick?"

Ben leaned back in his chair and tapped a pencil against the edge of his desk. "The abduction was a high-profile case. The media was all over Nick and Ashley Bale. I interviewed both of them, and there was something about Nick Bale that bothered me. You know, like a seed stuck between your teeth." He scratched the side of his neck.

"Are you saying you believe Nick might have had something to do with the abduction?"

He shrugged. "Just a gut feeling that still lingers in the pit of my stomach after all this time. I stayed on top of that case for over a year. I kept an eye on friends and family, but mostly I watched Nick. The guy made sure to always play the part."

"I'm not sure I understand."

"In my opinion, he was an emotionless, empty man. He rarely spoke. But stick a camera in his face, and he would become the grieving father the public expected to see. He seemed to crave attention and sympathy, and he got both in spades. Now, Ashley," he said, "was the real deal—a grief-stricken mother who wanted her child back."

Jessie made a mental note, then asked, "How does someone just walk out of a hospital with a baby?"

"Authorities discovered a grainy visual of a dark-haired woman leaving the hospital with a bundle held close to her chest. I know we had a copy of the video footage at one point since I watched it many times."

"I would love to get my hands on that."

"We might have a copy in our file room."

She frowned. "Ashley Bale gave me a binder filled with pictures and articles about the abduction, but there was only one article from the *Tribune*—written by Dustin Harrigan."

"Yeah, I took over the story after Dustin had some health problems. Between the two of us, there should have been close to a dozen articles."

"Strange."

Ben lifted a finger. "Hold on. Let me double-check." He grabbed his cell, chatted with someone on the other line, and then hung up. "Shirley is going to check the archives for me."

"I owe you," she said. "Again."

"You owe me nothing."

"That's not true."

His expression grew serious. "No more of this nonsense about me saving your life. You would have done the same for me had circumstances been reversed. We're good."

"So, how have you been?" Judging by the dark shadows under his eyes, he'd been working too hard. "Are you still having flashbacks?"

He nodded. "Everyone is convinced I'm seeing images from old crime scenes."

"You sound doubtful."

"Do I?"

She nodded.

Ben exhaled. "I have been wanting to talk to you about that day."

Jessie waited for him to continue.

"I guess you could say I've been struggling with everything that happened. I could have let the Heartless Killer go. I didn't have to kill him. I could have detained him and waited for the police. In fact, maybe that's what I should have done." He scratched the side of his neck again. "I saw you watching. I knew what I was doing, and yet I didn't stop."

Jessie looked him square in the eye and said, "I wanted to kill him, too."

"Thanks for that."

She shrugged. "It's the truth."

His cell phone buzzed again, and he picked up the call. When he was done, he stood and said, "Wait here. Shirley says she struck gold. I'll be right back."

After he walked away, Jessie got up and took a look around. She was surprised to see Colin through a glass wall. He wasn't facing her, but she had full view of his profile. He was inside a conference room with three officers and two men in suits. She figured the meeting had to do with the letters Ben had received.

Seeing him gave her an unexpected jolt as she remembered the way he'd held her in his arms on the dance floor. For a moment in time, she'd felt young and carefree. She knew he'd only been teasing about taking her through the car wash, but the idea had caused a fluttery feeling within. Both of their jobs required long hours. Colin had his daughter, Piper, to raise, just as Jessie had Olivia. It wasn't easy finding time for each other.

She looked away when she saw Ben returning with a large envelope. "Inside are copies of the pieces the *Tribune* published at the time. There's also a flash drive containing the video footage you wanted to see. If there's anything else you need, just give me a call."

"Thank you, Ben. I appreciate all your help."

She picked up her purse and pulled the strap over her shoulder. "I don't mean to stick my nose where it doesn't belong, but I get the sense that the images you see are causing you concern."

"No need to worry about me. I'm fine."

"I know you're okay, but if you ever decide to look into your past . . . you know, dig a little deeper, I would love to help. We make a good team. Together, we could visit the town where you grew up and talk to people, maybe even figure out what some of these images you're seeing are all about."

"You've got enough going on."

"I'm serious, Ben. Think about it."

THIRTEEN

With Higgins at her side, Olivia walked to Jessie's office to do some filing. Ever since her mother's funeral, she'd been feeling moody and depressed. She'd spent most of her life being angry at her mom for abandoning her only to find out she had been killed in a car accident on the night she'd disappeared.

The thought filled Olivia with guilt.

Sophie might not have been the best mother in the world, but she hadn't abandoned her after all. If she hadn't died that night, she would have come home, and they would have been a real family.

As soon as she unlocked the door and went inside, Higgins went straight to his bed in the corner and plopped down. The wire basket on top of the file cabinet was filled to the brim with papers. She left her bag on the chair in front of Jessie's desk. Before she could even get started, her phone vibrated.

There were text messages from her friend Bella. The usual stuff: **What are you wearing tomorrow? Did you hear about Noah and Mara? They broke up. Can you believe it?**

Without bothering to reply, she shoved her phone in her back pocket and grabbed the paper on top of the pile. It was a letter from an insurance company regarding an old workers' compensation claim.

Filing was a boring job, but it was the price she had to pay if she wanted to earn an allowance.

She thought about Bella. What her friend didn't know was that Olivia had been hoping Ryder would ask her to the upcoming dance. She felt bad about not telling Bella that she liked Ryder, especially since they used to tell each other everything. But Bella had been acting weird lately. The last time Olivia told her she liked a boy, Bella had blabbed her private business to half the school. When Olivia asked her why she'd done that, Bella had lied and sworn she never told a soul. But Olivia had seen the text Bella sent to another friend. She and Bella were still friends, but it just wasn't the same. She didn't trust her anymore.

"What are you doing?"

Olivia jumped at the sound of a voice and bumped her elbow on the filing cabinet. "Ouch!"

Higgins was on his feet, standing at attention, ready to attack. Olivia recognized the girl at once. It was Zee Gatley. Olivia had helped Jessie find Zee after she went missing. She felt as if she knew Zee even though they'd never met. According to Jessie, Zee suffered from a mental disorder. She experienced hallucinations and could be unpredictable at times.

"Hi. I'm Olivia, Jessie's niece."

"Oh. Cool," Zee said, her shoulders visibly relaxing. "I've heard about you."

"I've heard about you, too."

Higgins went to Zee, his stump of a tail moving side to side. She patted him on the head. "Did Jessie tell you I was crazy?"

Having no idea what to say to that, Olivia froze.

Zee laughed. "It's okay. I have schizophrenia, along with millions of other people in America. It's not as bad as everyone makes it out to be."

"That's good," Olivia said, at a complete loss.

Zee looked around the room. "Where's Jessie?"

"She's working another missing person's case—a baby snatched from the hospital seven years ago."

"That sounds exciting," Zee said, her eyes rounding.

Olivia nodded. "I heard you're working for Jessie now."

"Yep."

"Do you like it?"

"I'm watching a woman who claims she was injured at work. It's not as exciting as looking for a missing kid. Mostly I sit in my car all day. But, yeah, I like it."

"It's got to be a hundred times better than filing papers."

Zee glanced at the clock. "I have to go watch the woman's house for another hour and a half. Why don't you come with me?"

Olivia chewed on her bottom lip. She thought about calling Jessie, but then she remembered how busy she'd sounded when they had talked earlier. They would just be sitting in the car. What was the big deal? "What about Higgins?"

"Bring him along."

"You don't mind bringing me back here afterward?"

"No. Come on."

Olivia grabbed her bag and the dog, locked the office door, then followed Zee outside and across the street. She pointed to a blue Honda with a bent fender. "Is that your car?"

Zee looked that way. "No. Mine is the other blue car."

Olivia's mouth dropped open. "Is that a Tesla?"

Zee nodded. "My dad likes to spoil me."

The Tesla was a ridiculously sweet car. As soon as the door was opened, Higgins jumped into the back seat. Olivia slid into the passenger seat and hardly had time to fasten her seat belt before Zee sped off.

Higgins jumped between the seats and onto Olivia's lap. She rolled down the window so he could enjoy the air against his face. Less than ten minutes later Zee drove slowly down a residential street and pulled to the curb.

"Is that where the woman lives?" Olivia asked.

"No." Zee pointed straight ahead. "It's up the street a ways." She then climbed out of the car while it was still running, walked around the front, and opened the passenger door.

"What are you doing?" Olivia asked.

"I thought you might want to drive the car the rest of the way."

Olivia shook her head. "I don't even have my license yet. Besides, if something happened, Jessie would not be happy."

Zee snorted. "It's only a few blocks. Nothing's going to happen. You'll be fine."

Olivia wasn't sure what exactly possessed her to listen to Zee, but the next thing she knew she was sliding into the driver's seat and caressing the steering wheel.

Zee transferred Higgins to the back seat while she explained how everything worked.

Olivia's heart pounded as she released the brake and rolled slowly onto the street. By the end of the second block, she could come to a complete stop without jerking forward. Despite Zee's constant muttering, driving was surprisingly easy. She wasn't exactly sure what Zee was saying, but every sentence sounded as if it started or ended with "motherfucker" or "holy fucking shit."

If Olivia wasn't concentrating so hard on what she was doing, all the jibber jabber might have freaked her out. But she figured Jessie never would have hired Zee unless she trusted her.

"Oh my God," Zee said. "There he is!"

"Who?"

"Norton's weirdo neighbor. He's the one driving the four-door black Ford F-150 up ahead." Zee leaned forward. "Does he have someone in the truck with him?"

"I don't know," Olivia said, wondering why Zee thought he was weird but quickly deciding she really didn't want to know.

Zee pushed the button on her seat, making it move slowly backward until the headrest nearly hit the back seat.

Olivia's breath caught in her throat. "What are you doing?"

"I don't want the man driving that truck to see me. You need to follow him."

Olivia spotted the truck up ahead. "No way."

"Just a little farther so I can see who is in the car with him."

Olivia did as Zee asked, inwardly scolding herself all the way to the end of the road. "There is definitely a young girl in the car with him."

"How young?"

"I don't know. Fourteen or fifteen," Olivia guessed. "Oh, shit."

"What is it?" Zee asked.

"I'm coming up to a stoplight. No way am I going onto the main road." When she slowed down, a car that suddenly appeared behind her honked, long and loud, making her nervous. She stepped on the gas and followed the truck through the green light. "This is insane." She swallowed. "I'm going to crash. We're all going to die."

"You're doing great," Zee told her. "Pull over whenever you can, and we'll switch seats."

The car directly behind Olivia honked again before finally moving to the other lane and speeding around her. By the time they got to the next light, Olivia came to a stop right next to the truck. The young girl in the back seat looked out the window. Her eyes looked sad. As soon as the light turned green, the truck sped off.

Olivia kept going straight, looking ahead, hoping for a turn lane. "The truck is long gone. You can straighten your seat." It seemed every few seconds somebody found a reason to honk at her.

"If you don't speed up, you're going to get a ticket for going too slow."

Olivia sped up. Her heart was racing. By the time she pulled into the turn lane at the next light, she was feeling a tiny bit better. But then she made the mistake of looking to her left, where she saw a familiar face exiting the corner market, looking right at her. It was Grandpa! If he told Jessie he saw her driving, she would be grounded for life.

The second the light changed colors, Olivia stepped on the gas. The tires squealed as she made the turn. Less than a minute later, she pulled to the side of the road, shut off the engine, and said, "I'm done. Never again."

FOURTEEN

Jessie's meeting with Owen Shepard lasted thirty minutes. After he was called away, she spent an hour with his assistant, who was able to print copies of the letters that had been sent to Ben. The sheer number of complaints filed against DHI in the past three years alone would take months to sort through, but Owen had agreed to give her temporary access to their files stored online while she worked the case.

As she drove home, Jessie worried that she might have taken on more than she could handle. Not only did she have the usual requests to locate ex-spouses, do background checks on nannies, and find adoption records, but she was also working on the Ashley Bale case.

And what about Ben? She'd offered to help him, too. Ben had been having dark recollections since she'd first met him. Clearly he was conflicted. What struck her as odd was that he would remember dead people but not his own family. He had no idea if he and his sister had been close when they were growing up. He couldn't recall a thing about his parents or teachers or school or hobbies.

He'd once told her that after his accident he wasn't interested in looking back. But everything had changed after he'd strangled the Heartless Killer. It seemed he thought he might possess killer instincts. She'd been there when Ben killed the man. She could still envision the determined look in Ben's eyes, as if nothing could stop him, as if maybe he'd killed before.

But Jessie knew better. She'd worked side by side with Ben, and somewhere along the way they had formed a bond. She trusted him, and she was eager to help him so he could move on with his life.

She parked her car in the alley and then walked around to the front of the old house surrounded by a wrought iron fence with a rusted gate that no longer worked. Everything about the house shouted, "Help me!" But there was nothing she could do since she didn't have the time or the money to fix it. She had made a deal with the landlord. She wouldn't ask him to fix anything, and in return, he wouldn't raise the rent. Despite its condition, she was grateful to have a roof over her and Olivia's heads.

The front door creaked when she opened it. Nothing a little WD-40 couldn't take care of. Halfway up the stairs she smelled something wonderful. At the top of the landing, Higgins wagged his stump and ran over to greet her.

She put a hand to her chest when she saw that the table had been set and Olivia was cooking at the stove. "Am I in the right house?"

Olivia whipped around and shook the spatula at her. "You scared me! Everyone keeps creeping up on me today."

"Everyone?"

"Oh." She blushed. "Yeah, you and Zee."

"Zee Gatley?"

"How many Zees do you know?" She laughed. "Zee came to your office while I was filing and scared me just like you did."

"You were filing?"

Olivia made a face.

Jessie put her things on the coffee table. "I'm teasing. What did Zee want?"

"Nothing really. We introduced ourselves, and then we talked a little. I really like her. She even said she could take me shopping tomorrow after school if that's okay."

Jessie crossed her arms. "Zee Gatley offered to take you shopping?"

Olivia snorted. "What's wrong with that? I thought you liked her."

Jessie anchored her hair behind her ear. "I do like her. But Zee isn't like most people. In fact, she doesn't enjoy other people's company."

Olivia let out an exasperated puff of air. "Well, I guess she's changed. She knows you're busy, so she offered to take me to the mall. It's not that big of a deal."

"I don't think it's a good idea. She hasn't been driving very long."

"If her dad trusts her with a brand-new Tesla, I think I'm safe."

"How do you know what kind of car she drives?"

"I looked through your office window and saw her drive away in it."

Olivia's eyes narrowed. "Why are you so suspicious lately?" She turned back to the stove.

"You're right. I'm sorry. I've had a crazy day."

"So I can go?"

"Sure, fine, but text me when you're back home."

"Where will you be?" Olivia asked.

"I need to interview some people about the Ashley Bale case."

"Is that the woman whose baby was taken?"

Jessie nodded.

"That's so sad. What sort of person would take someone else's baby?"

"I wish I knew," Jessie said.

Fifteen

After dragging Brad Elton into the warehouse, he'd been so exhausted that he'd gone home to sleep and take a shower.

He'd returned five minutes ago and now stood a few feet away from the dark-haired executive, watching him struggle to get his hands free from the ropes.

"Let me go," Brad pleaded. "Please."

Without any of the passion he'd had when he'd first come up with his plan to teach DHI a lesson, he ignored the man. He walked over to his bag and pulled out his camera. He set up his equipment on the table that he'd left there after videotaping Tyler McDonald.

He scratched his head, looked around, then dragged the metal fold-up chair to the table and sat down.

"Please don't hurt me," Brad said, over and over again. "Why are you doing this?"

That's a very good question, he thought.

So many emotions had been running through him since Hannah died: Rage. Frustration. Confusion. At the moment, though, he was numb.

He stopped what he was doing and finally met Brad's gaze. His shoulders fell as he decided not to bother videotaping him. He didn't want to deal with him at all. But he also didn't want to leave the man here all day. Best to get it over with now.

"My family and coworkers are probably looking for me," Brad said, as if he sensed something had changed. "If you let me go now, I'll write you a check. Name your price, and I'll write the check." His eyes flashed. "Better yet, we can go to an ATM. You pick the place. Somewhere private. Just tell me how much money you need, and the cash is yours."

"I don't want your money."

Brad's head fell back against the cement wall.

"You're all the same. Greedy bastards who think everything can be taken care of with a wad of cash. Money isn't going to help you, Brad. What do you think about that?"

"What do you want with me?"

"How long have you been with DHI?"

"Thirteen years," Brad said.

"That's a long time. Did you ever meet any of your clients?"

"You mean DHI's clients?"

"Yes."

"I work in finance, but, yes, I believe I met a few."

"I'm sure the only clients you ever met were CEOs of large corporations."

Brad Elton's face paled. His arms began to shake.

"Am I right?"

Brad nodded. "Yes."

"You don't have a wife or kids."

"No, but I have a girlfriend and a brother and both parents. Please don't do this. Let me go."

"Did anyone you know ever suffer from cancer or any sort of illness that would require long-term care?"

"No," Brad said. He quickly added, "Not that I know of."

He shut off the camera. He was done. Tired of talking. Tired of listening. Just plain tired. He wanted to go home, wasn't sure if he'd ever come back to this place. He stood, went to his bag, slipped on his gloves, and then picked up the SIG.

Brad began to struggle with his bindings again. "What are you doing? Don't hurt me. I'll do anything you ask."

Ignoring him, he attached the suppressor as the man rambled on, begging for his life just as he'd once begged for Hannah's life. Stepping closer to Brad, he raised his gun and fired. One shot in the head. It was over.

After he turned away, he stopped, closed his eyes, and began gulping air. His anger had subsided. His hands shook as he put the gun to the side of his head. He could be done with it all right now. One shot. And it would be over.

But then he thought of Hannah.

How she'd suffered.

Shooting himself before he'd accomplished what he'd set out to do would be the coward's way out.

And then it struck him—an idea. He wasn't sure why he hadn't thought of it before. Adrenaline took over, pumping his body up with renewed energy. He put the gun away, pulled off the gloves, and rushed over to the laptop on the table. Once it was booted up, he searched the Internet.

Hannah had taught him everything he knew about computers. She'd always been an exceptionally bright child. He knew most parents felt that way about their children, but Hannah was gifted. At a young age she'd had a highly developed vocabulary and the ability to learn new words easily. She could read before she entered school. Her brain had been like a sponge, easily absorbing and incorporating everything brought to her attention. They'd had her tested, just to be sure, and the chances of a child her age having her IQ were one in five thousand.

She certainly hadn't acquired her abilities from him, he thought as he typed with one finger.

Once he had the keywords plugged into the search bar, it only took twenty seconds to find what he was looking for—pictures of Owen Shepard's family. He and his wife, Catherine, had three children. Two boys and a girl. His daughter, Emily, was in her early twenties and had recently started her second year at UC Davis.

He needed to know more about Emily Shepard.

Social media.

Hannah always said that everything you needed to know about anyone was on Facebook, Instagram, and Twitter. It didn't take him long to learn that Emily Shepard shared an apartment with two others. She also walked to campus every day.

He used Google Maps to find directions from the house he was renting to the university. The fastest route, despite the usual traffic, would take him about twenty-five minutes.

For the first time since Hannah's death, he knew exactly how to get Owen Shepard's attention. But first he had a body to dispose of.

SIXTEEN

Jessie knocked on the door of Apartment 6B at Woodlake Apartments off Marconi Avenue and then waited, hoping Kendra Sue Foster was home. At the time of Dakota's abduction, Kendra Sue had been a volunteer at the hospital.

The door cracked open, and Jessie saw a pair of dark eyes peering out at her.

"Who is it?"

"My name is Jessie Cole. Are you Kendra Sue Foster?"

"Maybe I am, but I'm not the one knocking on your door."

"I'm a private investigator, and I have a few questions about the Dakota Bale case."

"Are you kidding me?"

"No," Jessie said. "It's important that I talk to you."

"Go away."

Jessie quickly recalled one of Ben's favorite tactics and used it. "Twenty dollars for five minutes of your time."

Seconds ticked by. Jessie waited for the door to be slammed in her face. Instead, it came open. Before Jessie could step inside, the woman put out a hand, palm up.

Jessie dug out her wallet and handed the woman a twenty.

Kendra Sue peeked outside and looked from left to right. "Come inside. I don't want anyone to see you hanging around my place."

Jessie did as she said. The door closed behind her.

"Your five minutes have begun."

Jessie wanted to get a look around. She pointed at the misshapen couch. "Mind if I have a seat?"

Kendra Sue crossed her arms over her chest. "Have at it."

Jessie looked at the wall of bookshelves and at the knickknacks on the coffee table before taking a seat.

Kendra Sue remained standing. "Three more minutes."

"Do you have any idea who took Dakota Bale from the hospital seven years ago?"

"You think I wouldn't have told the police if I did?" Before Jessie could respond, the woman added, "You people are something else."

"I'm not sure what you mean."

"I was a volunteer at the hospital," she said, her tone sharp. "A *volunteer*. When was the last time you volunteered to do anything at all?"

"I can't remember."

"Exactly. I loved my work at the hospital. I used to bring booties that had been hand-knitted by my grandmother and give them to sick kids. Volunteering gave me purpose." Her eyes welled with tears. "And then Ashley Bale's baby was stolen, and my life was turned upside down."

"I'm sorry. I didn't mean to upset you."

"Then why did you come? Do those people still think I had something to do with their baby's disappearance?"

"No. But they are still searching, and I wanted to talk to everyone involved at the time."

"It was a witch hunt," Kendra Sue said. "Ashley Bale may not know it, but I saw her watching me 24-7. For a half a year she was my shadow. Do you know what that feels like to be sentenced without any proof?"

Jessie shook her head.

"She ruined my life. For whatever reason, that woman was convinced I had something to do with her—"

Jessie and Kendra Sue looked to the front door when it opened. A man stepped inside.

"What's going on?" he wanted to know.

He was big. His long, dark hair was streaked with silver. He wasn't much taller than Jessie, but he had a barrel chest and thick arms and legs.

"Are you crying?" he asked Kendra Sue.

"No," she said nervously, shaking her head for good measure.

He turned on Jessie. "Who are you?"

Jessie didn't like the way his fingers had rolled into fists at his sides. "I'm Jessie Cole. I had a few questions for Kendra Sue, but we're finished. In fact, I was just about to leave." She stood.

"That's right," Kendra Sue said.

Jessie headed for the door, but the man was standing in front of it. "Hold on," he said, refusing to move out of the way. "You had questions about what?"

Jessie forced herself to stay calm. "I'm investigating the Ashley Bale case. The only way to do that is to interview people who knew Ashley Bale or who happened to be at the hospital that day."

His eyes narrowed as he shoved a meaty finger into her collarbone.

Jessie tried not to panic. In a stern voice she said, "Keep your hands off me."

Kendra Sue tried to get between them. "Stop it. She's leaving!"

He grabbed hold of Kendra Sue's shoulders and began shaking her like a rag doll. "You never should have let her inside!"

Jessie grabbed his arm and tried to pull him away. It was clear he was hurting Kendra Sue, and she had to do something.

He let go of Kendra Sue and turned his attention on Jessie. Before she could make a run for it, he picked her up by the waist and tossed her into the bookshelf. She experienced a jolt of pain as she fell to the ground. Books and picture frames toppled over and rained down around her. She used her arms to shield her head.

Kendra Sue grabbed the man's arm and pulled him away.

There was glass everywhere. Jessie picked up the bigger pieces, along with a broken frame, and then pushed herself to her feet. As she set the picture aside, she saw that it was a young girl, two or three years old. She looked at Kendra Sue. "Is this your daughter?"

"Yes. She died from leukemia."

"She thinks that's the fucking Bale baby," the man growled. "Don't you get it? They'll never be through with us. Never. I'm done with this bullshit." He stormed away and disappeared into the other room.

Kendra Sue rushed to the door and opened it wide. "You need to get out of here, quick. He's going for his gun."

Jessie heard a closet door open and close. "What about you?"

"Don't worry about me. It's you he wants outta here. Hurry," she said. "Run!"

Jessie rushed out of the apartment and down the stairs to the parking lot. Voices sounded behind her as she unlocked her car and climbed in behind the wheel. Afraid he might fire at her, she crouched low as she started the car and drove off, not bothering to fasten her seat belt.

Once she was out of harm's way, Jessie buckled her belt. It took her a while to calm down. She thought about calling the police but decided against it. Kendra Sue seemed adamant about staying, and Jessie didn't want to cause her more problems than she already had. But who the hell was that child in the picture?

She'd read through the file Ashley Bale had given her. She'd also searched her databases for anything she could find regarding Kendra Sue Foster. There had been nothing noted about the woman ever having a child of her own.

———

With binoculars in hand, Zee focused in on the Norton house. The curtains on the front window had been pushed to the side, but so far nothing was happening.

At least not in the front room. Zee shifted the binoculars to the right until she could clearly see the sixteen-pound rock she'd left at the curb earlier that morning. She rotated the focusing ring until the corner of the fifty-dollar bill she'd stuck under the rock as bait came into focus.

She chuckled at her genius.

What better way to get someone to lift a heavy object than to stick money under it? Sure, she could have left a five or even a twenty, but she figured a fifty would guarantee at least an attempt on Lindsay Norton's part to lift the rock. A few minutes later she set the binoculars aside and reached for the brown paper bag sitting on the passenger seat. Her neighbor, who also happened to be Dad's girlfriend, had packed her a lunch. Zee hadn't wanted to take it from the woman, but Dad had given her one of his you-better-do-it kind of looks, and so she'd had no choice.

She looked inside the bag.

It was only ten thirty in the morning. She had eaten leftover lasagna for breakfast. She should be full.

Of course you're hungry. Everyone gets hungry when they're bored out of their minds.

"I'm not bored," she told the voice in her head as she reached into the bag and pulled out a sandwich, three chocolate chip cookies, and a small can of apple juice. She lined everything up neatly on the console. The sandwich was lumpy peanut butter slathered between two slices of wheat bread. She took a bite and chewed as she stared straight ahead. Before she had a chance to swallow, she nearly choked when she recognized the truck coming down the road. It was the neighbor, the same guy she'd seen grabbing that woman.

After he passed by, she sat up and watched him through the rearview mirror. His garage door slowly opened. As he pulled in, she saw not one but two small heads pop up. And then the garage door closed, and she couldn't see a thing.

What the hell was going on?

Who were those kids? If they were his kids, wouldn't she see them running around outside every once in a while?

Mind your own business, the voice said. *You want to keep your job, don't you?*

She fidgeted in her seat, wondering what she should do. Jessie had said she shouldn't do a thing unless there were signs that someone was in danger. She hadn't seen the kids' actual faces, not that it would have made a difference. They could be his niece and nephew visiting for the day.

What does the man do for a living? she wondered. And just as that thought crossed her mind, she saw Lindsay Norton's door open.

About time, Francis said.

There were many voices floating around inside her head, but she'd named only the three loudest. Francis was the troublemaker. Lucy was the bitch. And Marion was the clever one.

Zee grabbed the camera and fumbled around with it, her heart pumping fast as she readied the camera, pushed the lever to video, and began shooting.

Lindsay Norton did what she'd done every day that Zee had watched her. She headed for the mailbox. Today, though, Lindsay Norton appeared to have a bit of a bounce in her step, which was unusual. She had done her hair and was wearing a flowery dress. Zee had never seen her wearing anything but sweat suits. After she got her mail, she headed back toward the house.

Zee groaned.

Told you it wouldn't work.

Lindsay Norton stopped suddenly and made an about-face. She was looking right at the rock.

Bingo!

The woman walked slowly as if she wasn't sure what she was seeing. With the mail in her hand, she bent over and tugged at the money, but it didn't come free, so she set the mail on the ground, then lifted the rock all the way to her chest as if it weighed two pounds instead of sixteen. After setting the rock aside, she was finally able to grab the money, gather her mail, and then hurry back to the house.

Lindsay Norton didn't appear to be injured at all. Zee pushed "Rewind," then hit "Play."

It was blank. She'd hit the wrong button.

You're an idiot, Lucy said.

"Yeah," Zee said. "I think you might be right."

SEVENTEEN

After looking for Jessie at her office, Ben walked to her house and knocked on the door. Before he could knock a second time, he saw Jessie pull up to the curb. He sensed something was wrong when he saw her grimacing as she climbed out of the car. As he approached, he noticed scratches on the side of her face and neck. Blood seeped through her shirt on the back of her shoulder, but he figured it best if he kept that to himself since she had a severe aversion to blood. "What happened?"

"I made the mistake of paying Kendra Sue Foster a visit."

The name sounded familiar, but he couldn't place it.

"She was the volunteer at Mercy General when Dakota Bale was kidnapped," she added.

"Ahh."

After she grabbed her purse, he followed her to the front door. Limping along, she fumbled with the keys.

"Let me help you." He took care of opening the door, then held on to her elbow as she made her way up the stairs. "Sit down and I'll get you a glass of water." He knew Jessie well enough to know she was a stubborn one, and so he was surprised when she let him take over.

Through the kitchen window, he could see Higgins in a small gated area in the backyard. He handed Jessie the water. "Where do you keep your bandages?"

"Why?"

"No reason."

"How bad am I bleeding?"

She saw right through him. "Barely a nick on the back of your shoulder. Where's the first aid kit?"

"In the bathroom. Top shelf."

It was easy enough to find. He returned to the main room. "I'll need you to pull your shirt a few inches off your right shoulder."

She tried to take a peek over her shoulder.

"Don't look. I don't want you fainting on me."

"Okay, Dr. Morrison." She turned back the other way.

"I'm married to a nurse," he informed her. "I know my way around antiseptic and a bandage."

She tugged on her shirt and kept it out of his way while he worked. "How bad is it?"

"Hardly a nick, like I told you."

"You're such a liar."

"You can't handle the truth. Now let me clean this up while you walk me through exactly what happened."

"Kendra Sue didn't want anything to do with me," Jessie told him. "Thanks to a little trick I learned from you, though, I offered her a bribe, and she let me right in."

"Glad I could help. What were you hoping to accomplish?"

"I just wanted to take a quick look around the apartment, ask her a few questions, see what sort of vibe I got from the woman. But then her husband came home, or maybe it was her boyfriend—I really have no idea. As soon as he discovered I was there to ask questions about the Bale case, he went ballistic."

"He hit you?"

"Ouch."

"Sorry."

"He picked me up and tossed me into the bookshelf. All sorts of knickknacks fell on top of me."

"And then you left?"

"I made the mistake of commenting on a framed picture of a little girl."

Surprised, he asked, "Foster had a child?"

She nodded. "According to Kendra Sue, their daughter died from leukemia. The man didn't like Kendra Sue talking to me. After he rushed off to find his gun, I thought that might be a good time to get out."

"Good idea. How old was the child in the picture?"

"Two or three." She glanced over her shoulder at him. "Are you thinking what I'm thinking?"

"Absolutely."

"It shouldn't be too difficult to find out if there are any records of the woman giving birth," Jessie said.

He nodded his agreement. "Did you have your gun on you when you decided to pay her a visit?"

"No. I'm still on probation."

"For how much longer?"

"Until the end of the month."

Finished applying first aid, he stepped away. "All done. You're good as new."

She covered her shoulder.

"I wouldn't get it wet for a few days. Have Olivia look at it tomorrow and change the bandage then."

"What do I owe you?"

He knew she wasn't serious, but it made for a good segue as to why he'd come to see her. "That's why I'm here."

She looked him square in the eyes. "Really?"

"Really. Let me put this stuff away, and then I'll explain." When he returned, he sat on the edge of the chair across from the couch where she sat. Elbows propped on knees, he leaned her way. "I need your help with a missing person's case."

"Okay."

"But only if you promise that when we're done, you'll consider us even. No more talk about 'owing' me anything."

She stuck out a hand. "Deal."

"Deal," he said as he took her hand in his and shook it.

"So what's this case all about?"

"Me."

Jessie gave him a bemused smile. "Ahh. I see." It was quiet for a moment while she appeared to mull things over in her mind. "What if—" She stopped midsentence. "Never mind."

"No holding back," he urged. "If we're going to do this, I want everything on the table right from the beginning."

She rubbed her chin between her thumb and index finger. "What if I discover something about you that I don't think you'll like?"

"It doesn't matter. We both know how this works. There were plenty of details you learned about your sister that I'm sure you wished you'd never found out." He shrugged. "If we're not truthful with each other, what would be the point?"

"Okay. You're absolutely right. I'm going to treat you like any other client, which means I need to know everything you already know about your past. Family, friends, schools you attended, where you grew up."

"I'll put everything I know about my past on paper. It won't take long. I know both of my parents passed away before I turned thirteen. A coworker recalled my telling him that I was raised by my grandmother. But I don't know her name, and I don't recall anything about her." He raised his hands. "That's about it."

"You've told me more than once that you were fine not knowing about your past. What made you change your mind?"

"Last night I got a call from my sister."

Jessie's brows arched in surprise. "I thought she had no interest in getting reacquainted?"

"I never knew why she pushed me away. The few times I met with her after the accident it was clear she wasn't comfortable being around me."

"And you have no idea why?" Jessie asked.

"No."

"What did she say on the phone?"

"That she'll be in Sacramento this weekend and wants to meet my children."

"Interesting."

"Very. I invited her to stay with us, but she declined. She'll only be spending one night at the Hyatt Regency downtown. She wanted to make sure my wife would be at the house on Saturday when she visits."

"I wonder why now, after all this time?"

"I wondered the same thing," Ben said.

"The Hyatt is right around the corner," Jessie said. "Mind if I try to talk to her?"

"You're reading my mind."

"Perfect. Any questions that you would consider to be off-limits?"

"No. But it might be best if you hit her up on Sunday after she's visited with the kids," Ben said.

"I agree. Maybe after she meets your family, she'll be more willing to talk about you."

"Let's hope," he said. "I should have more details later, flights, etcetera, so you'll know when she might be leaving the hotel. I'll text you with that information if that works for you?"

"Perfect."

He stood and then snapped his fingers. "I almost forgot. I got my hands on something that might be of use to you in the Ashley

Bale case." He pulled a folded piece of paper from his coat pocket and handed it to her.

She read it, then looked at him. "What is it?"

"After Dustin Harrigan at the newspaper found out Ashley Bale had hired you to continue the search for her daughter, he gave me Rene Steele's phone number. She was a nurse at the hospital when Dakota Bale was taken. As we discussed, Dustin had been keeping tabs on most of the key players for months after the baby was taken. The last time he talked to Rene, he said she came across as skittish and was unwilling to talk. Dustin told me he did everything he could think of to get her to open up, but she remained tight-lipped."

"I haven't seen her name come up in Ashley's files. Why did Dustin consider her to be a key player in the first place?"

"He said there was something about Rene Steele that wasn't right. Journalists write about the facts, but we get there by feelings and instinct." Ben exhaled. "Dustin said authorities interviewed every nurse at the hospital that day, whether they worked in the nursery or not. Rene was not being singled out, but she acted as if she were. A little digging revealed she'd been working twelve-hour shifts, so Dustin figured she might be suffering from burnout."

"But then?"

"But then she began to act erratically."

"How so?"

"Late to work and then missing work altogether, which, according to her coworkers, was unusual. A few months after the abduction, she got a DUI. In Dustin's opinion, that changed everything."

"How?"

"Because she'd been sober for thirteen years. Dustin's question was and still is, why did she start drinking after thirteen years? Did it have something to do with the Dakota Bale abduction?"

"I'm assuming Dustin talked to authorities about his suspicions?"

"Many times," Ben said. "Investigators kept an eye on her and questioned Rene and her mother more than once. But ultimately the police believed Rene was innocent. A nervous Nellie, perhaps, but innocent. She was also well liked by the hospital staff and had recently won the Daisy Award given to nurses who stand out in their field."

Jessie held up the piece of paper. "Tell Dustin thanks. It won't hurt to give her a call."

He nodded. "After the DUI, Rene retired," Ben added. "She was fifty when she moved to Auburn to live with her mom. And that's all I've got."

Jessie pushed herself to her feet and walked Ben to the top of the stairs that led to the main door. "I'll let you know how it goes," she said as she watched him leave.

"Take care of that shoulder," he said. "I'll text you later about my sister's schedule."

Eighteen

Olivia was in the car with Zee. Thankfully, Zee had not asked her to drive. They were on the highway, headed home after shopping. They had spent the first hour at a gothic clothing store. Olivia had tried on jewelry and leather pants, and she really liked a red-plaid and black-lace party dress, but she knew that would never fly with Jessie. After that, they'd gone to the mall, where Olivia had ended up with a simple look that Zee thought was boring: jeans, a sleeveless top, and a pair of flats.

"If it's a Halloween dance, you should go all out and dress up."

"Nobody dresses up at these things, trust me."

"Well, you should at least get a nose ring before the dance," Zee said.

Olivia laughed. "Jessie would yank it out the minute I walked through the door. Besides, nose rings look like they would hurt."

Zee muttered something indistinguishable under her breath. It sounded a lot like "Boogie boogie boo." Although Olivia was getting used to Zee's outbursts, she wondered what it must be like to be Zee. She decided to ask. "What's it like to have schizophrenia?"

"I don't know. What's it like to be a skinny fifteen-year-old with freckles?"

Olivia made a face.

"This is just who I've always been," Zee said. "My behavior confuses most people, but it's all normal to me. I have good days and bad days. If I don't take my medicine regularly, the anxiety can be overwhelming, and sometimes I get depressed." She giggled. "I do have a lot of voices swirling around in my brain: Lucy, Marion, and Francis. Some people think that if you have schizophrenia, you have split personalities, but that's a myth. I'm not Jekyll and Hyde."

Olivia remembered reading about the voices when Zee went missing and Jessie was hired to find her. "Are the voices talking to you right now?"

"Yep. They have no idea why you're here, since I'm basically a loner and don't hang out with too many people."

"Must be sort of cool having built-in friends," Olivia said.

"I never thought about it that way. But I would have to say they're more like sisters. They get on my nerves most of the time." Zee laughed.

"What's so funny?"

"Francis thinks you're a spy. She doesn't trust you."

"What about the others?"

"Lucy doesn't care one way or another, and Marion isn't sure what to think about you."

"Well, I'm certainly not a spy," Olivia said.

"We'll see."

Olivia had no idea what Zee meant by that, but she decided it probably wasn't a good idea to ask too many questions. At least until she noticed that Zee took the wrong exit. "Where are we going?"

"There's something I need to check on. It will only take a moment."

Minutes later, they were driving down a residential street lined with houses that all looked the same. Zee pulled to the side of the road and shut off the engine. She pointed at the two-story house across the street.

"Does that house belong to the person you've been watching every day?"

"No," Zee said. "Remember the weirdo we were following the other day?"

Olivia would never forget. "What about him?"

"That's his house," Zee said.

"Why are we here? What if he sees us?"

"I did some research. His name is Rudy Archer, and he's the person we *should* be watching."

"How do you know?"

"I'm an investigator now. I know these things."

Olivia rolled her eyes. Zee wasn't making any sense.

"Seriously. I signed up for more than one database that markets to the investigative industry. I have a bucketload of information right at my fingertips. Social media is helpful, too, telling me more about the guy than I wanted to know."

"Like what?"

"For starters, Rudy is into ferret racing."

"I like ferrets," Olivia said.

Zee mumbled something under her breath. It took Olivia a second to realize she was singing a tune.

"Rudy Archer is forty-two, an only child, and he has never been married."

"Why is that weird?" Olivia asked.

"Because every time I see the guy, he's with people much younger than him. The first time I saw him, he was grabbing a girl by the arm. She didn't look happy, but before I could do anything about it, they disappeared back inside his house."

"Did you tell Jessie about the man?"

Zee nodded. "She said if he wasn't harming anyone, to let it be." She opened the car door.

Olivia's heart dropped to her stomach. "What are you doing?"

"I want to see if he's home. I might be able to peek into his garage on the way to his front door."

"What if he sees you?"

"I'll say I'm looking for an old friend."

Before Olivia could protest, Zee shut the door and ran across the street. Unsure of what to do, she looked around the neighborhood. A car passed by and then made a left at the stop sign. Farther away, she saw two people on bikes before they disappeared down another street. She glanced at her phone, then jumped when it buzzed. It was Jessie. She sighed and picked up the call.

"Hey there, kiddo. Where are you guys?"

"We're on our way home now."

"How did it go?"

She watched Zee disappear. From where she sat, Olivia couldn't see the front door. "Um, yeah, it was fun."

"Glad to hear it. Would you ask Zee if she wants to have dinner with us tonight?"

"Oh, um, okay." Olivia pressed her phone against her chest and pretended Zee was in the car with her. "Hey, Zee, Jessie wants to know if you want to join us for dinner?"

Flustered, Olivia looked around the inside of the car, grabbed a receipt sitting on the console and crumpled it in her fist as she answered in a very bad imitation of Zee's voice. She then raised the phone back to her ear. "Bummer. She can't join us tonight. Her and her dad are doing something."

"Are you sure everything is okay?"

"Positive. I'll be there soon. Love you!" She disconnected the call, feeling sick to her stomach when she couldn't see where Zee had gone. What was she doing? She was going to get them both into a lot of trouble.

Annoyed, Olivia climbed out of the car, shoved her phone into her back pocket, and walked briskly across the street. Zee wasn't at the door or behind the shrubs lining the walkway. This was insane. Her adrenaline spiked as she walked up the pathway leading to the front door and tried to peek through the decorative glass. She thought she saw movement. And then the door opened, and she completely lost her ability to speak, or think, or do anything other than stand there like an idiot.

"Can I help you?"

It must be him, the man Zee was worried about. He was creepy-looking. Bug-eyed, with a bad comb-over, and sweat marks under his armpits. A camera hung from a strap around his neck.

Zee wasn't the only one with voices in her head. The voice inside her head shouted, *Get out of there!* "Oh . . . gee . . . I thought this was my friend's house. Sorry to bother you."

He leaned against the doorjamb as if he wanted to have a long conversation. "Who's your friend?" he asked before she could do an about-face and run off.

"Oh, nobody really," she said.

"Your friend is nobody?"

She forced a smile, since she was pretty sure he was trying to be funny, but instead he came across as even creepier. And then he lifted his camera and looked through the lens at her.

She didn't move. Her feet were like lead weights as he pushed a button. She heard a click.

"Did anyone ever tell you that you have a beautiful smile?"

She wasn't even smiling. Finally, her brain kicked into high gear and told her muscles what to do. She backed away from the door, nearly tripping over her feet to get away from him.

"You were born to be in pictures," he said, making no move to go back inside.

Without another word, she turned toward the road. She was going to be sick. There was no way she was going to cross the street and climb inside Zee's car and just sit there, so she made a right. Walking as fast as she could, she stayed on the sidewalk. Her heart pounded against her chest. She kept glancing over her shoulder. When she couldn't see the man or the house any longer, she broke into a run.

By the time Olivia pulled out her phone, ready to call Jessie, Zee drove up beside her. She put her phone away, opened the door, and climbed in.

Zee sped off. "That was close."

Close? Olivia buckled her seat belt, then crossed her arms and said nothing.

"Are you okay?"

No. She wasn't okay. She was angry and scared and frustrated all at once. "I don't want to talk about it."

"Are you a Cancer?"

Olivia scrunched her nose. "What?"

"Your sign. You're a Cancer, aren't you?"

Olivia ignored her.

"I only ask because Cancers are usually sensitive, too cautious, moody, and emotional."

Olivia narrowed her eyes. "What are you? A Leo?"

Zee became suddenly animated. "Are you into horoscopes, too?"

"No," Olivia said, still annoyed by what had happened. "I just took a guess. Sounded like a sign that might fit your personality."

Zee laughed. "You're a very funny person."

"That ferret lover took a picture of me," Olivia blurted. "I think he's a real creeper, and you should stay away from him."

They drove the rest of the way in silence, which suited Olivia just fine.

When Zee finally turned onto the street leading to Olivia's house, she nudged Olivia's arm. "Is that Jessie standing outside on the curb?"

Oh, crap. Olivia sat up and inhaled as she smoothed her hair in an attempt to look as if nothing was wrong. Zee was oblivious to it all. Apparently she didn't have to follow rules set by her father or anyone else.

Jessie opened the passenger door for Olivia. "Are you sure you can't stay for dinner?" Jessie asked Zee.

"What are you having?"

"Pork chops and mashed potatoes."

"No-go. I don't eat meat. I don't do dairy, either. I'm a seagan."

"A seagan?" Jessie and Olivia asked at the same time.

"Vegan, but I eat fish sometimes."

Olivia grabbed her packages and would have shut the door, but Jessie held tight to the frame and leaned into the car. "I might need to pull you from the Norton case," she told Zee.

"Why?" Zee asked. "I'm about to crack the Norton case wide-open!"

Olivia inwardly groaned.

"I need your help with locating someone," Jessie told her.

Zee straightened. "The missing baby?"

"No. A new case. It will be tedious work, but it's important that we find this person."

"Is he or she dangerous?"

Jessie nodded.

"I'm in."

"Can you meet me here at noon on Sunday?"

"No problem," Zee said. "But if it's okay, I'd like to spend one or two afternoons next week wrapping up the Norton case."

"That's fine. I'll see you Sunday." Jessie shut the door, and Zee sped away.

"Is there something I can do?" Olivia asked after Zee drove off.

"I could use all the help I can get," Jessie said, seeming glad to see that Olivia wanted to get involved.

Nineteen

He wiped sweat from his brow as he took a moment to observe the work he'd done. Since he planned to keep his next victim much longer than the other two, he'd spent the past few days using the back corner of the warehouse to make a small room with four walls. He'd always been handy with a hammer and a nail.

The end result was striking: a clean and simple design. The two back walls were made up of the original cinder block. The other two walls were mostly wood, although each wall had a large section of paned glass that would allow him to view his prisoner at all times. Since the twelve-foot walls didn't come close to reaching the ceiling, it would be easy to have conversations with his prisoner.

Inside the ten-by-ten space, he'd constructed a wooden bench that could be used as a place to sleep. Also included were a portable toilet and two large coolers packed with Gatorade and yogurt.

The perfect "home away from home" for Owen Shepard's daughter, Emily Shepard.

He picked up a simple side table he'd made from leftover wood and moved it next to the futon, which he'd set up a few feet away from one of the windows. This area would serve as his own personal space when he visited.

Feeling satisfied with how things were progressing, he grabbed a water bottle and a bag of potato chips and plopped down on the cushioned seat, staring at the room as he ate. He ate the last chip, smacked his lips, then glanced at his watch.

Time to go home, take a shower, and get some sleep.

If everything went as planned, Emily Shepard would soon be wishing for him to end her life, and her father would get to witness every second of her demise.

TWENTY

Ben carried a pile of dirty dishes into the kitchen and began to wash them in the sink.

Melony came up beside him holding a dish towel, and together they watched through the large window overlooking the backyard as his sister, Nancy, played Frisbee with Abigail and Sean.

Back and forth the plastic disc went until Nancy tossed it too high. The disc wobbled through the air and landed in the middle of the pool. The dog jumped into the water, making them all laugh.

It had been a perfect day.

Earlier, they had enjoyed a picnic lunch at the school where Abigail played soccer. Her team won. Back at home, Ben and Melony had left Nancy alone to hang out with the kids. Abigail and Sean had been on their best behavior, excited to meet their aunt Nancy for the first time. They showed her around the house, told her stories about their hobbies and friends. Abigail played Aunt Nancy a song on the piano, and then Sean tried to upstage his older sister with an exciting card trick he'd been practicing.

"It's hard to believe your sister hasn't been a part of our lives for the past ten years," Melony said, breaking into his thoughts. "She fits right in, and the kids adore her."

"I was thinking the same thing. And yet she's definitely done everything in her power to keep her distance from me."

"I noticed that," Melony said. "At the school, I did get a chance to sit alone with her for a few minutes. I asked her about her life in Florida. She said her husband was in construction, and she was a legal secretary for a large firm. They are happy. That's all I got out of her."

Finished with the dishes, Ben dried his hands. "I am going to try to talk to her on the drive back to the hotel. Who knows if or when I'll ever see her again?"

"If you put too much pressure on her, she might not return."

"Then so be it," Ben said. "She can't even look me in the eye, Melony. If I can't have a real conversation with my sister, then I don't see any reason for her to ever come back."

The kids ran into the house just then, asking if Aunt Nancy could spend the night. Melony tossed the towel on the counter. "Of course she can."

Ben rushed to the sliding door to stop the wet dog from coming inside. "We're going to have dry you off first, buddy."

Nancy squeezed through the door. She wasn't yet forty, but her face had a hardness to it that made her look much older. It wasn't the fine lines or the hint of sadness in her eyes, but the unyielding way she carried herself and the hard set of her jaw and shoulders that made him think she'd seen her fair share of tragedy.

When she caught him looking at her, she quickly turned the other way.

He slid the door shut.

"We really would love to have you stay," Melony said over the children's heads as she dried them with a towel. "The guest room is ready for you."

"I appreciate the offer," Nancy said. "I've had a lovely time, but I have an early flight, and I'm eager to get home."

The kids moaned and groaned while Melony cheered them with promises of ice cream. Nancy didn't waste any time gathering her things. "I'm going to head outside," she said. "I have a car coming in a few minutes."

"I thought I would drive you back to your hotel," Ben said.

She ignored his offer and went to hug the kids goodbye. He and Melony shared a long look, but he wasn't ready to give up. After waiting for his sister near the front entry, he walked her out, shutting the door behind him.

"Melony and I are very happy you took the time to come and spend a day with all of us, and I don't want to come across as pushy, but can you tell me why you're so put off by me?"

Nancy stopped halfway across the walkway leading to the sidewalk. For the first time all day, she looked directly into his eyes. "I'm sorry about your accident and the amnesia, but in my mind you are the lucky one."

"I'm not sure what you mean."

"I wish I could erase all of my childhood memories."

The few times he'd talked to her, she'd been as vague as she was being now. Frustrated, he asked, "Why is that?"

She shook her head. "It doesn't matter any longer. The important thing is that your kids are great, and you and Melony seem happy. You were smart to bury the past and move on."

"I don't think I can do that anymore."

An owl hooted in the distance.

He could see by the way she kept glancing toward the street that she was eager to end their conversation and leave. "I really hope you change your mind," she finally said, "because if you start digging into your past, I can guarantee that you won't like what you find."

Weighed down by helplessness, his shoulders fell. He didn't just want to know where he came from; he *needed* to know. "I realize it's impossible for you to know what it's like to suffer from amnesia. But I'm asking you, as your brother, if you can somehow find it in your heart to tell me one thing?"

When she met his gaze again, he stared at her, unblinking, wishing he could merely look into Nancy's eyes and remember—something, anything at all. But there was nothing. No jolt of awareness. No glimmer of recognition from his past. "Were you and I ever close?"

She seemed to ponder his question before she answered. "Not really. I don't think you were capable of being close to anyone. I know, in your own way, that you cared about me, though." She closed her eyes, making it clear she'd already said more than she intended.

"Is this about Mom and Dad?"

Her eyes snapped open, and she wiped a tear from her cheek. "Our parents were not good people."

A car came around the corner. Her body slumped in obvious relief, her posture losing its rigidity. As she turned toward the street, he settled a gentle hand on her shoulder. "Please. Give me something. Help me understand. Did they hurt you?"

Her gaze fell on his hand before moving back to his face. "I don't want to go back there. I can't. I'm sorry."

Before she climbed into the car, he said, "Will we see you again?"

Another long pause followed. "I don't think so. You have a beautiful family, Ben. Enjoy every moment with them. I wish you nothing but the best."

She climbed into the car and disappeared as quickly as she had come.

When Ben walked into the house, he looked at Melony, who was in the middle of dishing up a treat for the kids. He gave a subtle shake of his head, letting her know Nancy wouldn't talk. "I'm going for a drive," he said. "I won't be long."

"We're having ice cream, Dad!"

Someone, most likely his wife, had dried the dog and let him inside. Abigail and Sean looked happy. This was his family, he thought, and he loved them. Why couldn't he let his past go? "You guys enjoy. I'll be back soon."

Melony didn't look pleased, but she didn't try to stop him.

He walked to his van parked on the street. It was only six thirty. The sky was bluish gray, the air a soothing sixty-five degrees. He climbed in behind the wheel and started the engine. He wasn't sure exactly where he was going, but he knew he needed to get out and clear his mind.

By the time he merged onto Highway 80 heading west, he was more certain than ever that he had done the right thing by asking Jessie Cole to help him look into his past. Good or bad, he needed to know where he came from.

It bothered him that seeing Nancy and talking to her had failed to summon memories from his past. Why would he recognize Jessie's sister, Sophie, after seeing her image on *Cold Case TV*, but not feel even a stirring of recognition when he looked into his own sister's eyes?

Twenty-five minutes later, for the second time in a matter of days, he found himself driving down a now-familiar street. In the distance he saw the brick building covered in graffiti. As he approached the tract development where cookie-cutter housing had been built over more than a few square miles, something odd happened. A spasm above his left eye quickly turned into an uncomfortable tingling in his forehead. It was as if something was stabbing his frontal lobe with dozens of needles. Unable to drive, he pulled to the side of the road, turned off the engine, and closed his eyes.

Thirty seconds later, the pain in his head subsided. When he looked up, he saw a man walking backward, struggling as he dragged a limp body across what appeared to be a construction zone. The cookie-cutter houses were gone. In their place were rows of homes in various stages of construction; some with only a cement foundation, some framed, while others were nearing completion. Barricade tape surrounded the area.

Slowly, Ben climbed out of the vehicle. The man walking backward looked like a young version of himself. How could that be?

He blinked a couple of times, but nothing had changed. He was losing his mind. Glancing around, he hoped someone would drive by so he could stop them and ask them what had happened to the houses that were here just minutes ago.

The man dragged the body around the side of a house that had a finished exterior. The vision was nothing like anything he'd seen before. It wasn't a film clip in his mind's eye. It was real.

Ben shut the van door and followed the same path the man had taken. By the time he came around the corner, he saw the younger version of himself standing near a hole close to the house. He'd left the limp body lying on the ground nearby.

Was the other man dead? Ben wondered. Horrified by the thought, he moved close enough to recognize the unmoving body as DJ Stumm.

This was absolutely crazy.

He didn't know whether to call the police or his therapist, but before he could pull out his phone, DJ's hand shot out and grabbed hold of younger Ben's ankle, yanking him to the ground.

They rolled around in the dirt, wrestling until younger Ben kicked DJ in the head, giving him time to get to his feet and grab the shovel. The other man tried to scramble away, but younger Ben stomped down hard on DJ's leg.

"You're crazy!" DJ screamed.

"You killed your family." Young Ben's voice sounded calm.

"My wife was a controlling bitch. She needed to die. Why do you care? Were you fucking the whore?"

Young Ben didn't flinch. "You tortured and killed your own children."

"Their mother needed to be taught a lesson."

"And so do you."

Ben gripped the sides of his head and squeezed as Young Ben lifted the shovel and came down hard, crushing the other man's skull. Young Ben picked up his pace, stripping the clothes from DJ and then dragging him by the feet to the hole. The hole wasn't wide enough. Young Ben disappeared and promptly returned carrying an ax.

Ben watched in horror as he chopped DJ into pieces so he could fit the man into the hole before filling it with dirt. When he was done, he wiped his brow with his forearm, put the shovel away, and scooped up DJ's clothes.

Ben followed Young Ben back to the street. His skin tingled when he saw Young Ben open the back of a van identical to the one he still drove, lift the hatch to the compartment where the spare tire was kept, and place the ax inside. Still carrying DJ's clothes, he went around to the front of the van, climbed in, and drove off.

Heart racing, Ben stood unmoving in the middle of the street. When he looked at the construction zone, everything was back to normal. The barrier tape and hazard signs were gone. Cars and mature trees lined the street.

Lights were on inside the homes. He could see movement and the flickering lights of TVs through many of the windows. Ben turned. His gaze settled on his van.

He jogged that way, opened the rear doors, lifted the metal lid, and breathed a sigh of relief when he saw the spare tire. He took a moment to calm his nerves. About to shut the rear doors and get going, he paused. He lifted the tire out and put it to the side. Underneath he saw a tattered and stained rag. He reached for the rag. There was a hard object wrapped inside. It was heavy. Slowly he unraveled the cloth until there was nothing left but a bloodied ax.

Working fast, he wrapped up the ax, shoved it back inside the compartment, and placed the tire on top of it. He shut the rear doors, walked quickly back to the front of the van, and got in. For a moment he wondered if the ax had been a hallucination. Surely he would have seen it before now?

Climbing out of the van, he walked to the back and flung open the doors. Again he dug out the tire and then reached inside and felt the ax beneath the cloth. He swallowed. He didn't know what to do or what to think. But he knew that he wanted to get as far away from this place as possible.

Back behind the wheel, he started the engine and drove off. Until recently, he hadn't thought he had a violent bone in his body. Not once had he put a hand to either one of his children; the idea had never crossed his mind. But instinct told him that what he'd just witnessed was not a supernatural event. What he'd seen was his past, a stored memory that hadn't decayed with age.

He made a left and then a right at the stop sign. Before he merged onto the main road, bright lights swirled behind him.

Shit. All he could think about was the ax. What if they found the ax? His heart rate spiraled out of control as he pulled over. In the side mirror he watched an officer walk toward him with a flashlight. Ben rolled down his window and was greeted by a blinding light.

"Ben Morrison?"

The light disappeared. Through narrowed eyes, Ben saw a face. It was Jessie's friend. "Colin Grayson," he said. "Is there a problem?"

"Why don't you step outside?" Colin told him.

His instinct was to question the officer. Instead, he opened the door, stepped outside, and followed Colin to the back of his van. Did he know something?

Ben's shoulders tensed as he grabbed hold of the handles to the back door. He couldn't recall whether or not he'd closed the cover to the spare tire.

"What are you doing?" Colin asked.

Ben gave him a puzzled look. "I thought you wanted to have a look inside."

"No. I just wanted to show you that not only do you have a taillight out, but it looks as if your back tire is extremely low. I thought you'd want to take a look for yourself."

Breathe, Ben told himself. *Breathe.*

"Are you okay?"

"Yeah. No," Ben said, shaking his head. "It's pretty safe to say that I've had a crazy day." The puzzled look on Colin's face worried Ben, so he added, "I met my sister for the first time." He shook his head again when he realized Colin wouldn't know what he was talking about.

"Your amnesia," Colin said, catching on. "Jessie has mentioned bits and pieces here and there. I guess your reunion didn't go so well. I'm sorry."

"Thanks." Ben gestured at the taillight. "So, what do we do now? Do you need to write me up for the taillight problem?"

"No need. Just try to take care of it in the next few days." Colin pointed at the tire. "Want me to help you change your tire?"

"No. No. I'll take care of it."

"What are you doing out this way, if you don't my asking?"

Again Ben had to collect himself. "It's sort of a long story, but it has to do with an old case. The killer has been on the Most Wanted list for twelve years, but recently they discovered his bones."

"DJ Stumm," Colin provided.

"That's the guy. Killed his wife and two kids. Larry said I was obsessed with the case, but I have no recollection of it." He raked a hand through his hair. "After the debacle with my sister, I needed to clear my head, and here I am."

"Did it help?"

Ben thought of the ax in the back of his van. "Not in the least."

TWENTY-ONE

Jessie picked up her phone. According to Ben's text, his sister's flight was at 11:25 a.m. out of Sacramento. On the off chance Nancy would eat an early breakfast before checking out of the hotel, Jessie had been sitting in the front lobby for the past hour.

She glanced at the clock above the reservation desk. It was eight o'clock. If worse came to worst, she figured she could jump in a cab with Nancy and talk to her on the way to the airport. But she was glad she wouldn't have to resort to trapping the woman in a cab when the elevator door slid open and Ben's sister, Nancy, stepped out and made her way to the coffee shop. Jessie kept her distance as she followed her that way. Since she didn't want her to head right back to the elevator, she would wait until she had ordered her meal.

After the server took Nancy's order and filled up her coffee cup, Jessie approached her. "Hi, Nancy. My name is Jessie Cole. I'm an investigator in the area, and I was hoping I could talk to you. I will only take a few minutes of your time, I promise."

The woman's face paled, and in that moment Jessie noticed that she looked a lot like her brother. The eyes and mouth.

"What is this about?" Nancy asked.

"Your brother."

"Is he in some sort of trouble?"

"No. He's asked me to help him look into his past, and I knew you were going to be in town, so I thought I'd stop by and see if I could find you."

Nancy looked around worriedly. "Is he here?"

"Who?"

"My brother."

"Oh no. Just me. I promise."

"You make a lot of promises."

Jessie thought about that for a moment. "Yeah, I guess I do."

Nancy waved a hand toward the empty seat. "Don't let me stop you."

Jessie hooked the strap of her purse on the chair across from Nancy and took a seat.

"You didn't just happen to run into me, did you?"

Jessie raised a questioning brow.

"How long have been waiting for me to make an appearance?"

"Over an hour."

Nancy took a sip of her coffee. "Well, at least you're honest."

"I try to be."

"Did Ben put you up to this?"

"No," Jessie lied. "It was my idea. In fact, he didn't want me to bother you. He was afraid I might compromise any chance of you two getting reacquainted."

"Have you talked to him since yesterday?" she asked.

"No." And that was the truth.

"Well, he did ask me why I've been avoiding him, and I told him the truth. That he should be glad he has no memories from his child-hood. They were grim years," she said before taking another swallow of her coffee. "I also told him to let it go. He has a lovely family, beautiful kids, so why screw it all up by digging into the past?"

"Did he mention that he's been having flashbacks?"

"No. What sort of flashbacks?"

"He sees what he calls film clips or film reels of people and scenes he believes could possibly be memories from a time before the accident."

"I see."

When Nancy failed to say anything more, Jessie asked, "Is there anything you can tell me that would make me understand why you're so dead set on keeping away from him?"

Her shoulders slumped forward. "As I told Ben last night, I always thought he cared about me. But overall, he was never the touchy-feely sort. In all those years I don't think he ever tried to have a conversation with me. He was four years older than me, so I've always tried to keep that in mind, but I can tell you that the man I met yesterday was not the same Ben Morrison I once knew."

Before Jessie could ask her to explain, she continued. "I'm going to tell you a story about Ben. For me it sort of sums him up. Do with it what you wish. Maybe it'll help you understand who Ben is or was—maybe it won't. We grew up in a small town called Clarksburg about twelve miles from here. Ben had few friends." She released a cynical laugh. "Who am I kidding? Ben had no friends. He was twelve at the time, and I was eight. On this particular day, one of the neighborhood moms left their son to play at our house while she went to run an errand."

Nancy stopped talking when the server brought her food. After he left, Nancy resumed where she'd left off. "I remember the day vividly. I think I was fascinated at the idea of Ben talking or playing or doing anything at all with another human being, so I watched the two boys from a window. Not five minutes went by before I saw the other boy break two good-size sticks from a tree and hand one over to Ben. The boy then appeared to explain something to my brother in great detail.

The way he held the stick and jabbed it this way and that, it seemed he was telling Ben that their sticks were swords, and they were going to have a sword fight. It started off well enough. The boy took a playful jab at Ben, missed, then took two steps back.

"I was more than pleased when Ben did the same. This went on for a couple of minutes. The whole thing was very entertaining, and for the first time ever, I really thought Ben was enjoying himself."

"He wasn't a happy child?" Jessie asked.

"That's the thing," Nancy said. "I really couldn't tell you. Ben didn't have a lot of expression in his face. I never knew if he was happy or sad. But on this particular day, I could tell that he was feeling something."

Nancy ate some of her breakfast while Jessie wondered where this story might be going. She used her napkin to wipe her mouth and then sipped her coffee before she said, "And then the boy poked Ben in the eye." Nancy closed her eyes as she inhaled. Clearly she was having a difficult time.

"Was Ben hurt?"

Nancy shook her head. "I don't think so. Ben dropped his stick and held his eye, but he wasn't crying."

"What did the other boy do?"

"He attacked my brother. First he used the stick to jab Ben in the stomach. When Ben did nothing to protect himself, the boy kept at it. Jabbing, jabbing, jabbing. It was awful."

Nancy's head fell forward slightly as she collected herself. Jessie felt responsible for the pain Nancy was experiencing, but she didn't try to stop her from going on.

"I wanted to stop it," Nancy said, "but I was afraid."

"Of the boy?"

"Of everything. The boy, Ben, what would happen if Mom or Dad found out. So I just kept watching. And it was the very next jab that changed everything."

Jessie had no idea where Nancy's story was headed, but the color had drained from her face, making Jessie tense. "What happened?"

"Ben ripped the stick from the boy's clutches and whacked him across the neck and the face and then every part of his body, over and over again. When the boy fell to the ground, Ben tossed the stick to the side, jumped on top of him, and began to strangle him."

"Oh no."

Stuttering, Nancy choked out the words. "I was frantic. I used my fists to pound the window, but he never looked over at me." She held Jessie's gaze. "I had to do something, so I ran outside and tried to pull Ben off the boy." She swallowed. "Finally, Ben saw that I was crying, and that's when he let go."

"And the boy? Was he okay?"

"I thought he was dead. Next thing you know, I hear sirens in the distance." She clutched her stomach. "Turned out Mom had watched it all but never did anything to stop it."

"But she called 9-1-1," Jessie said.

"Yes. She did that. And the boy lived, but only after spending a long time in the hospital—critical condition. He nearly died. Ben was kicked out of school. Social Services made a few appearances."

"How awful it must have been for you to witness that."

Nancy waved away any sympathy. "I told you that story because for me that sums up the brother I once knew. That was the day cold, emotionless Ben came alive," she said flatly.

Jessie had wondered what the point was, but the story didn't tell her much. One event, no matter how horrible or wrong, did not make a person. It certainly didn't give Jessie any idea of their family life. "Do you believe Ben's behavior had anything to do with his environment?"

"If you're talking about our parents, yes. I'm sure of it. As I told Ben last night, our parents were not good people, and I refuse to talk about either one of them." Nancy picked up her fork and picked at her food but didn't take another bite.

"So what made you come to see Ben now, after all this time?"

"I'm pregnant." She folded and unfolded the napkin in her lap. "I wanted to meet Ben's children and find out if I should be worried about possibly giving birth to a demon child."

Jessie was left speechless. *Demon child?* She could never tell Ben what she'd heard this morning, and she had a feeling Nancy knew she wouldn't.

"I'm not a bad person," she said.

"So your meeting with Ben's family was a test of sorts?"

She nodded. "I needed to know if his children showed any telltale signs of what I saw growing up. Not just in my brother but also in my mother and father."

Jessie was overcome with a sudden protectiveness toward Ben. "As you mentioned before, you were so much younger than Ben at the time. I don't see how one or two events could frighten you enough to want nothing to do with him. He's a loving father and a good man."

"I lived it. I was there. Ben did not suffer from mood changes and depression. What I'm talking about had nothing to do with hyperactivity or acting out. Ben was simply Ben, cold and emotionless. I can't describe him any better than that."

"What about holidays or birthdays? Was he different then?"

Nancy's shoulders slumped, and Jessie knew she was testing her limits. "I think you're asking me if there were happier times for Ben and our family."

Jessie nodded.

"The answer is no. Holidays brought out the worst in my mother." Nancy's mouth tightened before she blurted angrily, "When Mother got frustrated, she kicked the dog. If I protested, she'd kick harder. So I learned to bite my tongue and pretend not to care."

Jessie's stomach tensed.

"Nothing was ever good enough for her. It would usually start with a complaint. She'd say the house was a pigpen and then start throwing things, whatever she could get her hands on. On one particular Christmas, she broke the dog's legs, or ribs, or maybe both. I don't recall. When the dog yelped, she simply got meaner, did things to the poor animal that still keep me up at night."

Nancy looked down at her plate. "That was the only time I saw Ben stand up to our mother. He was big for his age and had been towering over her for a while. He came between her and the dog, put his hand on Mother's face, and pushed her slowly away from the dog until she was up against the wall. He then turned around, scooped the poor animal into his arms, and left the house."

No wonder Nancy had avoided talking to Ben about their childhood. It was the stuff of nightmares. "Did Ben get the dog help?" Jessie asked.

"I only know that I never saw my dog again." She wiped a tear from her face. "I haven't told my own husband what went on back then. I can't talk about this any longer. I'm finished."

"I understand. I'm sorry. Before I go, I was wondering how your visit went. I've never met Ben's children. What did you think?"

Nancy perked up a little bit. "They're lovely. And I can't wait to get back home and share the news with my husband."

"That you met your brother's children and thought they were great kids?"

"Oh no. He thinks I'm in Sacramento on business. I'm excited to tell him that I'm pregnant and that we're having a boy."

"I see," Jessie said, although she didn't see at all. "Congratulations." Jessie stood, thanking her again before she walked away. Jessie's insides roiled as she made her way to her car.

Ben's sister was pregnant, but she'd been too terrified by all that had happened growing up to tell her husband the news. Not until she made sure Ben's children had turned out okay.

For the first time since meeting Ben, Jessie wondered if leaving his past in the past would be the better choice. What if his sister wasn't being melodramatic? What if his memories did finally return, and the ugliness of his childhood brought him nothing but pain?

TWENTY-TWO

Jessie, Zee, and Olivia all sat in front of their laptops at the dining room table in Jessie's house. Jessie had logged each of them into DHI's database using her temporary log-in.

"There are thousands upon thousands of complaints, grievances, and appeals," Olivia noted. "Are we going to read all of them?"

Jessie nodded. "We're going to skim through every complaint and look for clues." She reached for the whiteboard and held it up. "We'll start by making a list of keywords. For instance, after reading the letter, we know that this father's grievance concerns his daughter, who was ill. So *daughter* would be a keyword." She wrote the word *daughter* on the whiteboard, and then *female*.

"How do you know the father wrote the complaint and not the mother?" Olivia asked.

"Because within the body of the letter he talks about losing his wife in an accident."

"Ahh. Got it."

"Let's all read the letter again and then brainstorm other keywords we might look for while reading."

After a few minutes, Olivia said, "'Diagnosed at twenty-one' and 'lumps and swollen joints.'" Jessie wrote them on the whiteboard along with two of her own: "suffered for months" and "died too young."

"Experimental drug," Zee added.

"Great. If you come up with more, write them down. There were approximately sixteen hundred grievances in the past two years. Each grievance has a link." Jessie pointed at Olivia. "You start with the first five hundred. Zee can take five hundred and one to one thousand. And I'll take a thousand and one to fifteen hundred."

"What about his signature, MAH?" Olivia asked.

"Good point. If we find a complaint written by anyone with the initials *MAH* or *MH*, then add them to the list and highlight the initials. Anytime you find a complaint with one of the keywords, write down the name of the person who filed the complaint along with the number assigned by DHI."

"The first three complaints on my list," Olivia said, "are Medicare hospital discharge appeals."

"That makes our job easier," Jessie said. "As soon as you see that, move on to the next. I also see a lot of policy cancellations due to nonpayment."

Surprised by Zee's silence, Jessie looked that way and saw her lips moving rapidly as she read through the complaints. Jessie was grateful to have her help.

For the next six hours, they worked quietly. A few hours in, Zee had moved to the couch. Olivia had only stopped on two occasions to take Higgins outside.

At eight o'clock Jessie told them it was time to call it quits. Olivia had school in the morning, and Zee had a thirty-minute ride home. The good news was they had worked their way through nearly one-third of the complaints. The bad news was that between all of them they had over three hundred names that would need to be looked at once they were finished going through the list.

———

The next morning, Jessie rubbed her temple as she pondered her workload. Although the DHI case was a current threat, the police and the feds were working hard to find the killer. Not only had Jessie agreed to help Owen Shepard, she also had an obligation to Ashley Bale to continue working on the abduction of Dakota. She would spend the mornings interviewing people who had worked at the hospital at the time Dakota was born. And at night, she and the girls could continue to work through DHI's list of complaints.

Jessie looked through her file on the abduction case. There were three women she'd wanted to talk to: Rose Helg, Kendra Sue, and Nick's cousin Wendy Battstel. According to her notes, Wendy had never married. DMV records showed her living in Colfax off Highway 80. She was a Realtor and worked from home. It took Jessie a minute to find a website with her picture. She had curly red hair, green eyes, and a friendly smile. Jessie grabbed her purse and headed out the door. Across the street she noticed a man sitting in his car. The engine was running. When he saw her looking his way, he sped off before she could get a good look at him. Strange.

An hour later, she turned onto Grass Valley Street in Colfax, a city that covered 1.4 square miles of land and sat at the crossroads of Interstate 80 and State Route 174. Wendy's house was a log cabin surrounded by pine trees. As she passed by, looking for a place to park, she saw the garage door open. In her rearview mirror, she watched an old Ford truck pull out and drive away.

Jessie made a quick U-turn and caught up to the truck. Although she couldn't see who was driving, she decided to follow the vehicle. Colfax was a small town. If it was Wendy, Jessie hoped she wasn't going too far.

Moments later the truck pulled into the Village Market. Jessie found a parking spot and watched the door open and the driver jump to the ground. It was definitely Wendy Battstel. The curly red hair was hard to miss.

Instead of making her way into the market, Wendy walked around to the back seat and opened the door. The last thing Jessie expected to see was a little girl, about three years old, climb out of the car. Hand in hand, Wendy and the child disappeared inside the market. Jessie thought about following them inside, but she decided to wait and follow them home instead.

Fifteen minutes passed before they exited the store with a paper bag filled to the brim with groceries. Wendy opened the back door, and the little girl climbed inside.

Jessie was about to start her engine when she saw a bright-colored rubber ball roll out of the car and into the parking lot. The little girl jumped out and set off after the toy just as a car parked across from Wendy began to back out. Jessie's heart skipped a beat when she saw that the driver wasn't looking.

Jessie jumped out of the car and yelled, "Stop!" as she raced toward the little girl, waving her arms above her head. The driver's windows were closed, and he was oblivious. She knew she had to do something. Still shouting, Jessie scooped the girl into her arms at the same moment the driver slammed on his brakes. The tires squealed in protest, and the little girl began to cry.

The driver got out of his car, apologizing and explaining that he hadn't seen her. Wendy was frantic by the time she realized her daughter had run off. She ran toward them. The little girl reached out pudgy arms for her mother.

"What happened?" Wendy asked as she took her daughter and held her tight.

The driver got into his car, and Jessie ushered Wendy back to hers so the man could safely back out.

"I had just pulled in," Jessie told her, "when I saw your little girl chasing after a ball that had rolled across the parking lot."

Wendy's face paled. "Thank you. I don't know how I failed to see her leave the truck." She raked a hand through tangled hair, then glanced at her watch. "Shit. I'm late for an appointment."

"I'm just glad everyone's okay." Jessie gestured across the parking lot. "I see her toy. Let me grab it for you." By the time she returned to the car, the little girl was strapped in her seat. Jessie handed the woman the ball. "Here you go."

"For Thithy," her daughter said, reaching for it.

"Thanks again," Wendy said as Jessie headed back to her car.

Once Jessie settled in behind the wheel, she inhaled and took a moment to calm down. Seeing that car so close to hitting the little girl had been horrifying. Wendy was obviously busy. Jessie decided she'd have to come back in a few days and try again.

Back on the highway, Jessie called Zee.

"Jessie Cole Investigations," Zee said. "How can I help you?"

Jessie smiled at Zee's greeting. "Are you in the car?"

"Yes, I am. What can I do for you?"

"I need information on two women. Since you mentioned having access to new and improved databases, I figured—"

"Give me the names and tell me what you need?" Zee said, cutting her off midsentence.

Jessie spelled out both names. "I need to know if Kendra Sue Foster ever married, gave birth, or adopted a child of her own. Same goes for Wendy Battstel."

"Is that it?"

"That's all for now. Call me if—"

The call was disconnected.

As Jessie drove along, she saw a blue Honda in the rearview mirror. It looked like the same car she'd seen outside her office earlier that morning. A minute later, the Honda exited the highway. Her shoulders relaxed.

It wasn't until she was nearing her exit forty minutes later that she spotted the Honda a few cars back. "Not cool," she said aloud. Instead of getting off the highway, she stayed at a steady sixty-five miles per hour, heading west.

The Honda continued on her same path.

Her phone rang. It was Zee. Using voice activation, Jessie picked up the call.

"Kendra Sue Foster was briefly married at nineteen years of age," Zee said. "To James Foster. That lasted six months. Although it appears she kept his name on most official documents, she was born Kendra Sue Cunningham, and she—"

"I'm being followed," Jessie said. "I'll call you right back."

"Who's following you?"

"I don't know. The windows are tinted, and I haven't been able to get the number on the plate."

"Are you close to home?"

"Yes. Why?"

"I'm in Sacramento in front of Norton's house, which isn't far from your office. If you can come this way, you could pull over. If he passes you by without stopping, I'll take over from there."

Not a bad idea, Jessie thought. "Okay, what's your exact location?"

After Zee gave her the address, Jessie plugged the information into her navigator. "Let's both stay on the phone," Jessie told her, "so I know what's going on. Okay?"

"Ten-four," Zee said. "Since I have you on the phone, Kendra Sue Cunningham did, in fact, give birth almost two years after Dakota Bale was born. So the reason you couldn't locate any records was because of the name on the birth certificate."

"Impressive," Jessie said.

"Yeah. I'm good at this. I'm not sure how long minimum wage will cut it."

"We'll discuss your pay at another time," Jessie told her.

"The other person you asked about, Wendy Battstel, adopted a kid. My guess is that it was one of those illegal transactions."

"How could you possibly know that?"

"E-mails. Lots of back-and-forth correspondence between Wendy and a sleazy lawyer who has since been disbarred. She paid the man a hefty sum."

"How could you have possibly gotten hold of that kind of information?"

"The easiest way is phishing, you know, fooling people into giving you account information so that you can log on to their PC. But I didn't even need to bother with all that. People like Wendy are pretty lackadaisical about passwords. Got it on the third attempt—12Wendy34. You've never hacked into someone's e-mail or bank account?"

"Please tell me you've never done that," Jessie said.

"I've never done that."

Jessie sighed. She couldn't worry about that now. "We'll talk later." She glanced at her rearview mirror as she took the next exit and pulled to a stop at the light. The Honda had fallen back, and for a few seconds she thought he might have continued on the highway. No such luck. There he was. As the Honda drew closer, the light turned green, and she hit the gas.

"Are you there?" Jessie asked Zee.

"Yeah. How close are you?"

"Another minute or two, depending on the lights."

As Jessie arrived at her destination, she could see Zee's car parked at the side of the residential street. "I'm going to go to the next block and then pull over."

"I got an idea. Maybe I should pull out immediately after you pass and let him hit me."

"Absolutely not. Don't do anything to put yourself in danger. Do you hear me, Zee?"

Silence.

"Zee?"

"Okay. Okay. I'm not a child. Oh, there you go. Hey there!"

Jessie did not glance Zee's way as she passed by. In fact, she questioned her decision to get Zee involved in the first place. "Do not pull out immediately," she warned Zee.

"Don't worry. I've got this."

Jessie rolled down her window, pulled to the side of the road, and readied her pepper spray. If he pulled over, too, she would get out of the car and attempt to talk to the driver to see what was going on. But the Honda sped up and passed her right by. Zee passed by a few seconds later.

"I didn't get a look at him," Jessie said. "Follow him, but don't get too close."

No response.

"Zee, are you there?"

She looked at the dashboard and saw that Zee had disconnected the call. *Damn.* She decided to sit there for a moment and see if the Honda came back around. Five minutes went by before she called Zee again. No answer.

Twenty-Three

Emily Shepard opened her eyes. She was on her side, lying on cement flooring. Her head throbbed, and drool slid down the side of her mouth. Groggy, she pushed herself from the ground until she was sitting up.

Her stomach roiled. She was going to be sick. Looking around, she crawled to the Porta Potty, opened the lid, and barfed until she was dry heaving. Every part of her shook as she pulled away from the toilet, then scooted backward until she was leaning against the wall. She pushed loose strands of hair out of her face as she looked around. Where was she?

The last thing she remembered was being late for class and rushing from her apartment. Across the street, she'd spotted a gray-haired man, maybe early sixties, with crutches, struggling to lift a package. It was obvious he was having trouble, and so she'd offered to help. He'd graciously accepted.

He'd made a big deal about whatever was inside the box being fragile. When she'd leaned into the trunk, trying to be as careful, she'd taken a blow to the back of her head and blacked out.

She reached a hand to the spot where she'd been hit and grimaced. There was a knot the size of a small peach. It was tender to the touch. Looking around, she saw two windows, one to the left and one to the right. From her worm's-eye view, there was nothing but gray cement walls beyond.

From the looks of it, a room had been built inside a bigger room, possibly a warehouse. The space she inhabited was about the size of the apartment room she shared with a roommate. There was a built-in bench and a cooler to her right. On the other side was the portable toilet. As her brain assessed the situation, panic set in, clogging her throat and making it difficult to breathe. That man had planned the whole thing. He knew someone would try to help him out. It was obvious he'd gone to a lot of trouble preparing the room. He meant to keep her here for a while. How long? A few days? Weeks? Maybe even months?

Oh, God, no.

Pushing herself from the floor, she held still until she was steady on her feet. She walked slowly to one of the windows and peered out. There was a futon and a table. Her backpack sat on the floor nearby. Inside her backpack was her phone and pepper spray. She needed to get her things.

The window was a large pane of glass. It didn't open. She went to the door situated between the two windows. There was no handle. She launched her body into the door, putting her weight into it, but it didn't budge. Above her head, she saw nothing but rafters at least twenty feet overhead.

She moved along the walls, pushing all the while, looking for a way out. When she found none, she'd had enough. "Let me out of here!"

Back at the window, she pounded her fists on the glass, hoping it would break. She screamed, long and loud. "Where are you? What's going on? Why am I here?"

There could be a front lobby. If she screamed loud enough, somebody would hear her. By the time she gave up, her throat burned. She went to the cooler and tossed open the lid. Inside, she found Gatorade and yogurt. She kicked the cooler, then turned it upside down, emptying the contents onto the floor. Lifting the cooler, she used it to try to break the glass.

It was no use. Another idea struck her. She grabbed the cooler, placed it on top of the built-in bench, then climbed up on the cooler and reached above her head. She would need to jump at least three feet to reach the top of the enclosure. She bent her knees, readying herself. The cooler creaked beneath her weight.

"You're going to hurt yourself," came a voice.

She got off the cooler and peered through the glass. It was the same man who had pretended to be injured. He was walking fine. "What happened to your crutches?"

"I think you know the answer to that. The crutches were an act to get you here."

"If you come near me, I'll scratch your eyes out."

He nodded.

"I will," she said. "I'm stronger than I look."

His silence made her angry. "Who are you? Just another old pervert acting out his kidnapping fantasies? Is that it? Your wife won't fuck you any longer, so you had to find someone young enough to be your daughter?"

She didn't wait for a response. Instead, she grabbed one of the yogurts from the floor, peeled off the foil top, and used her fingers to smear it all over the glass in order to obscure his view. She didn't want to look at him. Neither did she want him to be able to watch her every move. Thick globs of yogurt slid slowly down the glass before dripping onto the floor.

"I wouldn't waste that if I were you," he said. "You're going to get hungry, and I won't be doing any more shopping for a while."

She opened another one and did the same thing until she could see only a hazy figure through the glass. "I want out! I'll starve myself. I'm not going to sit in here and let some creepy fuck watch me with his beady little eyes."

"I didn't bring you here for the reasons you're thinking. We'll talk when you've calmed down."

"I want to talk now!"

"If you want to clean the windows, there are paper towels under the bench."

"Fuck you."

Through the other window she saw him take a seat on the futon and begin to read a pamphlet.

She opened a Gatorade, sat on the bench, and drank the entire bottle in a few long gulps. Her stomach growled. Her boyfriend was fond of telling her she was way too trusting. She'd always thought he was too cautious, too untrusting. It pissed her off that she'd proven him right.

Under the bench, just as he'd said, were paper towels. Angry for getting herself into this predicament, she wondered how she was going to escape.

Out of the corner of her eye, she saw the creep standing right up close to the clean window, staring in at her, no doubt. With a quick glance his way she realized he was setting up some equipment. As anger turned to fear, she kept her gaze on the floor. She didn't want him to know she was scared. "Why am I here?" she asked without turning his way.

"Because of the president and CEO of Direct Health Inc."

She whipped around. "My father?"

He worked while he talked. "Yes. Owen Shepard is the reason I brought you here. He's also the reason my daughter is dead."

"My dad is a dick, but he's not a killer."

In an instant, his face reddened and the veins in his neck bulged, making him look like a crazed maniac. He jabbed a finger at her, hitting the glass. "Owen Shepard isn't just a killer. He's a mass murderer. Refusing to cover medication because it's experimental is a death sentence for many."

He was furious. Every word came out sharp and accusing.

"Had the roles been reversed, and he was forced to watch you die, would he have made those rules? I don't think so," he said, returning to the task at hand.

"My dad isn't the only one who makes those kinds of decisions at DHI."

"Maybe not." This time when he put down his tools, he reached into his pocket and pulled out a piece of paper, its edges old and tattered. He unfolded the paper and flattened it against the glass so she could read it. "Your father might not be the *only* killer at DHI, but he's the one who signed this letter, letting me know DHI would no longer be covering the cost of my daughter's medication."

She read the letter to the end and then came back to his name and address, where he'd used a black marker to cover any identifying information. When he saw what she was doing, he pulled the letter away from the window.

Emily and her father rarely saw eye to eye, she thought, but he was no monster. "What happened to your daughter?" she asked.

The fight seemed to leave his body as he folded the letter and slid it back into his pocket. He then walked back to the futon and took a seat. With shaky hands, he rubbed his face as if to wash away the stress. When he looked back at her, even six feet away, she took note of his bloodshot eyes. The man was exhausted.

"I was one of the lucky ones," he told her. "I had a decent job with benefits. I made a comfortable living. And then my daughter got sick. But I wasn't worried. I had health insurance." He snorted. "Hannah suffered for months before the doctors found the right combination of medications. She was making great strides, and we were all hopeful. And then the letter from DHI arrived. Signed by Owen Shepard."

"Maybe if you had tried talking to him, he could have done something to help you."

His head fell forward.

She wondered if he was pondering that, but then his head snapped up, and she could see that she'd only served to make him angrier. His face was a maze of deep grooves.

"Cattle are treated with more respect and care than my daughter received. All I asked from your father was an apology and assurance that he would change the policy as it applied to experimental drugs. But he didn't see fit to reply." He got to his feet, grabbed a duffel bag, and walked across the room, his back to her. Was he leaving?

"Let me out. Please."

"I'll be back," he said without stopping.

"Don't leave me here! Let me go!" He disappeared around a half wall. She couldn't see him any longer, but she heard a door open and close, followed by what sounded like a series of locks clicking into place. She didn't know what to do. How was she going to get out of here?

Her father might be her only chance. And that scared her. He was a busy man. She rarely saw him. She and her brothers often referred to him as Uncle Dad. By the time her father realized the seriousness of her predicament, if at all, it could be too late.

Twenty-Four

Zee made sure to keep a good distance from the Honda. She hadn't been following him very long when he made a sharp right.

Panicked by the thought of losing him, she stepped on the gas and made the same right she'd seen him take. The long road ahead of her was deserted. She'd lost him. Frustrated, she made a U-turn, and that was when she saw his car squeezed into a tight spot between a truck and a building.

"Think you're so smart," she said.

Don't do anything crazy, a voice in her head warned.

Or dangerous.

If the driver of the Honda wanted to get back on the road, there was only one way he could get out, and she was going to block his path. She pulled her car in front of the narrow opening, rolled down the passenger window, and tried to get a good look at his plates. He'd covered them. She couldn't see the driver's face because the spot where he was parked was well shaded.

His engine roared to life.

It took her a second to realize he was either trying to scare her or intending to ram right into her. Her first instinct was to let him do it. *Stubborn* was her middle name. He might ruin her car, but she would have him right where she wanted him. And then she thought of what Jessie had said about not putting herself in danger.

If she disobeyed, she would be fired.

"Merlin's beard!" Determined to see his face if and when he came forward, she stared at him. He wasn't fooling around. He gunned it and shot forward. She stepped on the gas and missed being hit by inches.

Gravel sprayed beneath his wheels as he made a sharp turn out of the alleyway. The chase was on again. And Jessie was calling.

"Hello," Zee said.

"I told you to stay on the line."

"Sorry about that. Not sure what happened."

You shouldn't lie.

"Shut up," Zee told the voice in her head.

"What?"

"Nothing. Sorry."

"Where are you?" Jessie asked.

Zee glanced at the map on the dashboard. "That's a 10-20. Advise to location. Victory Avenue."

"No need to use police codes."

"That's a 10-4."

"Victory Avenue is right around the corner from here," Jessie said.

"Correctomundo. He tried to lose me by hiding in an alleyway. I found him."

"Were you able to see his plate numbers?"

"That's a big no. The plates are covered with a bag. But I'm hoping to get a look at his face."

"I want you to let him go. Meet me at the office."

Zee bristled at the idea. "But why? He's right in front of me. I can see—"

"Let him go, Zee. He's seen you. He knows you're onto him."

Zee pinched her lips together.

"When you get to the office, there are a few things I need to talk to you—"

Zee disconnected the call. The Honda was in plain sight. There was no way she was going to just turn around and let him go. The second she saw him cut through a gas station, tires squealing, she knew that he knew she wasn't giving up anytime soon.

———

Jessie was getting worried. She'd been sitting at her desk for twenty minutes, and Zee hadn't made an appearance.

The phone rang. Hoping it was Zee, she picked up, surprised to hear Dad's voice on the other end of the line.

"Hi," she said. "What's going on?"

"I couldn't sleep last night. I thought I'd call to make sure you and Olivia were okay."

She frowned. "We're fine. Thanks for asking."

"Does Olivia have her permit?"

"To drive? No. She just turned fifteen."

"So she doesn't drive?"

"No, Dad." Jessie frowned. "Why are you asking?"

"No reason."

This was crazy talk. Jessie's office was located a block and a half from the house she rented. From her desk, she had a clear view of the street that ran between her home and her office. "I can see Olivia now," she told her dad. "No need to worry. We're both fine."

"Oh, good. She's a sweet girl. I worry about her sometimes."

He never called. Something was going on. "Dad, why are you calling? What did you see?"

"I've got dinner on the stove," he said. "I'd better go."

"Dad. Tell me. I can't help Olivia if I don't know what's going on."

"I was at the market the other day, and I could have sworn I saw Olivia driving a sleek new car on Park Avenue."

"But you didn't call until now?"

He stuttered and then cleared his throat. "I wasn't sure if it was her."

She could tell he was lying. He knew it was Olivia, but he didn't want to get her into trouble, especially now that he knew she was okay. "Was anyone in the car with her?" she asked.

"The female in the passenger seat had dark hair, and there was a dog in the car, too."

He sounded flustered, and Jessie didn't want him to regret calling. She knew Dad well enough to know that the real reason he hadn't called before now was because he'd probably been drinking. Olivia was his only grandchild. He loved her, but his addiction to alcohol won out every time. "Thanks for letting me know."

"Yes. Good. I'll talk to you soon."

The call was disconnected. *Damn.* She was angry and disappointed and also confused by Olivia's behavior because Olivia was smarter than that. Jessie set her phone aside at the same moment Olivia and Higgins walked through the door. "Hey, there," Jessie said. "Where have you been?"

"I took Higgins for a walk."

Before Jessie could question her about what Dad had told her, Zee pulled up to the curb just outside her window.

Olivia waved.

By the time Zee joined them, Jessie's anger was overriding all other emotions. "What took you so long?"

"His car was right there," Zee said passionately. "I couldn't let him go that easily."

Jessie exhaled. She was going to have to let the girl go. Zee refused to obey orders and had a tendency to act impulsively. There was also the possibility that she might be a bad influence on Olivia. "This isn't going to work."

Zee tilted her head in confusion. "What do you mean?"

"Yeah," Olivia chimed in. "What do you mean?"

"This has nothing to do with you," Jessie told Olivia. "Go home. I'll be there in fifteen minutes."

Olivia's body tensed. "No," she stated firmly.

"Keep it up," Jessie said, "and you won't be going to that dance."

"You would never do that to me."

Jessie didn't like Olivia's body language. It was as if she was testing her. "Try me."

"Why are you being like this?" Olivia asked, sounding a little less defensive.

"Let's see, where should I begin?" Jessie asked. "For starters, Dad just called to ask me if you had your driver's permit." Jessie looked from Olivia to Zee. "Now why in the world would he call to ask me that? Any ideas? Anyone?"

Olivia flinched. "Oh."

"Maybe I should go," Zee said. "I can stop by in the morning on my way to the Norton house."

Jessie turned to Zee. "Stay right where you are." Then she turned back to Olivia. "What were you thinking, driving Zee's car?"

"It was stupid, I know. But don't blame Zee. It was my fault. I'm the one who got in behind the wheel and drove without a permit."

"That's true," Zee said.

Jessie pointed a finger at Zee. "Stay out of this."

Zee said nothing.

"How far did you drive?" Jessie asked Olivia.

"Around an empty parking lot and then to a stoplight and back. Not very far at all."

"You're grounded," Jessie told her. "No dance."

"You can't do that to me."

"That's a little harsh, don't you think?" Zee asked.

Tired of being questioned, Jessie turned her ire on Zee. "You're fired."

Zee put a hand to her chest. "Me?"

"Yes, you."

"Don't fire Zee. If you do, I'll have nobody to talk to when you're not around."

That was the last thing Jessie had expected to hear. She'd been trying so hard to keep an open line of communication with Olivia. But once again she'd failed. "You can talk to me."

Olivia's shoulders sagged. "That's not true. You're always busy, and I'm pretty sure you know nothing about the opposite sex since you're not married, you never had a long-term relationship, and you don't even date."

"Trust me—I know about boys," Jessie said, sounding childish to her own ears.

"I really don't," Zee confided. "The last guy I was infatuated with turned out to be a serial killer, so I'm pretty much batting zero."

Jessie blew out some hot air. The conversation was getting out of hand. "We'll talk about this later," Jessie told Olivia.

Olivia snorted. "Fine." She attached the leash to Higgins's collar and left.

Alone with Zee, Jessie took a seat at her desk. "About today," she said. "Hanging up on me midsentence and disobeying my instructions was unacceptable. I don't know if this is going to work out."

"What do you mean?"

"This is my business. There are rules that must be followed."

Zee opened her mouth to speak, but Jessie raised a hand to stop her. "I hired you because I need help with my workload. If I have to spend a large portion of my day watching over you and making sure you're following protocol, then that means I'm not getting my own work done."

Zee walked over to the chair in front of Jessie's desk and took a seat. "I've done everything you asked me to do. It only took me fifteen minutes to find the information you needed today."

"I told you to let the Honda go and return to—"

Zee looked at Jessie with big, round eyes and then jabbed a finger at the open file on Jessie's desk. "That's him," she said, excitement in her voice.

Annoyed that Zee wasn't listening to a word she said, Jessie looked where Zee was pointing. It was an old newspaper clipping. The headline read:

BABY SMUGGLED OUT OF HOSPITAL

Below that was a picture of Nick and Ashley Bale with their new daughter soon after the birth.

"That's the man who was driving the Honda."

"I thought you didn't see him."

"Not right away. After I hung up with you, I followed the Honda around the streets of Sacramento for a while."

Jessie frowned. "Of course you did."

"How could I not? His car was right there! I admit I was ready to give up the chase, but then he had to stop for the light rail. Trapped between a UPS truck and me, he had nowhere to go. I got out of my car, walked over to his, and took a picture of him. I was so quick, he didn't have time to cover his face." Zee handed her phone to Jessie.

Stunned, it took only a glance for Jessie to see that it was definitely Ashley's husband.

Zee read the article and then asked, "Why would the father of the stolen baby be following you?"

"That's a good question."

"Looks like you have your work cut out for you," Zee said as she stood. "I'll see you tonight to work on the DHI case."

"Zee?"

"Yes?"

"I fired you, remember?"

"You were serious?"

"I was, but I realize I was being impulsive, reacting out of anger. And for that reason I've decided to give you a second chance—under one condition."

"That I don't, under any circumstance, allow Olivia to drive my car?"

"Yes. And you also must promise me you'll follow orders. If I tell you to drop a case or stop following someone, then you must do as I ask."

"Deal."

"One more question before you go."

Zee actually stopped at the door and waited to see what she had to say.

"It's about Olivia. When the two of you returned from shopping, Olivia appeared upset, and I was hoping you might know why."

"She's fifteen," Zee said as if that might be news to Jessie. "The problem, as I see it, is her birth month. I thought she was a Cancer, but I found out she was actually a Libra."

Jessie had no idea where Zee was going with this.

"Don't get me wrong," Zee said. "Libras are clever and can be fun and spontaneous at times, but they're also indecisive, unreliable, a tad naive, and way too nice for their own good. Does that help?"

Jessie had a headache. "Not at all. But thanks."

"Anything else?" Zee asked.

"That's it for now. I'll see you later."

Twenty-Five

When Jessie returned to the house, she found Olivia in her room studying. Her niece looked over at her and said, "I'm sorry I drove Zee's car. It was a stupid thing to do."

"Yes, it was."

"I won't do it again."

Jessie nodded. "I'm worried about you."

"Why?"

Cecil the one-eyed cat circled her legs. Jessie set her bag down and picked him up. "Because you're at that vulnerable age when peer pressure can become too much. I'm not just talking about boys, but alcohol and drugs, too."

"We've had these talks before," Olivia said. "I'm not stupid." She blushed. "Not usually."

"Ever since your mom's funeral you've been quiet. And then hearing from Dad of all people that you were out driving makes me feel as if I'm not doing my job."

"I think you're doing a good job. I always know you're here for me if I need you. But I don't think you trust me."

"Under the circumstances, I think that's warranted." Jessie finished petting the cat and set him back on the ground.

"Agreed, but I'm talking about before the car thing. I think you're so afraid I'm going to become a clone of my mom that you can't relax. Parents these days are too paranoid about everything."

"That might be true, but I don't think you're being fair," Jessie said. "I've always given you your space. I don't come into your room uninvited and try to shove my views down your throat, do I?"

"What if I told you that a boy asked me to the upcoming dance?"

Before Jessie could respond, Olivia added, "You would probably make it into a big deal and ask to meet him and his parents—am I right?"

"Maybe."

"See? That's what I mean about trusting me. It's a ninth-grade dance."

Jessie crossed her arms. "You do realize you sort of messed up the whole trustworthy thing when you got behind the wheel of Zee's car, don't you?"

Olivia blushed again. "True, but I said I was sorry."

Jessie decided to let it go for now. For once Olivia was opening up to her, and she thought it was important they find a way to discuss important issues. "So, did a boy ask you to the dance or was that hypothetical?"

"A boy asked me to the dance."

"Ahh, I see."

"But it doesn't matter anymore since I'm grounded."

Jessie thought about it for a moment. Her niece had a point about Jessie being afraid Olivia might turn out like her mother. Sophie and Jessie had been opposites. Sophie had been known as the wild one while Jessie was told she had a tendency to worry and come across as uptight. "I've decided to give Zee a second chance," Jessie said, breaking the silence. "So maybe I'll give you a second chance, too."

"Really?"

Jessie held up a finger. "Really."

Olivia jumped off the bed and came at her fast. She wrapped her arms around Jessie, making her laugh. When Olivia pulled away, Jessie said, "I do think it would be helpful for us to talk about things that could happen so that you're prepared to deal with any situation."

Olivia's shoulders fell slightly.

"What's wrong with that?"

"You make me feel like I'm ten instead of fifteen. There are kids my age who are having sex already. Relationships are a big deal at my age. It's all we think about sometimes, but having a relationship doesn't mean going all the way."

"Well, that's a relief," Jessie said.

Olivia rolled her eyes. "It's the same with alcohol, drugs, and oral sex. Some kids my age do all those things. I don't judge because it's none of my business. But most of the kids I hang out with are smart. They don't need their parents stopping them at the door and giving them a list of what not to do every time they leave the house."

"Okay," Jessie said. "I get it. I'm going to trust you."

"And I'll talk to you every once in a while and let you know what's going on."

They hugged again and Jessie's heart swelled. For the first time in a long while, she felt as if she and Olivia were headed in the right direction.

Jessie took a shower and then put together a platter of vegetables and dip. Ben and Zee would be arriving in the next fifteen minutes to work on the DHI case. With her cell phone in hand, she plopped down on the couch in the family room and called Colin.

"Hey there," he said. "What's up?"

"I haven't talked to you since the wedding, and I wanted to find out how your dad is doing."

"He's still in the hospital, but the doctors are hopeful he'll be discharged by the end of the week."

"I hope so, too."

"Hang on a minute while I hop in the car."

She heard shuffling and then nothing. She thought she'd lost the connection until she heard his voice again. "Are you there?"

"I'm here," she told him. "Where are you off to?"

"No rest for the weary."

"The DHI case?"

"Yep. I guess you heard about it from Ben Morrison?"

"Actually, it was Owen Shepard. He asked for my help."

"He didn't mention hiring outside help during our meetings. Have you seen the news?"

"No, why do you ask?"

"Another body was found near the American River. I'm on my way there now."

Jessie wondered why Owen Shepard hadn't notified her, but she kept her thoughts to herself. "Any idea who the victim is?"

"Male. Possibly in his forties. Another DHI employee. That's all I've got at this point."

"Two deaths in less than two weeks," she said quietly. "Considering how blasé Owen Shepard came across when he hired me, I'm just surprised this thing has escalated so fast."

"I thought you would have solved the case by now," he teased.

"Not yet," she said, "but I was hoping to pick your brain and see what you knew."

"I wish I could help you out, Jessie, but I've got the sergeant so far up my ass with this one he's probably listening to us right now. I'll be lucky to get four hours of sleep tonight."

"I'll let you go then. Good luck with the case."

"You, too." There was a long pause before Colin said, "Hey, Jess?"

"What is it?"

"I had fun dancing with you. I hope we can do that again soon."

"Me, too."

After disconnecting the call, Jessie sat there for a moment, thinking about Colin and relationships, and wondering if they stood a chance.

Olivia walked into the room. "What's for dinner?"

"There are some leftovers in the fridge," Jessie said as she grabbed the remote and turned on the TV.

"I finished my homework," Olivia said. "Are we going to work on that DHI list tonight?"

"We are," Jessie told her before she turned up the volume. On the television screen was a female reporter standing near the American River. Behind her was crime scene tape around an area being worked over by a forensic team.

"The body of Brad Elton, chief financial officer at the main offices of DHI located in Sacramento," the reporter announced, "was found a short time ago by a man walking the trail near American River. Authorities have not yet made a statement, but as you can see behind me they have cordoned off a large area. The eyewitness said that a message had been written in black lettering on the dead man's chest." The reporter read from her notes. "It read: 'Who's next? Ask Owen Shepard.'" She paused while the cameraman zoomed in on EMTs as they transferred the body bag onto a stretcher and then wheeled it to where an ambulance waited. "We called DHI, but we were told that Owen Shepard, the CEO at DHI, wasn't taking calls, and we were unable to get a statement."

Olivia placed a slice of pizza in the microwave and then came to the living room to watch. "Another DHI employee is dead?"

Jessie nodded.

"Everyone who works at that company must be freaking out."

"I would think so." Jessie wondered if this would change Owen Shepard's attitude about the whole thing. At the same time, she knew the killer needed to be stopped before he hurt anyone else.

A knock at the door sent Olivia running down the stairs. She returned with Ben and Zee.

After Olivia filled Zee in on the news, she gave her a quick tour of her bedroom. Jessie offered Ben a seat at the kitchen table. "Thanks for coming."

He pulled a wooden chair back from the table and sat.

"They found another body," she told him.

He nodded wearily. "I just came from there." He met her gaze. "Owen didn't call you to let you know?"

She shook her head. "You look exhausted."

"I am, but don't worry about me. I'm here because it's what I do. It's my job. And besides, I need to keep busy."

"The images?" she asked as she went to the refrigerator and then brought him back a glass of water.

"Yes. They're getting worse."

"I'm sorry."

"Don't be. Just know that I'm here for my own sanity."

"It looks like the feds are involved now."

He nodded. "They took my file, both letters, and the flash drive."

"But you have copies of everything?"

"Of course." He reached into his bag, pulled out his laptop, and set it up on the table.

Zee and Olivia joined them, bringing their computers, both taking the same spots where they had sat last night.

Ben raised a brow at Jessie, clearly surprised by Zee's and Olivia's presence.

"I need all the help I can get right now," Jessie told him.

Ben said nothing.

"We have two letters from the killer," Jessie told the girls. "But we're going to start off by watching a video."

"I was able to edit out the last few frames, but it's still graphic," Ben said. "Are you sure you're all okay with this?"

"I'm fine," Olivia said.

Zee nodded. "Me, too."

Ben turned his computer so they would all be able to watch it together.

The video began with the killer's muffled voice saying, "Testing, one, two, three." After watching the young man, Tyler McDonald, pleading for his life, it was Jessie who felt sick to her stomach and appeared to be having the hardest time keeping it together. Everyone else looked focused and ready to find clues.

After the third viewing, Zee held up a hand.

Ben hit "Pause."

"Could you replay the last bit?"

Ben rewound the video to the point where the victim was looking directly into the camera lens.

Tyler: "Why are you doing this?"

Killer: "You know why."

Tyler: "I told you. I've only been working for DHI for a short time. I never met Owen Shepard. He wouldn't know me if we bumped into each other."

A long pause.

Tyler, eyes wide, voice pleading: "I had nothing to do with Han—"

A gunshot sounded. Screen went black.

"I wonder what Tyler was trying to say?" Olivia asked.

"Can you replay that last sentence in slow motion?" Zee asked.

Jessie had to fight the urge to turn the video off. But this was the reason they had gathered here tonight. For the next few minutes they watched the last section over and over again.

HAN—BOOM!

HAN—BOOM!

HAN—BOOM!

"It sounds to me like he might be saying something like, 'I had nothing to do with *han*dling your case,'" Olivia said.

"I don't think that's it," Zee said. "Look at the expression on his face. He looks suddenly worried, as if he realizes his life is not going to be spared."

"It does seem as if the killer panicked, didn't want the viewers to hear what Tyler was about to say, which means it could be our biggest clue."

For the next fifteen minutes they tossed out ideas on what Tyler might have been saying.

"I think it's time to move on to the victims," Jessie said. "Tyler McDonald and Brad Elton. We know they both worked at DHI. Could you and Zee," she said, looking at Olivia, "focus on finding as much information on the two men as possible? Olivia can search social media. Zee, you can use your personal databases. While you two work on that, I'm going to show Ben our list of keywords and how we're going about narrowing the list we got from DHI."

By the end of the night, the only connection between the killer's two victims appeared to be that they were single and they both worked for DHI.

Tomorrow night they would get back to concentrating on DHI's list of grievances. After Olivia went to bed and Zee drove off, Jessie walked Ben to his car.

"I wanted to tell you that I talked to your sister before she left."

"I was wondering how that worked out, but I was at soccer games on Sunday and I never got a chance to call you. When I didn't hear from you, I assumed it didn't work out."

"I'm sorry. I should have called."

"She agreed to talk to you?" he asked, clearly surprised.

"Yes. I caught her as she sat down to have breakfast at the hotel. She was gracious, and yet, of course, guarded after I told her I was helping you look into your past. She advised against delving too deeply, claiming it will only bring you grief."

"When I cornered her, she mentioned as much," Ben said.

"She did tell me that she had a wonderful time with your family."

"It's true," Ben said. "Our day together went better than expected. Melony and I felt as if she'd been a part of the family for years. As great as she was with my children, though, she still did all she could to keep her distance from me."

"I'm sorry."

"So," Ben said. "What did you get out of her?"

"She told me your mother had a mean streak and used to be cruel to Nancy's dog. If Nancy intervened in any way, it only made things worse. Nancy said she basically steered clear of your mother whenever she was in one of her moods. But there was one particular instance that stood out."

"Go on."

"It was Christmas Day, and Nancy said your mother was unusually cruel to the dog. You came between the dog and your mother and made her stop."

"Did she say how I stopped her?"

"According to Nancy, you were much bigger than your mother at the time. You put a hand on her face and pushed her backward until she was up against a wall. And then you turned around, scooped the dog into your arms, and left the house."

His brow furrowed. "What happened to the dog?"

"Nancy didn't know. She just said she never saw the dog again."

Ben groaned.

"What?"

"It doesn't sound like a happy ending to me."

"Why?" Jessie asked. "You must have found help. Maybe one of the neighbors offered to take the dog in." When Ben failed to respond, she said, "Don't worry. We'll get to the bottom of everything."

"That's what I'm afraid of."

TWENTY-SIX

"Tell me about Hannah," Emily asked her captor. "I know she was athletic since you told me as much, but what was she like? Was she funny? Quiet? Argumentative? Outgoing?"

Emily was sitting on one end of the bench, her back against the wall, and she could see Hannah's dad through the glass. He was reading again. The man intrigued her. Not too strange considering she planned to major in psychology.

Every day she set the cooler on the bench and attempted to jump to the top of the wall, and every day she failed. She'd finally come to the realization that she might not get out of here. She hadn't been feeling well. Her body felt fatigued, heavy. She might die in this dank, depressing room.

She had tried everything she could think of to convince him to let her go. She'd gone from scared to angry to desperate. But the man kept trying to convince her he was on some sort of crazy-assed mission to make a change, and the only way to do that was to create havoc and demand that people listen. He wanted all experimental drugs to be covered. Odd to think that in trying to save lives, he was willing to take lives.

As far as she was concerned, Hannah's father wanted revenge. Why else would he have gone after Owen Shepard's only daughter? Deep down she knew her father wasn't to blame for Hannah's death since decisions at DHI were made by many people, not just one man.

Interesting, too, that the anger she'd felt toward her father for years had completely left her. It took being locked up in a cramped, uncomfortable room to find a way to forgive him. He might never know she'd had a change of heart, but that was okay. Doing so had been freeing. With not much else to do but think and analyze, she'd realized that even though her father had rarely been around when she was growing up, she'd always known he loved her. Holding on to her resentment had been her way of clinging to her father. Grasping on to the worst parts of him had stunted her growth.

"She had a beautiful imagination," her captor said. "When she was very young, she would draw detailed pictures of faraway castles, complete with moats and dragons. When her mother asked if she was the princess living inside the castle, Hannah would laugh." His expression softened. "You see, according to Hannah, a prince lived inside the castle. He'd been trapped there all his life. He wasn't handsome like Prince Charming, nor was he exceptionally clever. But Hannah was the one who was going to save him." He paused, swallowed, and added, "And she was going to marry him."

"Why would she want to do that?" Emily asked.

"Because the prince was kind to all living creatures, including those who refused to release him."

"I would have liked to meet her."

His head was bent forward, and at first she thought he'd gone back to reading. But then she saw his shoulders moving and realized he was crying.

TWENTY-SEVEN

Jessie was in her office by eight o'clock the next morning. She opened the file on her desk and found herself staring at Nick Bale.

Why was he following her?

More than likely, he knew his wife had hired her against his wishes. Was following her Nick Bale's subtle way of telling Jessie to back off? If so, that would mean he was worried about what she might learn. Otherwise, it seemed logical to Jessie that he would merely confront her.

Beneath the article with Nick and Ashley's picture was the piece of paper Ben had given her with Rene Steele's name, address, and telephone number. Rene Steele had been one of the nurses working at Mercy General when Dakota Bale was abducted.

She stared at the phone number and thought about calling the woman. But then, just as quickly, she decided to take a ride to Auburn instead. Sometimes it was best to try to catch a person off guard. Not everyone was good at making excuses or getting rid of someone they didn't wish to talk to. Jessie was counting on it.

On her feet, Jessie grabbed her phone and called Zee.

"Jessie Cole Investigations," Zee said in greeting. "How can I help you?"

"I'm taking you off the Lindsay Norton case. I need you to work on the DHI list since we only have a few hundred DHI complaints left to examine."

"Why don't I just spend a few hours on the Norton case and then the rest of the day on the DHI case?"

"Zee. What did I tell you about following orders? I need you to work on the list. I'm heading to Auburn to talk to someone, but I expect to see you here in the office when I return."

"Okay, if you say so."

"Thank you. I'll talk to you later."

———

Zee put her phone down and let her head fall back onto the headrest. Jessie was absolutely right. She had a difficult time following orders. She straightened as she remembered that Jessie was heading to Auburn. It wasn't as if Zee needed to run off right this minute.

She glanced at Lindsay Norton's house. The woman was committing fraud. She was sure of it. If Zee didn't find proof, like right this second, the woman would collect money she didn't deserve.

Zee's stomach growled. She'd left the house so early she'd forgotten to eat breakfast. Reaching for the brown bag her dad's girlfriend, Deanne, had made for her, she looked inside and then pulled out a Fuji apple.

She turned up the volume on the radio. There was nothing less inspiring than an apple. If Deanne had included a side of peanut butter or even taken the time to cut it into slices, that might be different. Putting the apple aside, Zee lifted a piece of Tupperware from the bottom of the bag. Inside, she found a spinach wrap stuffed with vegetables. *Nice.* At the very bottom of the bag was a note. She unfolded the paper and read: *If you work hard and do your best, you can do anything.*

She had to admit the woman was growing on her. Deanne was a Taurus, kind, dependable, and caring. She was also a tad possessive of Zee's dad, and a bit materialistic, but overall, she was okay. Recently, Deanne had plummeted into the world of *The Secret*, an old bestselling self-help book by Rhonda Byrne. It was all about positivity and seeing-the-glass-half-full kind of shit, which was both admirable and annoying at the same time.

About to take a bite of her spinach wrap, Zee stopped when she heard what sounded like a scream. She quickly put her food away and turned off the radio.

There it was again. A high-pitched, slightly muffled shriek.

It was usually a fairly quiet street. She would know since she'd been sitting here for over a week now. There weren't a lot of cars or pedestrians. A few bicyclists every once in a while, but that was about it.

As soon as she exited the car, she heard a distinct call for help coming from Lindsay Norton's neighbor's place—the creeper's house. Leaning back into the car, she grabbed her cell phone, then shut the door and hurried across the street. The last time she'd approached the house was when Olivia had gone to the front door and got all pissy after the creeper took her picture.

This time Zee reached over the side gate and realized there was a padlock. *Weird.* Another shout from inside got her moving. Holding on to the top of the gate, she jumped as high as she could, then pulled with her arms and pushed with her feet until she could get one leg and then the other over the top. She dropped to the other side.

She wanted to yell back to the person, tell whoever it was that she was trying to get inside, but that would only alert the neighbors to the fact that she was trespassing. The thought that she might be hallucinating or paranoid stopped her from calling the police or running to a neighbor for help. She needed to be absolutely sure something was wrong before she did anything rash.

Go back to the car and ignore the shouts for help! Francis said.

Call Jessie. She'll know what to do.

"Quiet," Zee told the voices. "Jessie said if I didn't see anyone getting hurt, I was supposed to mind my own business. I'll just take a quick look around, and if I don't see anyone, I'll return to the car and forget about it."

Once she got to the backyard, the cries for help grew louder.

Panicked, she ran from door to door, and then window to window, but the house was locked up tight. She stood in place for a moment. When she looked up, she noticed one of the windows on the second story was a third of the way open. Upon further analysis, she realized the only way to reach the window would be to climb the big oak tree. She wasn't exactly limber, but she'd gotten over the gate, hadn't she?

You can do it, came another voice inside her head. It was Marion, the voice of reason and sometimes compassion.

The first two branches were the easiest to climb, and for a minute or so Zee thought she was quite brilliant. But the next branch was a different story. It was too high for her to reach. She would have to straddle the trunk of the tree and inch her way up or jump for it. What if she jumped and then missed altogether? That thought worried her. Or what if she jumped, hung from the limb, and then grew too tired to swing her legs over the branch? She was already far enough up that she could break her leg.

Definitely a conundrum, Francis said.

Don't do it, Lucy warned. *You'll fall for sure and break your neck.*

Praying the voices would shut the hell up, Zee hugged the trunk of tree with her arms and legs and began her slow ascent. The tree bark poked at her arms and into the fleshy part of her inner thighs. Painful, but she wasn't turning back now.

The cries for help were coming less often, but that didn't stop her from continuing. When she reached the next limb and maneuvered her body so that she could stand on the branch, she laughed and jabbed a finger into the air. "I did it!"

If you work hard and do your best, you can do anything. "That's right, Deanne!"

Zee could see right into Lindsay Norton's backyard. And speak of the devil. *Beans and cheese!* What was Lindsay Norton doing? The woman was standing in the middle of the lawn, doing squats and lunges without any problem whatsoever.

Zee reached into her back pocket for her phone, set it to video, and began taping just as Lindsay Norton picked up a big ol' kettle bell and began swinging it between her legs.

Why hadn't the woman heard the screams, she wondered. And then she saw the wires hanging from her headphones. She was obviously working out to music.

If you're going to do this, Francis warned, *you better get in and get out.*

Zee had almost forgotten why she was in the tree to begin with. She quickly put her phone away and continued. It wasn't until it came time to scale the roof that she fully questioned her sanity, something she tried so desperately to hold on to. *What was I thinking?*

We warned you! Only a fool would try to crawl to that window.

Zee held on to a branch above her head as she stepped onto the roof. She stood still for a few seconds, trying to get a feel for the terrain. It felt like sandpaper beneath her shoes. That was good.

She looked at the window.

Only about five feet to go.

She would do a slow sort of crab-walk, she decided. With splayed fingers flat on the prickly roof, she took her first step, and then another, and another.

It's not so bad, she thought right as her foot slipped and she lost her balance. Flailing, she reached above her head, thankful when her right hand got a grip on the window frame.

Breathing hard, she hung sideways for a few seconds before pulling herself upward. When she finally managed to open the window wide enough to pull herself through, she fell to the carpeted floor, cursing herself for being so foolish.

After catching her breath, she lifted her head and looked around. The room she was in was maybe twelve by twelve. There were boxes stacked high against every wall. No furniture at all. After getting to her feet, she tiptoed across the room to the door, then peeked out and saw a long hallway.

There was a door on each end and a stairway. She'd made it to the first door when she heard the same cry for help. It was coming from downstairs. Whoever it was had grown hoarse and lost their ability to shout. Without bothering to check the other rooms, Zee ran for the stairs, taking two steps at a time until she was at the front door. She peeked out the window—she could see her car a block away. Turning away from the door, she walked hurriedly through a family room area and into a short hallway.

"Where are you?" she said in a loud whisper.

The cries led her to a bedroom. The man on the bed had been blindfolded and stripped naked. His wrists and ankles were cuffed to the bedposts. From the looks of things, he'd chewed off the duct tape that had once covered his mouth.

"I'm here," she told him.

"Please help me," he croaked.

"I'm going to do everything I can to get you out of here." Zee looked around. Goose bumps covered her arms. Five different cameras on tripods had been set up in the room, circling the bed. They were all at varying heights and angles. Weirded out by what she was seeing, Zee began opening and closing drawers. "Do you know where he keeps the key to your cuffs?"

"Around his neck," he said.

Fuck. That wasn't good. The cuffs were made of metal, not plastic. How was she going to get them off him?

And then she remembered Jessie's cop friend. She needed to call him. She pulled out her phone again and began to scroll through her contact list. After Jessie had given her the business card, she'd added him to the list, but she couldn't remember his name. Was it Rollin?

Rollin. She went to the names listed under *R*.

Nope. Not Rollin.

"La-la-la. Oh, my. Zippy-doo-dah. Help me."

"What are you doing?"

"Oh, sorry." Spotting a sweater slung over the back of a chair in the corner of the room, she grabbed it and used it to cover his man parts; then she took off his blindfold. "I can't get these cuffs off you. I'm going to call for help. *Colin!* That's it. Colin Grayson." She scrolled back up, found his name, and hit the "Call" button. "Pick up. Pick up."

"Hello."

"Colin Grayson?"

"Who is this?"

"Zee Gatley. Jessie told me I could call you if I ever found myself in danger."

Through the curtains, she saw shadows as a car pulled into the driveway. "Oh no! He's here. I've got to hide."

"What's going on, Zee? Where are you?"

She rattled off Lindsay Norton's address. "It's the house to the left, and it belongs to Rudy Archer. Inside the house I found a man cuffed to a bed. He's been screaming for hours, but I can't get him loose because of the cuffs. The creeper dude just got home. Oh my God. I hear the door. I gotta go." She hung up the phone, then hurried to the bed and put the blindfold back on the guy. Her heart was about to explode inside her chest. How did she get herself into these predicaments? If she had simply followed Jessie's orders and headed back to the office, she wouldn't be in this mess.

"Where are you?" the man asked.

"Shhh. Help is on the way. I promise!" She scrambled around the room, looking for a place to hide.

In the closet, Marion told her. *Hurry!*

"Don't leave me!"

Grabbing the sweater from his lower half, she tossed it back on the chair where she'd found it. She then forced herself to stop and think. Her gaze fixated on the closet door. "Everything is going to be fine," she told the naked man. "I'll be in the closet until the police arrive."

Twenty-Eight

Jessie knocked on Rene Steele's front door. When nobody appeared, she rang the doorbell. There was a car in the driveway, and she could see lights on inside the house.

She knocked again, louder than before. "Rene Steele," she said in case the woman was standing nearby. "My name is Jessie Cole. It's very important that I talk to you."

Nothing.

She waited a few minutes and then started off down the walkway back toward her car. When she heard the door open behind her, she turned around and saw Rene Steele holding a rifle, the barrel pointed right at her. *Oh, shit.*

"Getz youz off my property 'fore I shoot!"

Double shit. The woman's words were slurred, and her body swayed. She was drunk.

Jessie raised her hands in the air in surrender. "I was just leaving. I didn't mean to bother you."

"I don't like strangers here on my prop—look! Youz messing my grass."

Jessie looked at her feet, which were clearly on the sidewalk. Besides, there was no lawn, just brown, dried-up weeds. Jessie wasn't sure what to do. If she walked away, would the woman shoot? She was about to do just that when the skinny little gray-haired woman swayed to her right as if a strong wind was pushing her over. Rene lost her balance and tumbled to the ground, arms flailing as she tried to break her fall. The gun dropped and clattered across the stoop.

Jessie ran to help her. Rene was struggling to move. Blood oozed from her nose and the corner of her mouth.

Feeling queasy, Jessie looked away as she helped the woman into the house. "Come on. Let's get you inside so I can see if you need to go to the hospital."

"Not going to no hospital."

"Okay, that's fine. Just let me help you, okay?"

"I don't have money if you're meaning to rob me."

"I'm not a thief."

Jessie led her to the threadbare couch in the main room and helped her take a seat. Rene reached for a throw blanket that had more holes than cloth and put it over her knees. Jessie headed off to find something to clean her up with. The house smelled like mothballs. The kitchen sink was filled to the brim with unwashed dishes. Jessie found a rag in a bottom drawer and put it under the faucet. When she returned, Rene's head had fallen back onto the cushioned seat.

Rene's mouth was wide-open. She wasn't yet sixty, but the spider veins and the jaundiced skin made her look closer to seventy.

"Here you go," Jessie said, startling the woman.

Rene hardly moved as Jessie did her best to clean her up without making eye contact with the blood. She'd never done well with blood. If she ever found time, she planned to see a therapist and hopefully find a way to deal with her extreme aversion to it.

Jessie kept the cloth over Rene's nose. If she didn't, they would both pass out. "It looks like you chipped a tooth. Here—hold this to your nose to stop the bleeding. Can I get you some ibuprofen?"

Rene waved a frail hand toward the kitchen. "Just get me that bottle of whiskey by the stove. That's all I need."

Jessie did as she asked. She also brought Rene a glass of water, glad to see her nose had stopped bleeding when she set the bloodied cloth to the side.

As the woman sipped her whiskey, Jessie took the rag and held it low and out of sight as she carried it to the kitchen. She then retrieved the rifle from outside and was glad to see that it wasn't loaded. She set the gun against the wall by the entry, then shut the door and returned to the main room.

"Who did you say you were?" the woman asked, her head wobbling.

"Jessie Cole. I'm a private investigator. I came here to talk to you about the baby that was stolen from Mercy General seven years ago."

"Dakota Bale," Rene said under her breath before taking another swig.

The woman's hands were shaking.

"Are you hungry? I'd be happy to make you something—soup or maybe a sandwich? It's probably a good idea if you eat something."

Rene snickered as if she'd said something amusing. "If my mother were still alive"—she hiccuped—"she probably would have shot you just for asking about that baby 'cuz she don't like me talking about the Dakota baby."

"Why wouldn't your mother want you to talk about Dakota?"

Rene sat up another inch. Her face grew serious, almost sober-looking. "She doesn't want my name dragged through the mud again." Rene groaned. "She hates that."

"When was your name dragged through the mud?"

"Long time ago," she said with a wave of her hand. "When I was living in Los Angeles."

"Do you remember what happened?"

Rene put the glass on the side table. "Yeah. I do. The people at the hospital where I worked called me a child killer."

Chills crawled up Jessie's spine. "Why would anyone call you that?"

"They were jealous. I was boss of them, you know, what do they call it—oh yeah, the head nurse." She grew quiet before she said, "There was a boy. A sick boy. During my shift he'd been given the wrong medication. He died that night. I was blamed."

Rene looked at Jessie, her eyes bloodshot. "They accused me of being an alcoholic." She downed the rest of the whiskey. "Those TV people wouldn't leave me alone. Everybody said I was a lazy, no-good drunk." She wiped a tear from her cheek.

Jessie went to the kitchen and found a box of tissues. She also found some crackers and brought those, too, surprised when Rene ate one and washed it down with water.

"Is that when you came to Sacramento?" Jessie asked. "After the boy died?"

She nodded. "I came here to live with my mother."

"And at some point you got a job at Mercy General."

"Yes."

"There was speculation around the circumstances at the time the Bale baby went missing," Jessie told her. "Do you remember that?"

"Yes."

"After Dakota Bale was abducted, you started coming to work late and sometimes not at all."

"Yes," Rene said. "My mother wasn't well at the time. I had to take care of her."

"What was wrong with her?"

She waved a hand as if she were swatting away a gnat. "I don't remember." Her body sagged to one side as she sipped from an empty glass. She frowned and said, "Fill my glass, and maybe it'll all come back to me."

Jessie knew the woman didn't need any more whiskey, but it wasn't as if Rene was going to stop drinking once she left.

"So," Jessie said after she handed her a full glass that she'd watered down. "Is that when you started drinking? After Dakota Bale was abducted?"

Rene took a gulp, swallowed, nodded.

"Were you involved somehow in Dakota's abduction?" Jessie asked next.

"No," Rene blurted, staring at the liquid in her glass as a child might peer through the glass of an aquarium.

Jessie leaned forward until she caught Rene's gaze. "You saw something that night in the hospital parking lot, didn't you?"

Rene's eyes gleamed back at her.

"What did you see, Rene? There's nobody here but the two of us. Tell me what you saw."

As she sipped the amber liquid from her glass, her gaze never left Jessie's. When she finally moved the glass away from her lips, she said, "I saw the person who took Ashley Bale's baby."

Jessie's heart thumped against her chest. *Stay calm,* she told herself since she didn't want Rene to stop talking. "Why didn't you report whatever you saw to the police?"

Rene's face twisted. "Because Mother insisted I keep quiet. No dragging my name through the mud, remember?"

Jessie leaned forward. "Who took Dakota Bale?"

"I had just gotten done working my shift, and I was leaving work. It was hotter than hell as I walked through the parking lot. That's when I saw someone standing a few cars away from mine, wearing a big fat coat." Rene coughed and then reached for a tissue. She almost knocked her glass from the table in the process.

Jessie waited patiently, wondering if Rene had really seen Dakota's abductor.

"It was late at night, but there was enough light, and my car was so close that I couldn't help but notice the person. I was scared, which made it harder to unlock my car door. But right as I did, I heard a baby cry."

"What did you do?"

"I looked that way, and the person in the coat looked right at me. He had long hair, which I quickly realized must be a wig because it wasn't a woman. He had a five o'clock shadow and a very prominent Adam's apple."

Rene took another swallow. "At first I simply stared back at him. Like I said, the area where I was parked was well lit, except for the light above his car. I remember thinking that he must have broken the bulb somehow. Even without the extra light, though, I could see him clearly."

"Did he try to talk to you?"

"I didn't give him a chance. I scrambled behind the wheel of my car, turned the key, and sped off."

Jessie pulled a picture from her purse. "Do you think there's any chance you would recognize the man if you saw him in a lineup?"

"I know who he is." Rene's head fell back on the cushion. Her drink sloshed. "I know his name."

Jessie frowned. "I thought you didn't recognize him?"

"I didn't." She lifted her head, put her glass on the table again, and then looked right at Jessie. "I didn't know who he was until I saw him and his wife on the morning news pleading for the return of their daughter. Nick Bale was the man I saw in the parking lot. His face has haunted me all these years. All the whiskey in the world can't make it go away."

"I'm sorry," Jessie said, "but I don't understand why you didn't call the police."

"My mother begged me not to get involved." Rene wiped more tears away. "I wasn't going to listen to her, I swear. But then I began receiving death threats."

"What sort of threats?"

"Phone calls in the middle of the night. A muffled voice telling me he would kill my mother if I said one word to the police. A dead possum in my car."

Jessie thought about the phone records. If she remembered correctly, they only kept them for up to five years. Nick Bale had stolen his own baby, and now he was following her. He could be out there right now, watching. She stood and went to the window. No blue Honda. Nothing unusual. She pulled the curtains shut, then walked through the house, making sure doors and windows were locked tight.

Rene came up behind her and touched her shoulder.

Jessie jumped. "You scared me."

"What are you doing?"

"If what you just told me about Nick Bale is true, I'm worried about your safety."

"He hasn't called me in years." She shook her head as she shuffled back to the living room.

Jessie followed her. "Your rifle is by the door. It's not loaded."

Rene chuckled as she plopped down on the couch again. "No?"

Jessie shook her head. "Do you want me to load it for you?"

"Nah. I'm not afraid of dying."

"Are you saying that you think Nick Bale would hurt you?"

"Think about it," she said. "I'm probably the only person on this earth who knows what he did."

"I think I should call the police."

"No," Rene said, her voice firm. "Not yet. I'm tired and sore, and I just want to sit here for a while longer and enjoy my whiskey."

"I'll have to let the police know what you told me eventually."

"I know, honey. I know."

"Lock the door after I leave, okay?"

Rene finished the rest of her whiskey, gave her a wicked grin, and said, "I will."

Twenty-Nine

Zee was smothered between clothes that smelled like cigarettes and old shoes when Creeper Dude walked into the bedroom. Through tiny slits in the door, she could see bits and parts of the man she assumed was Rudy Archer. Caucasian. Bedhead. Funny-looking ears.

"You chewed off the tape," he said. "I hope you didn't make a nuisance of yourself while I was away."

"Let me go."

"Sounds as if you've lost your voice. Been busy making a racket?"

When the man on the bed didn't respond, Creeper Dude laughed. "I paid you up front. You owe me another hour of work."

"I never agreed to be drugged and cuffed to a bed. Let me go!"

"Cry me a river. You didn't agree to a lot of things I have planned for you. And if you go to the police after I release you, do you think they'll believe a male prostitute with a penchant for drugs, or a photographer with a thriving business?"

"They'll find pictures."

"I blindfolded you. You have no idea where you are. And if you think I'm stupid enough to store the digital pictures on the computers in my own house, you're dumber than I thought." He clapped his hands, making Zee jump. "Let's get started, shall we?"

"The police are on their way," the man on the bed told him.

Creeper Dude ignored him as he shuffled through a middle drawer in the tall dresser against the wall. Zee held perfectly still. The object he was holding when he turned toward the bed made her skin crawl. What the hell was he going to do with that?

"What are you doing?" the man on the bed asked since he couldn't see a thing.

"You'll find out soon enough. Looks like we're going to need some lubricant." He set the object down and began setting up the cameras. Then he walked back to the same dresser and slid on a pair of latex gloves. Zee was glad she couldn't see what he had planned. She had an overactive imagination as it was.

"If you relax, buddy, it'll be painless. If you want to keep fighting me, then go right ahead. The sickos who pay to see this kind of crap like to see the terror in a person's eyes. The funny thing is, they think it's all an act."

A few seconds later, the man started to scream.

Zee squeezed her eyes shut and prayed Colin would get here soon.

"Help me! Girl in the closet, please help me!"

Shit. Zee stiffened.

The room grew quiet. Then sure enough, she saw a shadow of a man coming her way. She was going to die. She was an idiot, just like Francis always told her. "Plenty of sunshine headin' my way," she sang under her breath. "Zip-a-dee-doo-dah, zip-a-dee-ay!"

Shut up! Francis shouted inside her head.

The closet door swung open. "What the hell?"

Head first, Zee rammed into him. He grunted and fell backward. On the way down, the back of his head hit one of the tripods and sent a camera flying into the wall.

"You dumb bitch," he ground out, grabbing hold of her ankle as she tried to jump over him to get to the door. She fell on top of him and clawed at his face. When he tried to twist away, she jammed her elbow into his side.

He wasn't very tall, and he was overweight, but he was strong enough to push her away and get to his feet in quick order. At the same time she heard a knock at the door, a pillow came down over her face, pushing her nose sideways. Arms flailing, she tried to reach over the pillow for his hand or his arm, but she couldn't find anything to grab on to.

He was putting all his weight into holding the pillow over her face. It was impossible to breathe. How much longer would she last? Lightheaded, she could tell that she was going to black out soon.

A doorbell sounded.

In a last desperate attempt to get away, she kicked both legs straight out and finally connected with Creeper Dude's shin. He stumbled backward, giving her a chance to draw in a much-needed breath of air.

And then the man on the bed found his voice again, screaming so loud, she was certain he'd just pierced both of her eardrums.

Creeper Dude made a run for it.

There was a lot of banging on the front door. Somewhere inside the house glass shattered. Another loud crash sounded before heavy footfalls pounded down the hallway, coming her way. She was still struggling to get air into her lungs when two men rushed into the room. A tall good-looking guy hovered over her. "Zee?"

"Colin?"

He'd come just in time. She was alive. Her legs wobbled as he helped her to her feet. She held on to Colin, glad when he used his arm around her waist to help her keep her balance. He smelled nice. "Creeper Dude went that way," she said, pointing at the door.

"We got him on his way out."

"Nice!" She glanced at the man on the bed. His blindfold had been removed.

"Thank you for coming to my rescue," he said.

She nodded, but a part of her wanted to lecture him for throwing her under the bus before the cops had arrived. But then her gaze fell on the object creeper dude had used on him. It resembled a medieval weapon with its long handle and sharp metal spikes covering the head. She realized she probably would have ratted him out, too, if their situations had been reversed.

"Come on," Colin said, ushering her out as another man with metal cutters entered the room. "Let's get out of here. We can talk at the station."

With an exaggerated limp, she leaned her head close to his chest as they walked. "Do you think Jessie will fire me?"

"Why would she do that?" Colin asked.

"Because I sort of disobeyed her orders . . . again."

"I think she'll be glad she had the insight to hire such a brave young woman."

"Do you know what month Jessie was born?"

"May. Why?"

Zee winced. "May what?"

"May 26."

"Dang. She's a Gemini. That doesn't bode well for me."

"No?"

Zee shook her head as they made their way to the entryway. "She's an air sign. Geminis can be superficial and uncompassionate. I'm screwed."

He chuckled.

He thought she was funny. She liked that. "Are you and Jessie still dating?"

"Why do you ask?"

She wasn't that much younger than Jessie. Maybe she stood a chance with him. "No reason."

Thirty

He watched Emily through the window. She was lying on the bench and clutching her sides. "Take your medicine," he told her. "It will make you feel better."

He knew she didn't trust him, but the way she'd been moaning all day, he figured she'd probably take it.

She looked to the ground and then reached for the bottle of medicine and the spoon. "When did you put this inside my room?"

"When you were sleeping." He walked away, then returned with his video camera.

"Hello, viewers," she said, forcing a smile. "In case you were wondering, yes, I'm feeling like shit." Her shoulders dropped as she looked away from the camera. "Why am I so sick? You've been putting something in the yogurt, haven't you?" She looked up at him. "This has been your plan all along." The color drained from her face. Emily jumped up and ran to the toilet to throw up.

"She doesn't look good, does she, Owen?" He zoomed in on Emily, catching the pain etched in her face as she rocked back and forth, her arms wrapped around her waist.

"This is your fault, Owen. You had all the power when it came to my daughter's health, but now I'm in control. I'm the insurance company now. Do you have any idea how many of your clients lost their homes and their life savings to try to save their loved ones? And you never gave a shit. But you give a shit now, don't you?"

Emily was vomiting again. That was more like it. She needed to suffer like his Hannah had suffered, and Owen Shepard needed to watch.

The medicine Emily had just taken was much more powerful than the poison he'd been putting in her yogurt. She'd already lost weight. Her shoulders looked bony; her face looked gaunt. A soft yellow circled her eyes. The cracks in her dry lips had deepened.

He thought of Hannah and scrubbed a hand over his face. "I hope millions of people see what you've done. I hope your company is destroyed when they find out how you treat the people who put their trust in DHI. Owen Shepard is not in the business of keeping people alive." Again he zoomed in on Emily, who was panting now, struggling to catch her breath.

She looked straight at him, which was as good as looking into the lens, and put a hand to her throat, her eyes wide. "Help me," she squeaked.

I wish I could, Emily. I wish I could.

Thirty-One

On her way home from Auburn, Jessie thought about everything Rene Steele had just told her. It was too soon to call the police regarding the Bale case, she decided, since she didn't have any proof Nick Bale had stolen his infant daughter. It would be Nick Bale's word against Rene Steele's. And it was clear Rene had an ongoing love affair with the bottle.

She thought about paying Ashley Bale a visit, but if Nick was home, that wouldn't work. He could be dangerous. As soon as she got back to her office, she would e-mail Ashley and let her know she needed to talk to her as soon as possible.

She was still on the highway when she got a call from Colin.

"Hi," she said.

"Where are you?"

"In the car, about fifteen minutes from home."

"You might want to stop by the station. Zee Gatley is here."

Jessie's first thought was that he got it wrong. Zee was at her house, working on the DHI case. And then she remembered that it was Zee they were talking about. "Why? What happened?" Her stomach dropped. "She's not hurt, is she?"

"Other than being worried about the possibility of you firing her, she's doing fine. But I think it's best if I let Zee tell you what happened."

"Okay, I should be there shortly."

After checking in at the Sacramento Police Department, Jessie was brought to a holding room, where she found Zee sitting alone at a table. When Zee looked up at her, Jessie's insides twisted. Zee's lip was bloodied. Her left eye was bruised and swollen shut. "Are you okay?"

"I'm fine. They gave me ice."

"What's going on, Zee? Why are you here?"

Behind Jessie, the door opened. It was Colin.

"I did exactly what you told me to," Zee said. "Once I knew for sure that someone was in danger, I called your boyfriend."

Jessie took a seat at the table across from Zee. "Tell me everything."

"Okay. I was sitting in the car, watching Lindsay Norton's house. 'Psychic City' by Yacht was playing, and I was about to turn up the volume. It's a great song, you should listen to it sometime. Although 'Water Fountain' by tUnE-yArDs is another good one."

"Zee," Jessie said. "Try to focus."

"Yeah, yeah. When I heard what sounded like a loud shriek, I turned off the radio and climbed out of the car. That's when I heard it again, only this time the voice was much more distinct. Someone was calling for help."

"And so you called Colin?"

"Not yet," Zee said. "I wanted to be sure."

Exactly what Jessie was afraid of. "So, what did you do next?"

"I walked across the street and made my way around the side of the house to the backyard."

"Whose house?"

"Lindsay Norton's neighbor—Creeper Dude's house. The guy I told you about."

Jessie's eyelid twitched.

"The screams for help kept getting louder and louder, so I ran around to see if there was a way inside."

"The door was unlocked?" Jessie asked.

"It was the next best thing—an open window."

"So you climbed through a window, and what did you find?"

"Well, I was quickly distracted by Lindsay Norton doing a vigorous workout routine. I knew that might be my only chance to catch her on video, so I used my cell phone to capture the whole thing." She slid her phone across the table so Jessie could watch.

Jessie watched the woman exercising, swinging a kettle bell between her legs. The video was sharp, the woman's face easy to see. "This looks as if it was taken from pretty high up. Where were you?"

"On the roof. The open window was on the second story."

Jessie glanced over her shoulder at Colin. He shrugged.

"Impressive," she told Zee.

"I know."

"So, what did you find inside the neighbor's house?"

"Empty rooms with boxes stacked against walls and a naked man cuffed to a bed with at least five video cameras circling the bed at various angles."

Jessie's heart dropped to her stomach. "So you called Colin?"

"Not yet. The poor guy was desperate to get away, begging and pleading with me to help him get loose. But the cuffs were metal, and I needed a key. And then I saw a car pull into the driveway. And that's when I called Colin."

Feeling a headache coming on, Jessie rubbed her temple. "Zee. Listen to me. You have no experience whatsoever, and yet you entered that house alone, knowing something wasn't quite right." Jessie folded her arms across her chest as she mentally checked off all the horrible things that could have happened to Zee. The thought of Zee being harmed made her insides twist in a knot. Instead of revealing how worried she was, though, Jessie hoped to scare her so she would never do anything like this again. "You could be arrested for trespassing."

"Colin said he'd take care of it."

Damn. "Fine," Jessie said, "but that's not the point."

Zee looked at Colin and said, "I never should have gone inside. I should have called you or Colin the second I heard the cry for help."

It sounded to Jessie as if it had been rehearsed. Before she could respond, Arlo Gatley rushed inside, his face lined with worry. "Oh, my baby. What happened to you?"

"I'm fine, Dad."

"I came as soon as I could." He looked at Jessie. "Is she okay?"

"She's one of the toughest people I know. She'll be fine." Jessie looked at Colin. "Can Arlo take her home?"

"I got her statement already. She's free to go. I want both of you to know that because of Zee's bravery, we were able to arrest a man on, so far, ten counts of pornography, including distribution of child pornography."

Zee looked at her dad. "See, I did a good thing."

"You did a good thing," Arlo said sadly. "Let's go."

After Zee walked away with her father, Jessie and Colin were left alone.

"Did your dad finally come home?"

"No. There were complications. He'll be in the hospital for a while longer."

"I'm sorry."

"Yeah, me, too." There was a long pause before Colin said, "If I can give you a bit of advice, it would be to stay away from Ben Morrison."

His warning caught her off guard. "Why? Ben is a crime reporter. He has contacts. He helps me and I help him."

"I don't trust him."

"You don't know him like I do."

"I'm telling you he's up to no good. I found him lurking around a crime scene last week at dusk. Too late for a crime reporter to be snooping around where he doesn't belong."

"What crime scene are you talking about?"

"He was in Lincoln, the area where DJ Stumm's bones were found."

Jessie crossed her arms. "Since when is there a good time to explore a crime scene? It's his job. It's what he's been doing for twenty years."

"I stopped him for a broken taillight. He looked nervous, like he might be hiding something."

"He's going through a lot right now. He and his wife are having problems. His sister, the only family he has left, wants nothing to do with him."

"Jessie, listen to yourself. You've always had a thing for the broken and downtrodden."

"He saved my life."

"He killed a man with his bare hands."

His phone buzzed. He glanced at it. "I've got to go, but I'd like to talk about this more later."

"Sure." Jessie watched him walk away. Ben was a good man. He was just confused and misunderstood.

On the drive home, Zee wasn't sure she heard her dad correctly. "What did you say?"

"I want you to quit."

"Are you kidding me? I'm just getting started." She pointed at the exit ahead. "We need to get my car," Zee said. "Take the next exit."

"No. We'll get the car another time."

"Why are you so upset? I don't see what the big deal is."

"Zee," her father said. "Look in the mirror. Your face looks as if it has been used as a punching bag. Your eye is swollen shut, and I saw you limping. Don't you dare deny it."

If he knew the half of it, he would burst a blood vessel—no doubt about it.

"You could have been killed," he went on. "I don't think you have any idea what I went through after I lost your mother. I can't lose you, too, Zinnia. I can't."

As her gaze fixated on her dad's profile, a weird calmness settled over her. There were no jolts of energy lighting up her brain. The voices had quieted. It was almost as if she was a "normal" human being. It was beautiful.

"Do you understand, Zee? I need you to do this for me."

"I love you, Dad. I don't think I've told you that nearly often enough."

He shifted in his seat and was about to say something, but she stopped him with a raised hand. "You have been my rock since the day I was born," she said. "You know me inside and out. But I can't quit. Not for you or anyone else. My entire life has been crazy town. If I could let you inside my head for an hour, you would never see me in the same light. I've always been different. I know it, and you know it."

"I'm different, too," her dad said. "I get it, but I won't allow you to put yourself in danger. It must stop."

"I know you've been bullied for most of your life," Zee said, surprised that Francis, Marion, and Lucy had not made one peep. "People think your big ears are funny-looking. We both know people can be cruel. But you don't know what it's like to have voices in your head, some of them shouting, all these voices telling you what to say, what to do, and how to act. The voices never stop."

"But you told the doctor that the medicine was working?"

"I didn't lie, exactly. The pills keep me calm, but the voices are always there." She paused. "Everything changed, though, once I started working for Jessie."

"The voices stopped?"

"No. Everything but the voices." For a moment she simply looked out the window and watched the trees and houses sweep by in a blur. Then she looked back at her dad, the one person throughout her life who always had her back. "Dad," she said, "I wish I could make you understand."

He said nothing.

"I've never felt so alive," she told him. "For the first time in my life, I'm seeing colors. My life isn't black and white any longer. People don't freak me out so much. I'm not afraid of living. Don't get me wrong. I still have moments—many moments—filled with overwhelming anxiety, as if I'm hanging by the tips of my fingers off the edge of a cliff. But they're fleeting. For the first time in as long as I can remember, I feel free. And happy."

"Zee."

"What, Dad?"

He opened his mouth as if to say something, but then clamped it shut. She couldn't stand to see him look so worried. "If you still want me to quit, I'll do it."

"You just got through saying you couldn't quit."

"I guess I lied. Because I would quit for you."

He huffed. "After everything you just told me, why would you do that?"

"Because I love you, and I can't stand to see you suffer because of me."

He took the next exit. He drove along for less than a half a mile and then made a U-turn at the stoplight.

"What are you doing?"

"I'm turning around. You're going to need a car tomorrow, aren't you?"

THIRTY-TWO

Olivia was having mixed emotions about having agreed to meet Ryder at the dance. He was two years older than she was. He had offered to pick her up, but she'd told him she'd rather meet him there. The notion that he might actually show up made her feel queasy.

Bella stood next to her, arms crossed, brow furrowed.

"You need to lighten up," Olivia said, "or no one is going to ask you to dance."

"Who cares? Look around. Most of these boys look like they belong in the sixth grade."

"I see Troy over there. I thought you sort of liked him."

"He joined the band."

"What's wrong with that?"

The gym doors opened wide, and Ryder walked in. Excitement shot through Olivia at the sight of him. He was so frickin' hot. One of the popular girls elbowed her friend and gestured his way.

Poor Bella was in the dark. Olivia should have told her what was going on, but she'd figured there was only a fifty-fifty chance he would show. The second his gaze connected with hers, his eyes gleamed, and he headed right for her.

Bella looked at Olivia. "What's he doing here?"

"What do you mean?"

"He's not the type of guy to go to a school dance. He and his friends are usually throwing a party. Why is he looking at you like that?"

"He asked me to the dance," Olivia said, "but I told him to meet me here since I was spending the night at your house."

"When did this happen?"

Guilt swept over Olivia. She'd known Bella would have a problem with Ryder, and she should have told her he was coming.

"Since when have you been talking to Ryder at all?" Bella asked when she didn't get a response to her first question.

"I don't know." Olivia squirmed. "A few weeks, maybe."

"And you never told me?"

"I didn't want everyone in the school to know."

"Oh, wow. Okay. I get it."

Ryder walked right up to them. "You look good," he said to Bella before turning to Olivia. "And you look beautiful. How about a dance?"

Olivia watched Bella march off. Bella was right. She should have told her.

Ryder offered her his hand, which made her forget all about Bella. Goose bumps skittered up her arms the moment her fingers touched his. As he led her to the dance floor, across the room she saw Bella gossiping with three other girls.

The song that was playing was a difficult one to dance to, but she remembered what Grandpa had said about moving her arms and legs and swinging her hips.

It was easy, and she was having fun.

Halfway through the song, Ryder pulled her close. He smelled woodsy, which made her wonder if he was wearing aftershave. When she glanced up, she noticed he was staring at her, making her feel sort of funny inside. It was weird because in that moment, all her troubles seemed to melt away. Suddenly she no longer worried about the way she looked or about the clothes she'd worn. She found herself romanticizing their relationship, making it into something more than it was. She inwardly laughed at herself. *Earth to Olivia. It's just a dance.*

Until it wasn't.

Hours later, the night was coming to an end, and Olivia wasn't ready to go home.

"Come on," Ryder said, pulling her toward the exit. "I want you to meet some friends of mine."

Olivia laughed as she pulled back.

He looked over his shoulder at her. "What?"

"I can't leave. I'm staying with Bella tonight. I should go find her."

"We won't be long, I promise. Two minutes. That's all I'm asking."

His smile was her kryptonite. How could she say no?

Outside the air was chilly. He put his arm around her, and she leaned her head into the crook of his arm. They passed by the music room and the library, then took a shortcut to the football field, where four guys and two girls were huddled in a circle, smoking weed and drinking alcohol straight from the bottle. "I really shouldn't be here," she told Ryder.

He took a swig from the bottle and then handed it back to one of his friends. "It's okay. One more minute."

Don't be a Debbie Downer, she told herself.

Ryder told everyone her name, but nobody seemed to care if she was there or not. Ryder handed her a joint. She shook her head, then watched him take a hit.

She pulled on his shirtsleeve. "I need to go."

And the next thing she knew he was kissing her, something she'd wanted him to do all night. But the kiss wasn't exciting or intoxicating. Instead it was sloppy and sort of gross. He smelled like a mixture of alcohol and weed.

His friends cheered. She tried to push him away, but he held tight.

Finally, she was able to shake loose from his hold. "I really need to go," Olivia told him.

"Stay with us, Ryder," one of the other girls said as she tugged his pants, prompting him to drop down next to her. The girl covered his mouth with her own as she cupped her hand over his crotch.

Disgusted, Olivia marched off.

What an idiot she'd been to think he was an amazing guy. She didn't even know him. She couldn't find Bella anywhere. She grabbed her phone from her back pocket, found Zee's number, and hit "Call."

Before giving Zee a chance to say hello, Olivia rambled forth. "Zee, I need help. The boy I told you about ended up being a jerk. He was all hands and tried to stick his tongue down my throat. It's a long story, but I need a ride."

"I thought you were spending the night at your friend's house."

"She's mad at me, and I can't find her anywhere. I think she went home."

"Are you trying to get me fired once and for all?"

"What? Of course not."

"I can't help you," Zee said. "I'm sorry. You need to call Jessie."

"Hello?" Olivia said. The phone beeped. Zee had hung up.

Thirty-Three

Unable to sleep, Ben crept out of bed and made his way to the garage. Using the step stool, he reached blindly for the top of the tallest cabinets until he felt the object he was looking for. He carefully unwrapped the cloth, then simply stared at the bloodied ax. After a moment he set the ax in the steel sink and then grabbed a bottle of bleach from another cabinet. About to scrub it clean, he stopped himself.

What am I doing?

You're not a killer, he reminded himself. *Your mind is playing tricks on you again.*

And yet the niggling doubt that had been tormenting him for days convinced him in that moment that he needed to find out for sure. All he had to do was take a sample of the blood from the ax and ask his friend at the lab to do a blood analysis. The technician would then check the DNA against criminals in the national database. If the blood matched DJ Stumm's profile, his work was done.

Ben went to the kitchen, grabbed a plastic bag and a knife, then returned to the garage and scraped off enough blood to take to the lab. He then rewrapped the ax in the cloth and placed it back on top of the cabinets.

He tucked the plastic bag into the pocket of his robe and stepped back into the kitchen, shutting the door behind him. His wife stood near the refrigerator, facing him, arms crossed. "What are you doing, Ben?"

He raised both arms in surrender. "Nothing. I couldn't sleep. I didn't mean to wake you. I'm sorry."

"You're doing it again," she said.

"What is that?"

"Shutting me out."

"Because I couldn't sleep?" He shook his head. He couldn't deal with this right now. Heading back for their bedroom, he walked past her.

She followed close behind him. "Don't shut me out, Ben."

He hung up his robe in the closet, then went to the sink in the bathroom and washed his hands and face. His reflection in the mirror revealed ashen skin and deep-set eyes shadowed in shades of gray. He hardly recognized himself.

Before he could climb back into bed, Melony was on his case again, jabbing his shoulder with a forefinger. He whipped around and grabbed hold of her wrist to stop her. "Enough, Melony. That's enough!"

She looked from his fingers wrapped around her wrist to his face. "What's wrong with you, Ben?"

He let go of her. "I don't know what you want from me anymore."

She rubbed her wrist. "I want the man I married back. What happened to the happy family man who couldn't wait until the weekends so he could spend time with his family?"

"I'm still the same man, Melony."

She shook her head. "We hardly ever talk anymore. You come home late and you leave early. The day your sister came to visit was the most time the kids and I have spent with you in months. After she left, you disappeared. When was the last time you asked me about my work?"

He swept his fingers through his hair. "Work at the *Tribune* has been stressful, and the fact that my sister won't talk to me after spending the day with us hasn't helped my state of mind. But I've been seeing the therapist just like you asked. I don't know how much more I can do right now."

She walked around to the other side of the bed, shut off the lamp, and climbed under the covers.

Ben did the same. He looked at his wife's silhouette, wanting nothing more than to reach out and comfort her. But he couldn't find the energy. How could he possibly convince her everything was all right when he knew that was a lie? Staring into the dark, he said, "I have to work this weekend."

Silence.

"I love you, Melony. That will never change."

Thirty-Four

As Jessie waited for the coffee to brew the next morning, she thought about last night. After picking Olivia up from the dance, she'd made sure Olivia called Bella to apologize and to make sure her friend had made it home safely. Jessie and Olivia had proceeded to talk late into the night about boys and friendships and life. Olivia had learned a tough lesson. Mostly, that friends needed to stick together, and another person's trust had to be earned.

Olivia was still asleep.

Ben had called thirty minutes ago to let her know that he and Owen Shepard were on their way to her office to talk to her. He didn't have time to give details. They would explain everything when they got there.

She filled a travel mug with coffee and then grabbed the leash from the hook on the wall. "Sorry, Higgins. No time for a run today, but you can come to the office with me."

Higgins wagged his stump, happy to follow her down the stairs and out the door.

As she approached her office, a low growl erupted from Higgins. "It's okay," she told the dog when she recognized Ben and Owen Shepard waiting for her down the street.

"Hello, Ben," she said as approached. She turned to Owen. "Good to see you, Mr. Shepard."

"Call me Owen."

Jessie nodded. "What's going on?"

"I was hoping the three of us could talk," Owen said.

"Sure. Let's go into my office."

The main entry door was open. Ben and Owen followed her to her office, where she unlocked the door and led them inside. Jessie pulled out a folding chair from the closet where she kept everything from pens to printers, and put it next to the cushioned chair in front of her desk. "It's the best I can do."

"Not a problem." Owen took a seat in the folding chair, which made sense since Ben was much taller and bigger.

After everyone was seated, Owen said, "I'll get right to it. I asked Ben Morrison to join us since both letters were addressed to him. Yesterday I finally had the chance to visit the police station and view the video concerning Tyler McDonald." He shook his head as if it saddened him to think of what he'd seen.

"If you had returned my urgent message making it clear this was a life-and-death situation," Ben said, angrier than Jessie had ever seen him, "we might have been able to save Brad Elton."

Owen sighed. "I'm sorry. Even if I had been in town, I don't know how I could have helped. It would have been impossible to get the board of directors to agree to the lunatic's demands."

"Did MAH send a second video?" Jessie asked.

"No," Ben said. "The first letter was a warning. No video. The second letter came with the video, letting us know he meant business."

Owen rubbed his temple. "There's more."

Jessie and Ben waited for him to go on.

"Owen, what's this about?" Jessie asked impatiently. "The police and federal agents are all over this case, and I'm doing what I can to help you find this man. Why are you here?"

Owen rubbed his hands over his face as if anguished by everything that had happened. He was acting much different than he had the last time she'd met with him. The man looked genuinely disturbed. "Did something happen, Owen?"

Owen's hands fell into his lap. "The monster has taken someone else."

"A third person?" Jessie asked.

He nodded.

Ben's eyes narrowed. "How do you know this?"

"Upon arriving home from work last night I found a letter in my mailbox and went straight to the police." His gaze met Jessie's. "The police and the FBI are working closely with DHI. They were able to secure a warrant and will have access to certain records, but we all know it's slow and tedious work. I wanted you both here," he said, looking from one to the other, "because I know you have worked together before, and I need all the help I can get."

"Who did he take?" Jessie wanted to know.

"My youngest child, Emily."

Her heart plummeted.

"Was there a postmark on the envelope?" Ben asked.

"No."

"What about a security camera outside your home?" Jessie asked.

Owen nodded. "Authorities are looking into it."

"Was there a video included with the letter?" she asked next.

"Yes," Owen said as he pulled a laptop from his briefcase. "The police took everything, but I had already saved it to my computer. I also took copies of the letter."

Owen Shepard, Jessie realized, looked as if he'd aged a decade since she'd seen him last. His face was pale and drawn as he set up his laptop. Dark circles framed his eyes.

Outside, Jessie saw Zee drive up and park at the curb. "Excuse me for a minute. I'll be right back."

Jessie and Zee had a lot to discuss, but now wasn't the time.

When Zee spotted her walking toward her, Jessie noticed that she lacked her usual confidence. Instead she looked sheepish. Her left eye was still swollen, and she had scratches down the front of her neck that Jessie didn't recall seeing at the police station yesterday.

"Hello, Zee," Jessie said. "How are you feeling?"

She shrugged. "I've been worse." Zee shifted her weight. "I wanted to let you know I e-mailed you the video I took of Lindsay Norton doing calisthenics."

"Thanks. I'm sure the insurance company will be pleased."

"I've known for a while that Lindsay Norton was faking her injuries."

"How so?"

"I slipped a fifty-dollar bill under a good-size boulder, and when she saw the money, she picked up the rock and took the money and ran." Zee exhaled. "Unfortunately, the video wasn't turned on."

Jessie frowned. "For future reference, that wouldn't hold up in court."

"Really? Why not?"

"It's sort of like planting a bribe or evidence to ensnare someone. It's not legal."

"That's stupid. Hey! Did you just say, 'For future reference, that wouldn't hold up in court'?"

Jessie nodded. "Why?"

"The word *future* sort of hints at the possibility that you and I might still be working together for a while."

"Is that a problem?" Jessie asked.

"You're not going to fire me?"

"No. In fact, I need you to go to the house and get working on the DHI list."

"Wow. Okay. That's awesome."

Jessie reached into her pocket for her key to the house, then handed it to Zee. "Here, take this. I'll be there to help once I'm finished talking to some people in my office." She didn't have time to explain any more than that. She also didn't have time to let Zee know that she was proud of her. Although many might see Zee's actions as foolish, she had proved herself once again to be a very brave young woman. Who knew what would have happened to the man tied to the bed or others down the road if Zee hadn't intervened?

Zee held up the key. "I'll get to work." She headed off.

Jessie watched her go and found herself wishing that life wasn't filled with so much madness. And then she thought about Owen Shepard and his daughter, and she pivoted on her heels and rushed back to her office.

Ben handed her a copy of the letter as soon as she swept through the door. "Read the letter, and then we'll watch the video."

> Dearest Mr. Shepard,
> If this doesn't get your attention, nothing will. After my daughter needlessly suffered only to die a horrible death, my objective was to see that DHI, and other insurance companies like it, made changes to their policies. But after the death of not just one but two of your employees failed to get an apology from you or anyone else at DHI, it became personal. I realized the only way to make you pay attention was to take your daughter. Emily will be with me for a while. She doesn't realize it, but her journey toward the end of her life has already begun. Her death will be slow and often agonizing, but nothing close to the torturous pain my own daughter endured.
> I will be satisfied only in knowing that you will finally understand my pain.

I have no requests since there is nothing you can do to save Emily.

Final recordings will be sent to local news outlets for public viewing so the world will know what you and DHI stand for.

MAH

"Are you ready to watch the video?" Ben asked.

Sickened by what she'd read, Jessie nodded.

Owen was staring mindlessly out the window.

Ben hit "Play." The image on the computer screen showed a young woman she assumed was Emily lying on the ground.

Jessie kept her eyes on the screen. Emily wasn't moving, and Jessie thought it was a still shot until Emily groaned as she rolled from her side to her back. She rubbed her eyes and then looked around before her gaze connected with the camera. After pushing herself to her feet, Emily took wobbly steps until she was closer to the lens, and all Jessie could see were two green eyes. Emily took a step back. "If anyone is watching this," she said, "my captor has sparse, stringy hair, brown eyes, and a large mo—"

The screen went black.

"The footage has been edited like that throughout," Owen said, looking at the screen now. "Emily is twenty-one years old. She's feisty and stubborn, too. She and I don't often see eye to eye, but she's always been m-my little girl." His voice cracked.

Jessie and Ben said nothing.

When the video resumed, Emily was sitting on a wooden bench inside a dingy, eerie-looking space with cement floors and gray cinder-block walls—just as Jessie had seen in the video featuring Tyler McDonald.

"Dad," Emily said, looking into the camera again. "This guy lost his daughter. She was my age at the time she was diagnosed. There was medicine that could have saved her life, but because it was experimental, DHI refused to pay. The doctors and nurses at—"

Cut off again. They waited.

"They sold everything they had," Emily continued, "including their house, to pay for the medication, but by that time she'd gone without for too long and she began having seizures. I feel like I know Ha—"

The screen went black again. Every time the video was cut off and then resumed, Emily was sitting in a new position. At the moment she was cross-legged on the floor.

"Dad," Emily said when the video came back on. "We argue more than we talk"—she winced, held her stomach—"but I want you to know that I'll always remember those special times when you would tuck me in at night and read the book *I Stink!* Those were great memories." She used the sleeve of her shirt to swipe at a tear. "I'm not scared. No matter what happens, I'll be—" Again the video was cut off midsentence. Thirty seconds passed. Nothing.

"Is that the end?" Jessie asked.

Owen nodded. "Yes."

"Ben has already been helping me with the case since he's covering the story for the *Tribune*," Jessie told him. "We've been working on narrowing down the list of DHI clients who have filed grievances in the past two years. I should have a final list by tonight."

"How many names left?" Owen asked, his voice hopeful.

"Hundreds," she said sadly before sucking in a cleansing breath. "I think we should watch the video again and see if we might have missed something the first time."

Just as she and Ben and the girls had done with the Tyler McDonald footage, they watched the video over and over again.

"She doesn't look well," Owen said, scratching his forehead. "She's very active, plays soccer, and has been involved in an outdoor type of group that goes hiking . . . things like that." He shook his head. "My point is, she's energetic. But you wouldn't know that by watching the film. She's definitely not well."

"He mentioned in the letter that she doesn't know her journey to the end has begun," Ben added. "He must be drugging her food or drink."

"That's what I was thinking," Jessie said. "She was off balance when she walked toward the camera."

"There was something else," Ben said. "Almost every time the video is cut off, I hear a faint noise, a sort of rumbling."

"I did hear something at the end," Owen agreed.

They watched the video again, pausing and adjusting the volume. In one particular section of the video, before Emily was cut off, there was definitely a rumbling sound. They all heard it. At the end of the video, instead of a rumbling, it sounded more like a distant horn, perhaps miles away.

"It sounds like the drilling or blasting I've heard on construction sites," Ben said.

"It could also be a train," Jessie said. "Maybe Emily is somewhere close to a busy highway."

Grimacing, Owen tapped a finger on Jessie's desk. "In the video Emily talked about a book I used to read to her. I wish it were true, but I never read to the kids. That's something their mother did."

"You never read her a book titled *I Stink!*?"

"Never."

Thirty-Five

Emily Shepard was grateful for the padding and pillow her captor had given her when he'd arrived that morning. The bench and the floor were hard and uncomfortable. Her neck hurt, and her spine was stiff. He came to watch her and record her every morning and usually left around seven at night. She knew this because he'd given her a radio. The radio kept her from going completely bonkers.

Feeling nauseous, she slid her legs off the bench and sat there for a moment, trying to steady herself. She'd been having difficulty walking. Convinced he was spiking the yogurt, she refused to eat it. She'd been surprised when he brought her soda crackers, but so far they weren't helping. Maybe the confusion and nausea were symptoms of stress.

Last night he had told her his name was Rickey. Why would he tell her his name unless he really did mean to let her die?

He was a tough one to figure out.

Sometimes he wouldn't stop talking. Other times he would not speak a word. The weird part was that he was getting to know her, and she was getting to know him. He didn't eat much, at least not in front of her, but he did have a sweet tooth. He'd already gone through an entire plastic jar filled with red licorice.

When he did talk to her, it was usually about his daughter, Hannah. He'd clearly put her on a pedestal.

Most of the time Emily felt sorry for him.

At the moment she hated him. Her knees wobbled as she walked to the toilet, lifted the lid, and threw up. Her life had quickly become a sad routine. Throw up, eat a cracker, drink some Gatorade, lie down, and then start all over again.

When she was sure she'd gotten rid of everything in her system, she sat up. A noise caught her attention. She turned toward one of the windows and saw that Rickey was back with his fucking video camera.

Yes, she hated him. Despised everything about him. He was a family man who had once loved his only daughter so much that after she died he decided everyone must suffer just as she had suffered.

The thought of her own father being overwrought with grief when it came to his children was almost laughable. And for some reason that made her hate Rickey even more. She didn't have a violent bone in her body, but if she had the opportunity to plunge the blade of a knife into his heart, she would do it.

She used her sleeve to wipe her mouth, then pushed herself to her feet. Her legs wobbled, and for half a second she thought she might not be able to take a step. But she could, and she did as she walked back to the bench to lie down. Her stomach gurgled. "Why are you filming me now?"

"I'd like you to look into the lens and tell my viewers what it's been like to be trapped with nowhere to go."

"Your viewers? What are you, some sort of weird-ass blogger?" She snorted. "That's it, isn't it? You probably have a million followers."

"Everyone needs to know what you're feeling," he stated firmly. "Tell them what it's like to feel as if you're deteriorating and there's no one to help you."

"I'd like your viewers to know that you're an asshole—a lazy, good-for-nothing asshole. If you really wanted to make a change," Emily told him, "you could have run for office. You could have written letters and started a movement. Instead you took innocent lives and allowed your daughter to die in vain."

"I think you've said enough."

"I'm just getting started," she said. "Instead of doing something about what happened to your daughter, you took the easy way out. Feeding your anger. It's easy to be violent, angry, and mad. It's a lot harder to fix something."

"You have no idea what I've been through."

"Are you kidding me? You talk more than all my roommates put together. Your daughter didn't die because she couldn't get her ridiculously expensive medicine—she died from listening to your endless chatter."

He said nothing.

For some stupid reason, she felt bad for being mean. *Ridiculous.* The man had kidnapped her, was probably going to kill her, and she felt sorry for him.

"My daughter should be alive," he said. And then his voice softened. "My entire life, I did everything right. I was a good son and a decent person. I never argued with my parents, seldom cursed, and always got good grades."

She was tempted to do a slow clap, but it probably wouldn't do any good to provoke him more than she already had.

"I married at a reasonable age," he droned on. "I bought a house, along with life insurance, health insurance, and car insurance." He paused long enough to give her a long, hard stare. "I bet your father never knew what it was like to leave a cart full of groceries in the market because he couldn't make his paycheck stretch far enough to feed his family."

"I wouldn't know," she said. "I don't know my father."

"I've seen pictures of you with your brothers and your parents enjoying the good life. Trips to the Caribbean, horseback riding through the lush mountains of Hawaii."

"Maybe you should do another Internet search. Those pictures were taken before my parents divorced. I was eleven, maybe twelve. But sure, whatever. I've been given everything I needed. I've never had to beg, borrow, or steal."

"What do you mean when you say you don't know your father?"

Her voice became flat. "Before my parents divorced, he was never home. He didn't teach me to tie my shoes or show me how to swim. I can't remember one word of advice. After they divorced, he never called or visited."

"What about on your birthday?"

She laughed but then began hacking instead. It took a few seconds for her to catch her breath.

"What's so funny?"

"You sound genuinely concerned."

"Maybe I am."

She tilted her head. "You seem too compassionate at times to be a killer. Why did you kill those men?"

"Because I had to."

Was he going to kill her, too? She thought of the first video he'd made and how she'd tried to send her father clues. She'd mentioned the book, *I Stink!* because not only had it been her brother's favorite book but also whenever the warehouse door opened, she got a whiff of an unpleasant odor that smelled exactly like the piles of waste at a dump site.

Her insides rumbled, and she held tightly to her stomach, then jumped up and ran to the toilet.

Thirty-Six

Ben knocked on the door to the apartment Emily Shepard shared with three other people. The apartment building was five minutes from the UC Davis campus.

His boss, Ian Savage, had agreed with authorities to hold off on publishing a piece regarding DHI for a day or two. Instead of focusing on DHI right out of the gate, Ben would begin his story with Emily Shepard and then bring it full circle back to DHI, thus revealing Emily's connection to her captor.

In Ben's opinion, *how* he told the story was more important than *what* the story was about. He needed to find a way to connect his readers with Emily and make them care. To do that, it was important that the story be comprehensive. The more sources and viewpoints, the better.

The door opened, and a young woman peeked out. Her long T-shirt skimmed knobby brown knees. The messy bun on her head was flattened on the top. Clearly he'd woken her up.

"Hi. I'm Ben Morrison with the *Sacramento Tribune*. I'm here to talk to you about Emily Shepard."

"Emily's dad was here yesterday. So were the police. We told them everything we know."

"Your friend was abducted. If you were the one taken, would you want your roommates to help in any way they could?"

Her chin fell slightly before she opened the door wide enough to let him inside. "Go ahead and take a seat on the couch. I'll go get the others."

Ten minutes later, all three roommates, in varying degrees of alertness, joined him. The apartment was small. The girl who had let him in said, "I'm Karen. And that's Teri and Brenda."

"Like I told Emily's dad, I really didn't know her that well," Teri blurted. "I've only been living here for a few months."

"Which one of you saw Emily last?"

Brenda lifted her hand. "It was the day she went missing. Emily was late for class, didn't even have time to eat anything before running out the door."

"Does anyone know if she made it to class that day?"

"She never got there," Teri said. "I know that for a fact because we're both in that class, and she wasn't there."

Ben looked at Brenda. "You saw Emily rush out the door and that was it? You didn't happen to be outside at the time, did you? See her talking to anyone?"

"She rushed out the door, and that was it. I was over there." She pointed to the kitchen area. "I haven't seen her since."

"Did any of you see her talking to a neighbor or someone you didn't recognize in the days before she was abducted?"

They all shook their heads.

"Which one of you would be willing to show me the exact route Emily usually took to school?"

"I'll do it," Karen said. "Just give me two minutes."

"Give me two adjectives that might describe Emily," Ben asked the other girls.

"Super sweet," Brenda said as Teri nodded in agreement.

"I thought she was fake when I first met her," Teri said. "But it didn't take me long to realize she's the real deal. Nothing phony about her."

"Does she have a boyfriend?"

Teri said yes while Brenda said no. Teri rolled her eyes as she explained. "Emily didn't want her parents to know she was dating anyone."

"Why not?"

Teri shrugged. "No idea."

"Her mother is strict," Brenda told him.

Ben used the app on his iPhone to take notes. "Did Emily usually walk to school?"

Brenda nodded. "She has a car, but she never uses it to get to class."

"No way," Teri chimed in. "Out of the four of us, she's the athletic one. She never drove to campus."

"What's her routine? Does she stop for coffee on the way?"

"She doesn't drink coffee," Karen said as she returned. She looked at Ben. "Are you ready to go?"

He stood, tossed a business card on the glass table in front of him. "If you think of anything that might be helpful to the investigation, give me a call, okay?"

They all nodded before he followed Karen out the door and toward the campus.

THIRTY-SEVEN

Emily had spent the past few hours with her head in the toilet, puking her guts out. She didn't have the strength to get to her feet, so she lay on the floor curled in a ball. Surprised to hear the door to her room open, she managed to turn her head just enough to see him enter her space. He'd come inside only once before. She regretted that she hadn't lunged for him, kicked him in the balls, or pulled his hair out.

And now she didn't have the energy to stand, let alone attack him.

She turned on her side, her head resting on her arm, and watched him drag the padding on the wooden bench out of the room and then replace it with something thicker. Same with the pillow. Next he stepped around her, took the toilet apart, and walked away, holding the section filled with waste.

It took a second for it to register that he'd left her alone and the door was still open.

This was her chance to escape.

She crawled to the bench and used it to pull herself to her feet. With her hands on the wall for support, she made her way to the door. The wide-open space before her was as tall as it was long and wide. Her heart beat hard and fast against her ribs. As soon as she let go of the doorframe, her legs shook from the effort it took just to stand without anything to hold on to. Her feet felt like twenty-pound weights. Each step took tremendous effort. She had barely reached the futon where her captor sat every day when her vision blurred and the room began to spin.

The exit had to be close. She couldn't stop now.

Arms outstretched, she took two more steps before her legs crumpled beneath her and she wilted to the ground.

Thirty-Eight

As soon as Owen and Ben left, Jessie walked back to her house, where she found Zee working quietly at the kitchen table. She looked around. "Is Olivia still sleeping?"

"Yep. She's probably traumatized after being attacked by that boy at the dance."

"How did you know about that?"

"She called me for a ride, but I told her to call you."

Jessie's shoulders fell at the idea that Olivia hadn't thought to call her first.

"Morning," Olivia said as she trudged past them to the kitchen with Higgins and Cecil following close at her heels. "What's wrong with everyone?" Olivia asked when no one responded to her greeting.

"My eye hurts a little," Zee said, "but other than that, I'm fine."

Olivia looked at Jessie and frowned. "What did I do now?"

"Nothing," Jessie said.

Zee snorted. "I think her feelings are hurt that you called me for a ride instead of her."

Olivia groaned. "Why are you so sensitive about that kind of stuff? I was upset, and to tell you the truth, I really wasn't thinking." Olivia walked over to Jessie and gave her a hug. "If I had taken a minute to think things through, I definitely would have called you first."

"It's not a big deal," Jessie said. "We're good."

"Okay," Zee said, clapping her hands for emphasis. "No time for family drama. We've got to find that girl."

Jessie took a seat next to Zee. She picked up the list of grievances, which had been narrowed down to 350 names.

"We've hardly made a dent," Zee said.

"Patience. It's a process of elimination." Jessie looked at the letters written by MAH and saw that Zee had highlighted words and phrases such as *sincerely, greed, needlessly suffered.*

Zee looked at Jessie. "I figured we might as well focus on word usage."

Olivia hovered over them. "Basically we're doing the same thing over again, only we're looking for new keywords?"

"Yes," Jessie said. "Until new information emerges, this is all we've got to work with."

Zee nodded. "Let's do this."

Before focusing on the DHI complaints, Jessie logged onto her computer and did a search for the book *I Stink!* Why would Emily make up a story about her father reading that particular book to her unless she was trying to tell them something?

A dozen links popped up. The book appeared to be an oldie but goodie, still popular, written and illustrated by Kate and Jim McMullan. It was written for ages five and under. There were lots of colorful pictures. The book was about landfills and waste material, how waste decomposes and gives off an odor that many people find offensive.

She wrote down the words *dump, landfill, bad-smelling odor.* What did it all mean? What was Emily trying to tell them?

THIRTY-NINE

When Emily opened her eyes, she was back inside the tiny room. How long, she wondered, had she been unconscious? Her mouth was dry, and her tongue felt like sandpaper. Her skin itched.

The man had made her a makeshift bed on the floor instead of on the hard wooden bench. Was he trying to prevent her from falling off the bench? He obviously knew she was weak. But the idea of him trying to make her more comfortable didn't make much sense under the circumstances.

Turning her head to the right, she saw a water bottle and a granola bar. Her hand shook as she reached for the water. It took most of her strength to open the lid on the plastic bottle, but it was worth the effort. The water tasted fresh and glorious. Cold and crisp on her tongue before it made a river down her throat. Up until now, she'd been given Gatorade, yogurt, and crackers. She was tired of eating and drinking the same thing, but desperate times called for desperate measures. She chuckled. Not because it was funny but because she had no more tears to shed. For the first time since she'd been brought to this place, she knew she was dying. She'd known from the beginning that it was a possibility, but she'd never imagined that she would just slowly disintegrate.

Were her brothers looking for her?

Did anyone know she was missing?

As she struggled to unwrap the granola bar, she saw the man looking through the window. "Am I dying?" she asked him.

At first he simply stared at her, then he nodded, slowly.

"I thought so. At least I won't die in vain, right?"

Nothing.

"I mean, maybe people will watch your videos and finally understand that people shouldn't have to die needlessly."

"Do you really believe that?"

"No. That's not how the world works. Most people are just trying to survive themselves."

"Maybe so, but people need to start caring. Your father and others at DHI need to hold themselves accountable. They're the killers, not me."

His voice shook as he spoke. This was the most angry she'd ever seen him. "You're right," she said, hoping to calm him. She didn't really believe her father and the people working for him were killers, but she also understood the man's frustration. He'd done everything he could to save his daughter, but it hadn't been enough. He wanted to blame someone. "In the short time I've been here," she said, "I thought I could forgive my dad. And maybe I have in some ways." Her voice cracked, and it pained her to talk, but she couldn't seem to stop. "I mean, I forgive him for not always being there, and for not being the best dad, but—" She stopped, unable to think straight.

Emily's gaze clouded. She was sick and she was dying and she truly felt bad for her abductor's loss. Maybe it was stupid of her to feel sorry for him, but she couldn't help it. Dizziness overtook her as the room began to spin. She wanted him to stop being angry. "If I were you, I would be angry, too."

He pointed a finger at her. "Stop trying to play me. You don't know anything!"

"I'm not playing you."

"My Hannah loved life. She was grateful for all she'd been given. She never asked for anything!"

"I had everything," she said, "and yet I never appreciated half of it." Her throat burned. "Cars were given to me. Insurance paid for. I wasn't anything like Hannah. I had it all. Does that make you feel better?"

He turned the other way.

"Don't walk away from me! Please don't go. I'm dying. I don't want to die alone." Her voice faltered. "Did you walk away from Hannah?"

He looked over his shoulder at her, muttered something under his breath, then grabbed his things and left her alone to die. In that moment, she didn't care. She was tired, and the pain wasn't going away. She only wanted to leave this horrible, ugly place even if she had to die to do it.

Forty

Jessie glanced at the clock before taking a moment to check her e-mails. Zee and Olivia had just left to take Higgins for a walk around the block. Ben had called thirty minutes ago to let her know he'd talked with Emily's roommates and checked out the UC Davis campus, but it was a dead end. He was on his way over. Jessie was worried about Ben. When she'd seen him earlier, he'd been quieter than usual, but she hadn't wanted to question him in front of Owen.

There was one message from Ashley Bale agreeing to meet Jessie Thursday morning at the coffee shop in Midtown.

Perfect.

If Nick Bale was keeping tabs on either one of them, Jessie thought it would be a good idea to meet at a coffee shop instead of her office. Best to keep him in the dark, if possible. Jessie planned to let Ashley know about the conversation she'd had with Rene Steele. She also wanted to tell her that Nick had been following her.

At the moment, though, her priority was finding Emily.

Ben arrived five minutes later. He looked exhausted, bordering on haggard. She ushered him to the kitchen table and poured him a cup of coffee.

When she sat across from him, she said, "What's going on? I didn't want to say anything this morning, but you look like you haven't slept in weeks."

"You are an observant one," he noted drily.

"I have my moments."

"Melony is upset with me. She thinks I'm keeping secrets from her."

"Are you?"

"I don't tell her everything that pops into my head. If that's considered keeping secrets, then so be it."

"You sound frustrated."

"I am."

Jessie didn't want to add to Ben's frustrations, but there was something she needed to talk to him about, and she couldn't think of any reason why she should wait. "Colin told me he ran into you recently."

Ben looked her square in the eye. "What else did he tell you?"

"That you were near Sun City Boulevard in Lincoln, within the vicinity of where DJ Stumm's bones were found."

"Your friend doesn't trust me."

"No. He said you seemed nervous."

"What do you know about the case?"

"The DJ Stumm case?"

He nodded.

"I know authorities believe he killed his family. Because of where they found his bones, they have determined that he was killed days later." She tapped her finger on the tabletop. "I guess now they need to figure out who chopped him up into pieces and buried him."

"It was me," Ben said.

Jessie laughed. She set her coffee cup down, saw the expression on his face, and realized he was serious. "What are you saying, Ben?"

"That I killed DJ Stumm. I don't think I can make it much clearer than that."

217

"That man was murdered twelve years ago. You don't remember anything that happened during that time, so how would you know if you were responsible?" She raised her eyebrows at him. "Can you answer me that?"

"After the visit from my sister, I went for a drive. I wanted to clear my head. For the second time in a short period, I found myself in front of the house where DJ Stumm's remains were found. As I sat there, staring out the window, wondering what had brought me there, I saw a tall man, my height and my build, dragging a limp body around the side of a building. I got out of the car and followed him."

Ben raked a hand through his hair, and Jessie could tell that what he was telling her was something that pained him.

"When I was finally able to get a clear view of the tall man's face, I realized it was me."

Jessie opened her mouth to protest, but he stopped her with a raised hand.

"I was the man who brought DJ Stumm's body to that location, chopped him up with an ax, and tossed him into the hole."

Jessie rubbed both hands over her face, trying to scrub all the nonsense he'd just told her away. Ben was tired. He didn't know what he was saying. "You do realize how ridiculous this sounds, don't you?"

"Yes."

"So, would you compare what you saw with having an out-of-body experience?"

"Definitely."

They were both quiet for a moment while Jessie soaked it all in. "Listen, Ben. You've been seeing images of old crime scenes for a while now. What makes this any different?"

"After the man buried the body, he left the shovel on the site and took the ax to the back of his van."

Jessie did her best to sit quietly and hear him out. "When did this hallucination end?"

"After he put the ax away, everything changed back to present time. All signs of new construction disappeared. The surrounding streets suddenly looked much different. There were a lot more houses, older houses. The trees had matured, and the sidewalks showed signs of wear and tear."

"What did you do?"

"I rushed to my van and opened up the cargo space. Beneath the spare tire, wrapped in a dirty cloth, was an old bloody ax." He exhaled. "Melony was right. I haven't been telling her everything."

"This is crazy talk." The worry she saw in his eyes broke her heart. He wasn't a killer. He was a good man, a family man.

"Early this morning I took a sample of the blood from the ax to a friend who works at a lab," Ben told her.

"How will you get your hands on a sample of Stumm's blood?"

"That friend I just mentioned has access to the national database. It's what he does. This isn't the first time he's been asked to do a blood comparison analysis on the side."

"Does he know where the blood came from?"

"No, and he didn't ask. He knows I work crime scenes. I should have an answer in the next few days."

"Even if the ax you're talking about turns out to be the one used to chop up DJ Stumm, anyone could have put it in the back of your van. According to the story in the paper, you worked that case. It makes sense that you would have been there."

"Ever since I recognized your sister on TV, things have changed, Jessie."

"How so?" She could see him struggling to deal with whatever was going on inside his head.

"I feel different inside."

Jessie waited for him to spit it all out and hopefully be done with such nonsense. He was punishing himself for reasons she didn't know.

"Sometimes I feel cold and emotionless," he said. "When that sensation comes over me, my toes and fingers go numb, almost as if I'm waking from a long, deep sleep. And it's as if I'm surrounded by an unnatural silence."

"But that doesn't make you a killer."

Ben was staring straight ahead, his body stiff. "When it happens, the only thing I feel is a need to dominate and control, maybe even a desire for vengeance."

Jessie swallowed. She didn't like what she was hearing, didn't want to admit that in the short time she'd known him he really did seem different. Serious. More intense. "I wonder if your sister was right in trying to protect you from revisiting your past."

"No," he said. "I'm not turning back now." His shoulders relaxed as he met her gaze. "Good or bad, I need to know." He gestured at all the papers on the table. "But it can wait. Right now, the only thing that matters is finding Emily."

———

On the news, after Zee and Ben had left and Olivia had gone to bed, Jessie saw a reporter standing in front of a mansion. There were at least forty people gathered on the street outside the gated property.

It took her a minute to figure out that it was Owen Shepard's residence. A group of protesters had gathered to demonstrate their objection to DHI's refusal to cover medications that had been classified as experimental. People held signs behind the reporter that read: Affordable Health Care For All and Fix It Don't Nix It.

The camera zoomed in on a distraught woman holding up a picture of a young man. "Owen Shepard and DHI killed my son, Tyler McDonald."

Jessie picked up the phone and called Colin.

"Hey there," he said. "Everything okay?"

She could hear noise in the background. He was still at the station. "I'm fine. It sounds like you're busy."

"Yeah, it's been crazy around here."

"I just turned on the news and saw the reporters and protestors outside Owen Shepard's house. Do you know what's going on?"

"The killer took it upon himself to send every local news station in the area a copy of the letter and video, including a statement letting the public know that DHI was not in the business of saving lives. He's managed to spark outrage in the community in a very short time."

"When did the news stations receive the package?"

"Late last night."

"Were there security cameras in the area?" she asked.

"Yes. Our people are looking through the footage now."

"Are you getting any closer to finding the maniac?" Jessie asked.

"Not close enough and time is running out."

Forty-One

Jessie entered the coffee shop on the corner of Sixteenth Street at exactly 7:50 a.m. the next day.

She approached the front counter, paid for her coffee, and then found a table near the entrance. By the time she'd taken a seat, the line at the counter had doubled. When Ashley entered the establishment, Jessie waved her over and offered to buy her a coffee.

"No, thanks," Ashley said, taking a seat. "I don't have long. The boys are only in school for a short time, and I have errands to run." She looked around. "Is there a reason we met here instead of your office?"

"Yes. Your husband has been keeping track of me, and I was hoping to stay off his radar."

Ashley appeared genuinely stunned. "Nick has been following you?"

Jessie nodded. "I'm not going to be able to work on your case for a few days, but I wanted you to know what was going on. And I didn't want to talk over the phone or put anything in writing."

With a pinched expression on her face, Ashley stiffened. "Okay. Go on."

"Do you recall a woman named Rene Steele?"

"Yes. She was a nurse at Mercy General when Dakota was born."

"You never mentioned her name, and she's not anywhere in your notes."

"That's odd. I'm sure there was something in the binder I gave you."

"Why don't you go ahead and tell me what you remember."

"Rene Steele refused to talk to me. In fact, her mother wouldn't allow me inside their house."

"If her mother were still alive," Jessie said, "I don't believe she would have agreed to talk to me, either." Jessie didn't know quite how to break the news, true or not, but she needed to get to it. "What Rene told me was quite shocking, actually, but I wanted you to know what she had to say."

"Tell me, please."

"She believes she saw the person who took Dakota."

"What?" Ashley looked horrified and hopeful at the same time. "How can that be? Any sane person would have come forward with that kind of news."

"According to Rene, her mother wouldn't allow her to speak to the police. Years before, she'd been working as a nurse in Los Angeles when she was accused of negligence. A young boy died, and her reputation was destroyed."

"But what does any of that have to do with being a witness to an abduction?" She shook her head in disgust. "That makes no sense."

"She told me she was being threatened."

"By who?"

"Your husband."

Ashley's jaw dropped. After a few seconds of awkward silence, she began to gather her purse. Her face paled.

"You're leaving?"

Her gaze darted around the coffee shop. "I must. Nick didn't want me to pursue this, and now I see why. Not only are you accusing my husband, an important businessman, of following you as if he has nothing better to do with his time, but you're blaming him for the abduction of our little girl." Ashley's hands shook as she pulled her purse close to her chest. "I'm calling this whole thing off."

"Ashley, please. I'm not blaming your husband for anything. I'm merely relaying what I've learned. We've come too far to stop now. You have to think about Dakota."

Ashley was on her feet. Her expression softened, and for half a second Jessie thought she might actually break down and tell Jessie that her husband wasn't the man she'd made him out to be. Maybe she wanted to tell someone the truth—that Nick was toxic. A bully who watched her every move and tried to isolate her from the outside world. "Is there something I should know about Nick?"

After a short pause, Ashley's spine stiffened. "You should know that a day hasn't gone by that I haven't thought of my daughter. I have to call the investigation off. Send me a bill."

As Ashley walked out the door, Jessie could've sworn she saw a blue car speed by and then disappear farther down the road. It boggled the mind to think Ashley wouldn't take two minutes to even consider what she had to say.

Was Ashley truly that blind, or maybe it was something else . . . maybe he *was* controlling and possessive, and she was scared to death of him.

FORTY-TWO

Back at her office, Jessie spread out all her notes on the Emily Shepard case as Emily's video played on her computer. There were no DHI complaints filed by anyone with the initials *MAH*. There were thirteen complaints filed by people with the initials *MH*, but not one of the four grievances written by men had anything to do with experimental drugs or daughters.

She let out a long, ponderous breath as she looked at the list of names she, Olivia, and Zee had compiled. There were still over a hundred names left. The killer could be any one of them.

Shit.

It could take them days to narrow the list down further. *This is like looking for a fucking needle in a haystack.*

As she tried to think, the rumbling sound from the video sounded much more distinct. She played it again as her gaze fell on the piece of paper where she'd written the words *dump, landfill, bad-smelling odor.*

Chills scurried up her spine. "Oh my God! Trains, dumps, and . . ."

Looking back at the video, she zeroed in on the cinder blocks.

"And warehouses!"

Emily was trapped inside a warehouse near a dump site. Her foot began to bounce beneath her desk. She was onto something, and she could barely contain her excitement. Opening a new window on her computer, she began searching for dumps and waste management sites in the Sacramento area.

The ringing of the phone broke into her thoughts.

"Ben! You need to get over here now."

"Where are you?"

"At the office. I have something I want to share with you."

"I'll be there in less than twenty."

As soon as Ben walked into her office, she explained her ideas regarding the book Emily had mentioned and the dump sites in the Sacramento area. "What do you think?"

"I like where you're headed."

"Remember the strange noise we heard on the video with Emily and what sounded like a horn or a siren?"

He nodded.

"Here. Listen. In the beginning, I think that's the sound of a train in the distance. At the very end you can hear the rumbling of train tracks."

She played the tape, watching Ben the entire time. When it was finished, he said, "I think you might be right."

"If it's a train we're hearing, and if Emily was trying to let someone know where she was, then we need to concentrate on warehouses in cities close to a railroad track and a dump site."

"I agree." He sat down across from her, pulled out his laptop, and waited for it to boot up. "Did you see Ashley Bale this morning?"

Jessie nodded as she made notes.

"How did she take the news about her husband?"

"Not very well. She fired me."

"Odd thing for her to do under the circumstances. What are you going to do?"

Jessie looked up at him. "Emily is more important at the moment. I'll give Ashley Bale a few days. Hopefully she'll come around. If not, I might pursue the case on my own."

"Because you have an idea of what might have happened to Dakota Bale?"

"No, but I'll bet you my life savings that Nick Bale knows."

Thirty minutes later they had a list of six waste sites. They'd used Google Maps to find sites near industrial areas that were also within two to five miles of the train tracks. It was the best they could do. Whether there were warehouses in the area, abandoned or not, was impossible to tell.

"I think we should divide and conquer," Ben said. "I'll go to one waste site while you go to another."

Zee pulled up next to the curb outside. The moment she walked into the office, she looked from Ben to Jessie. "You both look as if you've drunk too much coffee or seen a ghost, or maybe both. What's going on?"

"I'm going to get started," Ben said. He held up his copy of the waste sites and said, "I'll take the top two on the list."

"Good luck," Jessie said. "Keep in touch." After he left, she printed off another copy for Zee and then explained the plan.

Zee frowned. "If I go to one of these places, it could take twenty-fours before I even hear a train."

"Forget about hearing the train," Jessie told her. "We've already narrowed the list of sites down to the ones close to the tracks. What we need to do now is find a warehouse that looks as if it isn't being used much."

"With the economy going down the toilet, my bet is that there are plenty of unused warehouses in the Sacramento area." Her eyes widened. "According to Wikipedia, it's the sixth largest city in California. Just covering the warehouses around these six waste sites could take days if not weeks."

Jessie grabbed her bag and began stuffing it with files and notes.

"Emily could be anywhere," Zee went on. "What if she's not in Sacramento at all?"

"It's all we've got to go on at this time." Jessie stopped what she was doing and looked at her. "Do you have a better idea?"

"What about the list of grievances?"

Jessie shook her head. "Our list was whittled down from thousands to three hundred names." She lifted her hands in surrender. "We don't know where this guy is from. We don't know his or his daughter's names. Right now this is our best lead."

"Okay," Zee said with a sigh. "I guess we better get moving."

FORTY-THREE

Apprehension slowed his pace as he entered the building.

It was quiet. Too quiet.

Before he'd left the premises last night, Emily Shepard had been going in and out of consciousness. He saw her on the floor and wondered if she was dead. He didn't move. His stomach quivered. He had to force himself to forge ahead, unlock the door, and step cautiously inside.

Chills crawled up his arms. He'd known she was dying. Of course he had. But he didn't want her to die. "Emily?"

Nothing.

Kneeling down beside her, he felt for a pulse.

She was alive. *Thank God!* Adrenaline raced through him as he scooped her into his arms and carried her to the futon in the middle of the warehouse. He then rushed outside to the trunk of his car, grabbed a washcloth, and dampened it using the hose outside the main door.

The other day he'd removed the antifreeze-laced Gatorade and yogurt from the cooler in Emily's room. But every time she'd come to, she'd seemed confused, and her speech had been garbled. That was when he'd realized it was too late. She was dying.

That was the plan, he reminded himself.

That had always been the plan. To document her suffering and make sure the world, and especially Owen Shepard, experienced first-hand what it was like to watch an innocent child die a slow and tragic death.

But the pain and suffering was on him. Not Owen Shepard.

Racked with guilt, he brought a folding chair close to the futon, took a seat, and placed the cool washcloth on Emily's forehead. She stirred, muttering a string of nonsensical words.

He'd left one last video for Owen Shepard. This time he'd left it at the neighbor's house down the street, since reporters and protesters had begun to gather in front of Owen Shepard's estate. The video was intended to thrust one last dagger into the man's heart. That was, if he had a heart.

Watching Emily waste away through the lens of his digital video camera had begun to wear on him. After all he'd been through, he'd never thought this would be so difficult. The problem was he liked the girl. She reminded him of Hannah. She was young and feisty and unafraid to speak her mind. He hadn't enjoyed watching Emily suffer. He'd thought it would bring him relief, but it only brought him more grief.

Her eyelids fluttered. "Jacob. Is that you?"

Jacob was the older of her two brothers. During their time together, he'd learned a lot about Emily. She liked to talk about her brothers. More than once, she'd mentioned Jacob and how he'd been the strong sibling who had done everything he could to keep Emily's spirits high when their parents had divorced. Jacob was her best friend, and when she was gone she wanted her brother to know that she hadn't been afraid to die.

"Jacob isn't here," he told her.

Recognition came slowly. "It's you," she said, reaching for his hand. He pulled away, just out of reach.

"When your daughter was dying, was it like this?" She licked her dry lips, and he used the cloth to squeeze drops of water into her mouth.

"Isn't it strange that I feel close to you?" she said, her voice gravelly and low. "Do you think I'll be the catalyst for the change you're looking for?"

He nodded even though he knew the odds were against that. He drizzled more water into her mouth, then folded the cloth in a neat square and set it on her brow. She was too weak to hold it there herself. His shoulders quaked, and he could see his fingers tremble as he held the cloth to her forehead. *What have I done?* he thought as a keening pain sliced through his middle.

"I hope after I'm gone, things are better and you find the peace you're looking for. It might take some time." More licking of the lips. "I'm really thirsty."

He left her to get a bottle of water. The sick feeling inside him sat like a heavy brick in his gut. Returning to Emily's side, he put the bottle to her mouth and let the water trickle slowly down her throat.

"That's nice," she said when she'd had enough.

For a moment it was quiet. The quiet scared him because her eyes had closed, and he could no longer see the rise and fall of her chest beneath her cotton shirt. Panic set in just before her eyes opened, startling him. "Don't get angry with me," she said, her voice as creaky as an old rocker, "but I don't think your daughter"—she stopped to take a breath—"would want you to kill any more people. Let me be the last."

He couldn't do this—couldn't watch her die, couldn't bear to hear the hoarseness in her voice as she tried to make sense of what was happening to her. "What is wrong with you?" He set the water bottle aside. "You should be the one who is angry. You're too young to die. You're forgetting that I took advantage of your kindness. I did this to you to get revenge."

"You lost your daughter. You weren't thinking straight." She had a difficult time catching her breath, but she finally managed. "After I'm gone, you should turn yourself in."

He thought of Hannah then, and he realized she, too, would have helped an old crippled man. Hannah and Emily were so much alike. He jumped out of his seat, took the chair, and slammed it against the wall. The chair broke.

Hannah hadn't deserved to die.

And neither had the men whose lives he'd taken. He rubbed his hands over his face, agonizing over what he'd done. How had it all come to this? He dropped to his knees and began to rock back and forth.

He'd lost everything, including his soul.

His insides twisted.

What have I done?

What have I become?

FORTY-FOUR

Jessie saw that Zee was calling, so she pulled to the side of the road and picked up. "Zee," she said, "I'm going to call Ben and set up a three-way call so everyone can report their progress, if any."

Once she had Ben on, Jessie said, "Go ahead, Zee."

"There are no warehouses anywhere near this place," she said. "I've been down every road I could find, but so far, I've got nothing. If it's okay with you guys, I'm going to head over to the Roseville Refuse Collection in North Highlands."

"Sounds good," Jessie said. "We can also check off the Western Placer Waste Management Center in Roseville. I'm on my way to the landfill in Lincoln. What about you, Ben?"

"No luck so far. I'm in front of a warehouse right now that I'm going to check out, and then I've got to head back to the office for a few minutes. Call me if you find anything worth looking at."

"Will do."

They all disconnected.

A mile or so past Thunder Valley Casino in Lincoln, Jessie noticed an unpleasant odor. She'd been driving with her window down all afternoon, but this was the first time the smell of decay was overpowering. More than a mile down Athens Road she could see the landfill. The smell grew stronger.

It wasn't until she turned onto Fiddyment Road that warehouses and storerooms began to pop up here and there. The few warehouses she passed so far were occupied. Trucks in the loading dock areas. Lots of cars in the parking lots. People coming and going.

From there she headed down Moore to Nelson Lane. She drove slowly, watching and listening. Almost immediately after driving over the railroad tracks and finding herself on Beacon Avenue, her skin prickled. There was no traffic in front of her or behind her. She pulled over to the side of the road and got out of the car. She felt a low rumble beneath her feet. Retrieving her cell phone, she launched the camera app, swiped to video mode, and tapped the "Record" button. She wanted a video to compare the sounds with the ones in Emily's.

It wasn't long before a train passed by, its whistle blaring. Once the train could no longer be seen in the distance, she knew she was close even before she replayed the video she'd just made. Climbing in behind the wheel, she turned on the engine and merged back onto the road. There was nothing but dusty terrain and few trees on both sides. She turned onto an unpaved side road and drove for a mile before realizing it was a dead end.

Again and again, she drove down every road in the vicinity.

At the end of another dirt road, she sat still for a moment as she scanned the area. Something niggled.

HAN—BOOM!

HAN—BOOM!

In her mind's eye she could see the shape of Tyler McDonald's lips and the way his tongue slid under the roof of his mouth as he said, "Han."

"Han-nah," she said aloud as she looked straight ahead. "Hannah," she said again. Tyler had been saying he'd had nothing to do with Hannah's death. The killer's daughter's name had been Hannah!

She squinted as she leaned forward, her chest pressed up against the steering column.

In the distance was a building in the middle of nowhere. Looking from left to right, her heart racing, she realized she couldn't get to it from the road she was on. She put the car in reverse and sped backward, gravel popping beneath the tires as she drove over uneven dirt until she was on the main road again.

Keeping an eye on the building as she drove, afraid of losing sight of it, she made a left and then a right.

There it was. It was definitely a warehouse. Dust sprayed up from the wheels as she pulled closer. The building looked like an oversize gray stucco box. There was no loading dock. Only a double steel door and few windows.

Flooded with adrenaline, she circled the building, braking when she spotted a car, a silver Lincoln Town Car. She pulled up and got out to check it out.

She could hardly breathe. Was Emily inside the building?

Bent forward, she rushed over to the car and tried all the doors. Locked. Through the window she saw cases of Gatorade and water bottles. On the floor was a toolbox. She took a picture of the license plate and texted the image to both Zee and Ben, asking for assistance in finding out who the car belonged to. She also typed out the name *Hannah*.

Six minutes later, Zee responded with a text of her own: **Rickey Talbert. Daughter, Hannah Talbert.**

Five seconds after that, Ben called. "He's on the DHI complaint list. That's our guy. Where are you?"

She gave him her location, then asked, "What about the initials *MAH*?"

"It seems it's been right there in front of us all along," Ben told her. "In every complaint Rickey Talbert sent to DHI, he mentioned being mad as hell. In the first letter I received, he told me the same thing. He said he was Mad As Hell . . . MAH."

Jessie cursed under her breath. How had she missed that?

"Hold on," Ben said. She heard him set his phone down before muffled voices sounded in the background.

"The police have been called," he said once he was back on the line. "They're on their way."

"Thanks."

"We already know Rickey Talbert has proven to be a dangerous man," Ben warned. "You're not armed. Get out of there now."

———

Rickey Talbert paced the room, sickened by what he'd done. His anger had changed him into something he no longer recognized. Across the room, Emily reached out. Without hesitation, he went to her and sat in the chair beside her. "What is it? What do you need?"

"Dad," she said, her voice barely audible. "You're here."

Back stooped, chin trembling, he squeezed his eyes shut.

"Don't be sad," she told him. "Everything will be all right."

His chest ached. "I'm sorry." If he could take it all back, he would.

"You did the best you could." She gritted her teeth. When the pain finally passed, she said, "I love you. I'm sorry."

"I'm sorry," he said again before his head fell forward. He thought of his daughter then and choked out the words, "I'm so sorry, Hannah. I didn't mean to cause so much pain and suffering. I've missed you and your mother so much."

He lifted his head, wiped tears from his eyes.

Emily's face was so pale. She was so young. He couldn't stand it any longer. He got to his feet and moved the chair aside. He couldn't sit here and watch her die. It might be too late to save her, but the doctors and nurses could make her comfortable. No more pain.

He'd been wrong. So wrong.

She didn't have to needlessly suffer.

Drowning in despair, he lifted her into his arms and carried her to the exit. "Hang on. I'm going to get you help."

———

Jessie had never struggled so hard to do the sensible thing. More than anything she wanted to storm inside the building and try to save the girl—if Emily was in there and still alive, that was.

Yes, it would be a foolish thing to do since she was unarmed.

But what if there was a chance, any chance at all, that she could rescue the girl?

She glanced at her watch.

How could she possibly drive away and do nothing?

She got out of the car; gravel crunched beneath her shoes as she walked toward the building. Cars whizzed by in both directions on Highway 65; white noise unless she focused on it. Standing in place, less than ten feet from the steel doors, she stopped, breathed, listened. Her fingers flexed at her sides, curling and uncurling.

Far off to the right in the distance, she could see a row of warehouses. To the left she saw movement, merely tumbleweeds, rolling across an empty field.

Her phone buzzed. It was Ben. She hit "Talk" and held the phone to her ear at the same time as the steel doors to the warehouse opened.

Her breath caught in her throat. For a fleeting moment she thought she was seeing things.

A man walked out carrying a girl, her arms and legs bony and frail, her body limp.

He looked up, saw Jessie, and stopped in his tracks, his legs set wide apart as the doors clanged shut behind him.

Her adrenaline spiked as a compulsion to flee set in. But she held her ground. *Rickey Talbert,* she thought. Just as Emily had described him on the video, he had stringy hair and dark-brown eyes—sad eyes, not the eyes of a killer. And yet he had already killed two people, possibly three.

Seconds passed. Neither of them made a move. The phone was still pressed against her ear. "Jessie," Ben was saying. "Where are you now?"

"I never left."

"Are you in your car?"

"No. It's too late." She disconnected the call and shoved her phone into her pocket. Her heart pounded against her ribs. "Is she alive?" Jessie asked Rickey Talbert.

"Not for long."

What did he mean by that? Was he going to kill her? What was he doing with her? Why had he come outside? To dispose of her body?

Jessie could see the girl's face. It was Emily Shepard.

She looked from Emily to Talbert. The woeful expression on the man's face confused her.

"Will you take her to the hospital?" he asked.

It took half a second for his words to register. Jessie nodded, then turned and ran to her car and opened the back door so he could place Emily inside. The thought that it could be a trick floated through her mind. But what if it wasn't?

There was no turning back now. She didn't have a weapon. There wasn't a whole lot she could do if he decided to attack her. Jessie watched him walk toward her. The man looked frail, and yet he didn't appear to struggle with the weight of the young woman in his arms. His face was drawn, focused, as if he was intent on getting her help.

Nothing about this scene made any sense whatsoever.

It was difficult to tell if Emily was breathing. Every part of her body had gone slack. Her skin was pale, her eyes closed.

Sirens sounded in the distance. He placed Emily carefully on the back seat and shut the door. "Go," he said.

Jessie didn't need to be told twice.

She jumped in behind the wheel and drove off, gravel spitting and popping beneath the undercarriage. She stopped at the corner of the building as police cars streamed in, one after another. The moment she spotted the ambulance, she jumped out of the car and waved it down.

The paramedics didn't waste any time transferring Emily to a stretcher.

Jessie followed one of the EMTs to the back of the ambulance, where they were loading her on and assessing the situation. "Is she alive?"

"We have a pulse," he said.

Relieved, hopeful, Jessie stepped back so they could shut the doors and be on their way.

"Put your hands over your head," she heard an officer shout.

Jessie looked back toward Rickey Talbert, surprised to catch him looking right at her. She was too far away to hear what he said unless he shouted, but she'd been reading lips since middle school. The way he pronounced each word made it easy for her to decipher: "Don't let her suffer."

The ambulance backed out onto the street and sounded its alarms as it took off.

"Put your hands in the air!" came another warning.

Jessie watched with growing tension. *Don't do it,* she thought.

Rickey Talbert wasn't listening to the cops' continued shouts to put his hands up.

Her skin prickled as she watched the tension leave his body as he slowly, methodically, reached deep into his front pants pocket.

He whipped his hand out and pointed a finger at the officers closest to him. Shots were fired. Rickey Talbert dropped to one knee and then crumbled to the ground.

Something told Jessie Rickey Talbert had gotten exactly the ending he wanted.

FORTY-FIVE

Less than twenty-four hours later, Jessie and Olivia stared out the front window overlooking J Street. News vans were parked along the main street, and a line of reporters stood just outside the broken gate with their microphones and camerapersons.

"Did you call the hospital?" Olivia asked.

Jessie nodded. "Emily is still in critical condition, but she's hanging on."

"That's good. What about Hannah's dad? Is he going to make it?"

"No. He's gone." From everything Jessie was able to gather from Colin and Ben, Rickey Talbert was once just a regular guy from Missouri. Before he lost his wife and daughter, he was seen in his community as a good man, respected by those who knew him.

"It's probably for the best that he's gone."

Jessie agreed but wondered why Olivia would say that. "Why is it for the best?"

Olivia shrugged. "I don't know, really. I guess from everything I've overheard you telling Colin on the phone, it just seems like he sort of went off the deep end after losing his daughter. If he could have gotten help, you know, talked to someone, I don't think he would have killed those guys."

"And yet you think he's better off dead?"

"Definitely. He won't have to spend his life in a cell trying to figure out or explain to others what went wrong. He can be with his wife and daughter now."

"Hmm." Jessie had mixed feelings about Rickey Talbert. On the one hand, maybe he was better off dead. He'd obviously had no will to live without his wife and daughter. And yet it bothered her to think that he could have used that anger and drive to advocate for a positive change instead.

There was a knock on the door. From the looks of it, a brazen reporter had seen them looking out the window and figured it was worth a shot.

"How am I going to get to school?" Olivia asked.

Jessie ushered Olivia away from the window. "Call Bella and tell her I'm going to take you this morning. You be a good dog," Jessie told Higgins. "I'll be right back."

Olivia made the call, then grabbed her backpack and followed Jessie out the back door and down a long flight of narrow stairs.

When there were no parking spaces on the street, Jessie parked near the dumpster in the alley. A young reporter happened to peek down the alleyway and headed toward them.

"When we get to the car, just get inside and lock your door," Jessie told Olivia.

"Jessie Cole. One question, please!"

The young reporter was right on her heels. Jessie sifted through her purse for her keys, which was never an easy task considering she had everything from ChapStick to a plastic fork inside her bag.

"Everyone wants to know how you found the girl."

"It was a lucky shot," Jessie said, still walking, still searching.

"No, really. How did you know where to look?"

Ignoring the question, Jessie and Olivia kept walking.

When they got to the car, Olivia went to the passenger door and tried to get in. "Do you have the key?"

Jessie gave Olivia a look. "I'm trying."

"Were you working the case on your own? Did DHI hire you?"

"I had help," she told the reporter. "Ben Morrison with the *Sacramento Tribune*." She found the keys and held them up to show Olivia, who merely rolled her eyes.

"Once again you're being called a hero."

"I was just doing my job." She unlocked the door and climbed in behind the wheel. "Emily is still in the hospital," Jessie told the reporter, "and I only hope we were able to find her in time."

"It is kind of cool that people think you're a hero," Olivia said as they drove away.

Jessie was reluctant to take that label. "Heroes are doctors and nurses, firefighters and scientists. They change lives."

"And they also save lives," Olivia stated matter-of-factly. "This isn't the first time you've saved a life."

"I guess we all have it within ourselves to be heroes," Jessie said. "You're a hero."

"No, I'm not."

"You saved Higgins, didn't you?"

Olivia shot her a mischievous look. "I wish I could save a lot more animals."

"You also saved Cecil. Who else would have taken in an ugly one-eyed cat and saved him from death's door? You could have had any cat in the pound, and you chose Cecil."

"Cecil is *not* ugly. He would not be happy to hear you say that."

Jessie chuckled.

The next few minutes were quiet until Jessie said, "Have you talked to Ryder since the dance?"

"He's left a couple of messages apologizing for being a jerk, but I don't want anything to do with him. He has a lot of growing up to do."

Jessie's smiled as she pulled close to the curb in front of the school. It wasn't easy being a teenager. A developing brain and body. Mood swings and testing your limits. "I'm proud of you, Olivia."

Olivia climbed out, adjusted her backpack, and then shut the door and leaned into the open window. "Ditto."

Maybe she was doing a decent job raising her, after all, she thought as she watched Olivia walk off. She punched in the address of where she planned to go next. She wanted to stay far away from her home and office until the hoopla surrounding Emily Shepard died down.

Today she would go to Clarksburg, a small town located on the Sacramento River where Ben and Nancy had been born and raised. After their parents had died, they'd lived with a relative. Ben's knowledge of his childhood was limited. After the accident, the only information he'd gotten from his sister was that they'd grown up in Clarksburg, and that his parents' names were Lou and Dannie. That was it.

He'd spent months in the hospital, and when he'd returned to his apartment in West Sacramento, nothing was left but a room filled with garbage and a few broken dishes.

If Jessie hadn't been in such a hurry to get out of town, she would have called Ben and asked him for his social security number. A search of public records and private databases using the names *Lou Morrison* and *Dannie Morrison* had gotten her nowhere. In 2010 Clarksburg had a population of 418. With so few people, *somebody* had to remember Ben's family and hopefully be able to shed some light on who they were and what happened to them.

After taking Exit 510, Jessie glanced in the rearview mirror. Nobody was following her, which made her wonder what Nick Bale was up to these days. Did he know that his wife had called off the search?

A few miles down South River Road, Jessie turned onto Clarksburg Road. It was a beautiful area—sprawling vineyards next to a winding river. She had heard of the Old Sugar Mill before but had never been.

The building had a vintage country feel to it and featured thirteen wineries. Deciding to start there, Jessie pulled into the parking lot.

The atmosphere inside was casual and welcoming. The place had high ceilings and lots of natural light. There was a large outdoor patio and plenty of seating next to a grassy field. People were scattered about, enjoying wine and chocolates. Jessie talked to a woman behind the counter who had lived in Clarksburg for over a decade, but she had never heard of the Morrison family.

Jessie's next stop was the post office and then an empty church, and finally a small market on Netherlands Avenue. For such a tiny building, the market appeared to have everything you could possibly need. A friendly couple stood behind the checkout stand. Jessie found some snacks to buy before she headed that way and asked about Lou and Dannie Morrison.

"Never heard of them," the man said.

"Lou and Dannie," the woman repeated. "Those names sound familiar." She snapped her fingers. "You're not talking about Ben and Nancy's folks, are you?"

"Yes, I am."

Jessie paid for her snacks and then moved aside so the woman's husband could help another customer.

"Ben was in an accident ten years ago that left him with amnesia," Jessie explained. "Since he has yet to regain his memories, I'm trying to help him find out more about his childhood and his parents."

The woman's brow creased. "I heard about the accident." She offered Jessie her hand. "My name is Sadie Powers. Nancy and I are the same age. We went to elementary school together."

"So you knew Ben?"

"Not really. He was older."

"Did you ever hang out at Nancy's house? Anything like that?"

Sadie waved a hand through the air. "No way. We never went to each other's homes. My parents didn't like me being friends with Nancy, but I couldn't tell you why. I moved in the seventh grade, and I never saw her again."

"When did you move back?"

"About ten years ago." She looked at her husband and winked. "I just came back for a quick visit, but then I met Dennis, and I've been here ever since."

"Do you have any idea how Lou and Dannie Morrison died?"

She shook her head. "I had moved by then. To tell you the truth, I can't imagine Nancy caring about her mother's passing one way or another. They never did get along. But you're going to have trouble learning anything about Lou and Dannie Morrison."

"Why is that?"

"Because their name was Wheeler. Lou, Dannie, Ben, and Nancy Wheeler, not Morrison."

Jessie glanced around as if looking for answers. How could that be? At the very least, Nancy could have mentioned that her brother was using a different surname. "Well, thank you for that information," Jessie told Sadie. "You wouldn't happen to know anything about Nancy's father, would you?"

Sadie's lips tightened as she appeared to think hard on that. "I never heard much about him." She scratched her arm. "I'm afraid I'm not much help at all."

"If I were you," Dennis chimed in, "I would go talk to Ed Klein. He knows just about everyone who has ever lived in the area."

"Would you happen to have his address?"

"Hold on," he said. "Let me get it for you."

"Be careful of old Ed," Sadie whispered after her husband disappeared. "He can be a bit crotchety." She made a face. "I try to stay clear of that one."

"How old is he?"

"Oh, gosh, he's got to be tipping close to the nineties about now."

Dennis returned with a slip of paper. "There you go. He lives on the slough. If he's not in the house, he can usually be found on his boat out back."

"Thanks," Jessie said. "You've both been a big help."

"If you see Nancy, tell her I said hello."

"I will."

Sadie followed Jessie outside, waving to her as she drove off.

Jessie stayed on Netherlands Avenue for quite a while before she pulled onto a long drive. At the end was a single-story ranch house. Nobody answered the door, so she walked around the side of the house. There were no fences, and the property backed up to the slough, just as Sadie's husband had said. There was a twenty-foot boat tied to the dock. Through one of the windows she saw movement. "Hello. Anyone home?"

The sharp report of a rifle shocked her to the core, and she dropped to the ground. Gulping in air, Jessie looked around for cover but saw nothing but acres of grass and weeds. Prickly thorns bit into the palms of her hands as she scrambled back the way she'd come. And then laughter coming from somewhere behind her caused her to freeze in place.

Still on all fours, she looked over her shoulder at him. Definitely not the harmless old man she'd figured him for. Sadie hadn't been kidding when she said the man could be a bit crotchety.

With his rifle slung over his shoulder, he walked over to her and offered her a hand up. His hands were calloused, his nails as black as a coal miner's. That didn't stop her from putting her hand in his and letting him pull her to her feet. For a thin old man with deep grooves in his face, he was strong.

He let go of her, and she dusted off her jeans before she held out her hand to him, this time as a greeting. "My name is Jessie Cole. I was just at Holland Market. Sadie and her husband said you might be able to answer a few questions for me."

He ignored the hand, spit on the ground next to her foot, and headed for the house.

Figuring she better take a hint unless she wanted to get shot, she headed back the way she'd come.

"Where are you going?" he called after her.

Jessie looked over her shoulder at him. "I took that as a no."

"Sensitive, are you?"

"Not really."

"We'll have to agree to disagree," he said.

Crotchety might not be the best word to describe him, she thought as she turned and followed him across the yard. His jeans were caked with dirt like the rest of him. Thick gray hair was tied in a ponytail. He led her through a sliding glass door that was cracked from one corner to the other.

The inside of his house was tidy and clean, nothing out of place. Everything about the man confused her.

He pulled out one of the four chairs circling a wooden table in the kitchen and said gruffly, "Take a seat."

She plopped down.

"Now go ahead and ask your questions. I'm going to fix myself something to eat. I haven't eaten since breakfast."

She watched him take a plastic container from the refrigerator, remove the lid, and shove it into the microwave.

"I was told that you might know something about Lou and Dannie—"

"If I were you, I wouldn't go around asking about those two." He shook his head. "Bad news. Anyone who lived here in Clarksburg when they were around remembers them well enough to lie about ever knowing them."

"Why? What did they do?"

Bent over, Ed put his face right up close to the microwave so he could watch his food heat up. "I'll put it to you this way. Lou made me look like the nice guy around these parts."

"Was he abusive toward the children?"

He nodded. "And the wife. Verbally and physically. I never saw that woman around town without bruises or a busted lip."

"What about the kids?"

"I didn't see their daughter much, but it was the same for the boy. A broken leg here, fractured nose, busted-up lip, and bruised eyes there."

"Did anyone ever try to help the family?"

"One woman did. Good ol' Lexi Byrne. I don't think anyone tried to do more for that family than Lexi did, especially the kids. When Social Services finally made it out to their home, everyone was on their best behavior." He tapped his foot and glanced at the microwave. "But Lexi wouldn't give up."

After the bell rang, he removed his food, grabbed a spoon, and started eating.

"Did Lexi ever get anyone to listen?"

"Lexi disappeared a few months after Social Services showed up," he said with a full mouth. "For a long time, maybe still, it's one of the bigger mysteries around these parts."

Jessie tapped a finger on her chin. "I couldn't find any death certificates on file for Lou or Dannie."

"Well, I don't know why not. She's definitely gone."

"Cancer?" Jessie asked, hoping to pull it from him.

He snorted. "Dannie definitely didn't die of no cancer."

"Heart attack then?"

He put his food down and picked something out of his teeth. "My guess is that she died of the same thing Lexi died of."

"I thought you said Lexi's death was a mystery?"

"I have a good imagination. They found Dannie floating facedown in the slough. There are a lot of bodies in these here waters. Just sayin'." He slowly shook his head. "I'm telling you, Lou was as mean as they came. Still is."

Jessie frowned. "Still is?"

"Ol' Lou finally got what he had coming. If you really want to get the scoop, go pay him a visit at Folsom Prison. He got life in the slammer."

Ben's father was alive? How could Ben not know? *Because Nancy never told him,* she concluded. The thought of his sister keeping that from him pissed her off. She looked at Ed. "Did Lou go to prison for killing his wife?"

"Nah. They couldn't prove he killed Dannie, but during the investigation they found the body of a young woman buried on his property. The rope around her neck matched the rope in Lou's shed. His DNA was the clincher."

Jesus. Jessie knew she shouldn't be surprised, but Ben's past just kept getting worse. Ed's account made Nancy's Christmas story seem like a walk in the park. It was almost too much to take in. Ben would be devastated to learn that not only was his father alive but he was a killer. She wondered if life with his mother and father had anything to do with him becoming a crime reporter.

"Right up until he was carted off to jail," Ed went on, "the son of a bitch tried to put the blame for the dead girl on his son."

"He said Ben killed her?"

"Said his son killed the girl *and* Dannie—his own mother. I told you Lou was a cruel man."

Forty-Six

Before Ben climbed out of the van, his phone buzzed. It was Jessie. Through the window he could see his daughter on the soccer field.

"Hi," she said. "You called?"

"I've been trying to get in touch with you all day."

"It's been one of those days."

"Well, then I won't keep you. I'm at my daughter's soccer game, but I thought you might be interested to know that Rene Steele is dead."

"How?"

"I wasn't at the crime scene, but one of the guys I work with was. Suicide by hanging. He said it looked staged."

"Nick Bale," she said.

"I wish I knew."

"Okay," she said. "If you get a chance later, will you give me a call?"

"Will do." Ben climbed out of the van and headed for the area where parents watched their kids play. He spotted Melony sitting in the stands. For a moment, he simply stood there and wondered how he'd gotten so lucky. Not only was his wife beautiful but she was smart and funny—a wonderful mother and the kindest person he knew. What she'd seen in him all those years ago, he would never understand. A battered man without memories of his past or any foundation at all. A lost soul. It was Melony who had put Humpty Dumpty back together again, not the doctors.

Melony jumped to her feet and shouted when their daughter's team scored. His son was at her side. Sean looked his way, and when he caught his gaze, he waved and grinned.

His family meant the world to him. He didn't know what he'd do without them.

Ben gave his wife a quick peck on the cheek before he sat down, their son between them.

"We're winning, Dad! Abigail even scored a goal!"

Melony gave him a tight smile. Ever since their last argument, after he'd been unable to sleep because of the bloody ax, Melony had been distant. She'd been right about him not telling her everything. How could he tell her about the images he'd seen or about the ax being in his van? Not even his therapist knew that he'd been having urges . . . violent urges. The anger he sometimes felt was not a healthy sort of anger. It hijacked his body and mind.

"What's the score?" he asked, trying to get involved.

"Two to one," Sean told him.

"How was school today, kiddo?"

"Boring. Math gives me a headache."

Melony patted her son on the back. "Maybe Dad can find some time to sit down with you and help you with your times table and percentages."

Sean groaned.

Ben nudged Melony playfully in the arm, but she wasn't having it. Her gaze was fixated on the game.

It was dusk by the time the game ended. Abigail's team won. Sean ran down to the field. Melony was deep in conversation with a woman sitting nearby.

Ben watched the huddle, kept his eye on the coach. He didn't like what he saw. Coming to his feet, he made his way to the field, his gaze never leaving the coach's hands. One hand was wrapped around the neck of the girl on his right, and the other was rubbing slowly, up and down, the back of the girl on his left. The girl on his left was Abigail.

He kept waiting for the intimate contact to stop, but it didn't.

Ben tilted his head, heard it crack.

The asshole was giving his ten-year-old daughter a massage. He clenched his jaw; his stomach turned.

Watching the man's fingers rub against his daughter's flesh made his skin crawl.

One of the girls took notice of Ben and straightened.

The coach looked at him. "We're in a huddle. If you could go stand with the rest of the parents, we'll be finished in a minute."

"Take your hand off my daughter."

The coach's eyebrows slanted together. "What?"

When he failed to do as he asked, Ben stepped between the girls, took hold of Coach-Whatever-the-Hell-His-Name-Was's arm and twisted until the man grimaced and dropped to his knees.

Abigail turned on him. "Dad! What are you doing? Mom! Dad is going crazy!"

Ben could hear and feel the chaos happening all around him. An arm came around his chest, but he knocked the person away.

And then he heard Melony's voice. "What are you doing, Ben? Let him go now!"

"I called the police," another voice chimed in.

Suddenly Ben could see everyone and everything much more clearly. Melony had Abigail and Sean wrapped in her arms. The kids were crying. Melony was furious.

Ben let go of the coach. He looked from face to face. "Didn't any of you see the way he was touching the girls? They're ten years old, for Christ's sake. He shouldn't be touching them."

Nobody said a word. Everyone looked either shocked or scared.

He looked at the coach as the man was helped to his feet by one of the other parents. "If you ever touch Abigail again, I'll kill you." Ben walked over to Melony and the kids. "Come on. Let's go."

She kept walking until they were out of earshot. "Kids," she said calmly. "Go to the car. I'll be right there."

Abigail wouldn't make eye contact, but Sean peeked up at him. Ben patted him on the top of his head. "Everything will be okay. I'll see you later."

The kids walked away.

"Leave us alone," Melony said through gritted teeth. "I don't want you to come back to the house."

A sudden coldness hit him at his core. He glanced at the kids. "What are you saying?" With a shaky finger, Ben pointed at the coach. "That guy is a pervert. I can see it in his eyes. You could see it, too, if you looked!" His chest tightened. "Everyone here has their heads up their asses."

"Do not come back to the house," she said, her tone resolute. "You are not welcome there."

The way she looked at him made him realize she was serious about this.

"I need a break."

"A break from what?"

"From all your secrets, Ben. I'm tired of trying to pull emotions out of you. We hardly talk anymore. It's been months since I've felt as if I've had a husband and a partner."

Every muscle tensed. "I'm seeing a therapist just like you wanted. I'm doing everything I can to hold this family together, and this is the thanks I get?"

"I'm not doing this, Ben. I'm serious about needing a break from all this."

"From 'all this'?" he said. "Or from me?"

"From you." She lifted her chin. "If you refuse to go, we will."

"Melony—"

"Go!" she said.

Ben took a deep breath and walked back to his van. How the hell had it come to this? Why couldn't anyone else see what he was seeing? His own wife was ostracizing him for standing up to a man who was touching their daughter in an aggressive manner. He climbed into the van, slammed the door shut, and drove away.

FORTY-SEVEN

On her way home from Clarksburg, Jessie thought about what Ben had told her. Rene Steele had hung herself.

What a crock of shit.

Jessie didn't believe in coincidences. The only reason Rene had talked to Jessie the other day was because she'd been drunk.

But that conversation had obviously been enough to set someone off. Nick Bale? Why would he take such a big risk after all this time?

Because he can get away with it, she thought, *that's why.*

If Nick could kill, then he was certainly capable of abducting his own daughter. Had he killed Dakota?

She thought about his cousin, Wendy Battstel, and her darling little girl, the one who could have been run over if Jessie hadn't been watching them that day.

The little girl had a lisp. "That's for Thithy," she'd said when Jessie had returned the bouncy ball.

She hadn't thought much about it at the time. But she did now. What did "Thithy" mean? Was it someone's name?

The ball was for *Thithy.*

Jessie's heart began to beat faster. People with lisps often pronounced *s* with the *th* sound.

Sissy.

Why would Wendy's little girl say it was for Sissy unless she had a sister?

Had Nick Bale given his infant daughter to his cousin?

It was a crazy thought, but Jessie took the next exit just the same. She pulled into a parking lot and looked through her navigation system for previous addresses. She needed to drive to Colfax. The address came up. She pushed "Go."

Even going over the speed limit, it took her forty-five minutes to get to Colfax. She found a parking spot and shut off the engine. About to exit the vehicle, Jessie stopped when she saw Wendy's car come down the long drive and pull into the driveway.

The passenger door flew open, and a young girl stepped out onto the lawn. It definitely wasn't the same little girl who had been at the market.

Jessie guessed this girl was at least seven years old. She was holding a stick, waving it in circles, colorful streamers flying.

Wendy walked around the front of the car to the other side just as she'd done when Jessie watched her the last time. She unbuckled the smaller girl from her car seat in the back. As soon as she was free, the same little girl chased after the girl with the wand. "Give it to me, Thithy!"

"You have to catch me first." The older girl ran in circles on the front lawn, the little one doing her best to keep up.

Wendy headed up the stone path to the front door. "Stop it, Elizabeth. Give her the wand."

It took a few seconds for Jessie to snap out of the bizarre trance she found herself in.

The older girl was a mini Ashley Bale. She was tall for a seven-year-old, just as her mom had been at that age. Her blonde hair shimmered, and her flawless skin looked porcelain beneath the morning sun.

Jessie waited for Wendy and the girls to disappear inside the house. Only then did she take a breath. What the hell was going on? She reached for her cell and called Ashley Bale. No answer. She couldn't risk leaving a message. But this couldn't wait.

Almost an hour later, Jessie rang Ashley Bale's doorbell.

Relief fell over her when the door opened.

Ashley did not look pleased to see her. "What are you doing here?" In the living room behind her, Jessie saw a young woman playing with the boys. Ashley stepped out onto the porch, her face pinched.

"Two minutes of your time," Jessie said. "That's all I'm asking."

Ashley's pupils appeared dilated. She wasn't angry, Jessie realized. She was nervous. "I asked you never to come to my house. You know how my husband feels about my hiring you. Why are you doing this to me?" She looked over Jessie's shoulder, left to right. "Please go," she said. "Nick will be home any minute now."

"I would not have come if it wasn't extremely important. You must know that. I have to talk to you."

She crossed her arms over her chest. "Leave or I'll call the police."

"I found her," Jessie said.

Ashley wobbled slightly before placing a hand on the side of the house to catch her balance. "I don't believe you."

"I have no reason to lie to you, and you know it. Come with me," Jessie said, gesturing toward her car. "I'll show you."

Ashley hesitated.

"If you can look me in the eyes and tell me you have no desire to see your daughter or learn what happened all those years ago," Jessie said, "I promise I will walk away right now, and we'll never talk again."

"Are you still adamant that this has something to do with Nick?"

God. Why wouldn't this woman listen? "I don't know. I thought we could find out together."

Ashley rubbed the back of her neck and then finally nodded. "I'll be right there. I need to tell the nanny I'll be going out."

The ride back to Colfax felt interminably long, filled with awkward silence. Ashley appeared to be on the verge of having a mental breakdown. It wasn't until they arrived in front of Wendy's house that Ashley spoke. "Where are we?" she wanted to know.

Jessie pointed to the white house across the street. "That log cabin, the one with the bright flowers in the planter box, is where Nick's cousin Wendy Battstel lives."

Ashley shook her head. "It can't be."

"Why not?"

"Because Nick's cousin Wendy is a drug addict living in the Midwest somewhere."

"When was the last time you talked to Wendy?"

"We don't talk. After Dakota was taken, the police interviewed Wendy multiple times. She was already a little wacko by then, and she told Nick she was afraid of me. She said I didn't trust her, which was true to some extent. Hell, I didn't trust anyone at the time. Before Dakota was taken, I guess I thought we were friends. But then she moved and cut Nick and me out of her life completely." She grew quiet for a moment. "Dakota's abduction changed everything. I had to let more than a few relationships go."

Jessie stared at the house. She needed to find a way to get Ashley to come to the door with her.

"I don't know what sort of crazy-ass goose chase you're taking me on, but I'd like to go home. I never should have come with you."

"Your daughter is inside that house. I saw her."

"That's not possible," Ashley said. "It's not her."

Jessie opened the car door.

"What are you doing?"

"We've driven all this way. The least you can do is come to the door with me. If it's not Wendy, I'll make up a story about being a Realtor. I'll tell her we made a mistake, and then we'll leave."

A long stretch of silence followed before Ashley muttered an expletive under her breath. She opened the passenger door and climbed out.

Side by side, they walked to the front door. Jessie rang the doorbell.

"Come back here!" a woman shouted from inside the house. "Don't open that—"

When the door opened, the same little girl Jessie had seen earlier stood inside looking at them curiously.

Ashley's face paled as she stared at the girl. She looked past the child at the woman rushing forward. "Wendy?"

"What are you doing here?" Wendy looked from Ashley to Jessie. "I know you. You're the one I talked to in the parking lot."

Jessie nodded. "We're here to talk to you about Elizabeth."

"How do you know my older daughter's name? Who told you where I live?" Wendy took a gentle hold of Elizabeth's arm and said, "Take your little sister and go to your room."

"But we didn't do anything wrong."

"Go now," Wendy said. "Or no playdate this week."

Jessie looked at Ashley and watched how intently she observed Elizabeth as she stomped off. Ashley stepped over the threshold and into the house.

"You can't come inside," Wendy said, her voice low and gruff.

Ashley wasn't listening. Her focus seemed to be directed on the house—the furniture and decor.

Wendy followed her closely. Every time she reached out to grab Ashley's arm, Ashley shrugged her off and gave her an icy look.

"What are you doing?" Wendy asked. "You both need to leave."

Jessie and Wendy both watched Ashley walk slowly around the living room. Jessie had thought Ashley would become overwhelmed with emotion when she saw her daughter, but that wasn't the case. It was obvious to Jessie that Ashley was numb with shock. Something inside her was stopping her from believing that it could be true.

And that something was Nick Bale.

It was as if she couldn't comprehend the possibility that for all this time her daughter had lived only an hour away. Ashley had trusted Nick. To the point of being blind when it came to Dakota's abduction.

Ashley glanced at the pictures lined up on the mantel and then made her way to the kitchen. As if in a trance, and moving at a snail's pace, she studied the drawings and school papers held to the refrigerator with magnets. She even went so far as to open the refrigerator, pull out a Disney lunch box, and sort through its contents.

Wendy didn't try to stop her. Nor did she attempt to call the police.

Ashley found a scrapbook. She carried it to the couch, sat down, and began turning the pages. Finally, she looked at Wendy. "Dakota has been here all this time?"

Wendy merely nodded.

The front door opened and then slammed shut, startling all three of them. Nick Bale marched into the living room. His eyes narrowed as he looked at each one of them. Sweat covered his brow.

Jessie had kept an eye out on the drive over. She'd never seen his car in her rearview mirror.

"Where are the kids?" he asked Wendy.

"They're in their room. Keep your voice down."

"What's going on here?" he asked.

Wendy raised her hands. "I'd like to know the same thing. Maybe you should ask your wife?"

He looked at Jessie before his gaze settled on Ashley. "I told you to leave it alone. I asked you not to hire a private investigator, but you went behind my back and did it anyhow."

Ashley looked at her husband with pleading eyes. "Dakota is here! I don't know what to think. Please tell me you had nothing to do with this."

"You never should have come here." He reached behind him and pulled a gun from his waistband.

"Put that away," Wendy said, her voice firm.

Jessie assessed the situation. The children were her first priority. The only way to get to their room was the hallway behind Nick.

Ashley put the picture album aside and came to her feet. "Nick. Stop this nonsense. What are you doing?"

He raised his weapon, his hands steady as he pointed the barrel of the gun at her. "You should have listened when I told you it was time to move on. But you never listen, do you?"

"You need to calm down," Wendy told Nick. "I do not want you to scare the children."

Ashley's face twisted in pain. "Did you know your cousin was raising our daughter?"

"Wendy has done a fabulous job with the girls."

Ashley turned her attention to Wendy. "I don't understand. Nick told me you were a drug addict and that you had moved to the Midwest."

"He told me you were depressed and incapable of taking care of a child." Wendy put a hand to her heart. "I didn't think it was a good idea to take Dakota. Not at first. But he convinced me you weren't well."

"How could you let him hand over my child to you?"

"The awful things he said about you. I believed every word."

"What about the police and the FBI?" Ashley asked in disbelief. "They talked to you on more than one occasion. This makes no sense."

Wendy rubbed her temple. "For the first six months, someone else raised Dakota."

Ashley turned away in horror, her attention back on Nick. "Tell me the truth. Are you the one who took Dakota that night?"

He said nothing, but the smirk on his face was telling enough.

Ashley pointed an accusing finger at him. "How could you give away our baby?"

Nick's face morphed into a maze of deep lines and jagged crevices. "Because she's not mine!"

Ashley blushed. "What are you talking about?"

Jessie stomach turned as she recalled what Rose Helg had said about Ashley's rumored affair.

"Was it my face you saw when you were making love to another man?" Nick asked her.

"You're talking nonsense," Ashley said, her voice calmer than before.

His smile twisted. "Is he the one you think about when we climb into bed each night?"

Jessie thought about lunging for his gun, but she was too far away. He could easily get a shot off before she reached him. They needed him to calm down. "Nick," she said. "Don't do this. Think about the children. Put away your gun."

"This is crazy." Ashley pulled her phone from her pocket. "I'm calling the police."

Nick lifted his gun, then aimed and fired. A shot rang out, piercing Jessie's eardrums as Ashley wilted to the floor.

Wendy turned and ran, disappearing down the hallway.

Jessie stood still as her gaze swept over the room, looking for something she could use as a weapon. Lamps, vase, decorative elephant with trunk raised toward the sky.

Hovered over Ashley, Nick asked, "How could you? Doug Jenkins was my best friend."

Wincing in pain, Ashley clutched her stomach. "It was wrong," she said through gritted teeth. "A horrible mistake. We never saw each other after that night." The color had drained from her face. "That's why you gave our baby to your cousin?"

"Dakota isn't mine," he said.

Jessie was running out of time. She took slow, tentative steps toward the iron elephant.

"That's a lie," Ashley told him.

"I've had DNA tests done. She's not mine. Doug is her father." He pointed the gun at Ashley's head. "You're mine. In life and death you'll always be mine."

Now or never. Jessie grabbed the elephant by the tusks and swung hard, hitting Nick square in the shoulder. He stumbled and fell to one knee. His gun slid across the floor.

Jessie got to the gun first, grabbed it, and pivoted, keeping Nick in her line of sight. "You killed Rene Steele."

"I warned her not to talk."

He lunged for Jessie, but she was able to maneuver so that the dining room table was between them.

Nick did a quick two-step. "I was a loyal and loving husband. I did everything I could to make Ashley happy. I'm not going to jail."

Across from where Jessie stood, Wendy returned, holding a gun. "It's over, Nick. You've done enough harm."

He whipped around so that he was facing his cousin. "Take the kids and go, Wendy. This has nothing to do with you."

She shook her head. "It has everything to do with me. When your mother was drunk on the floor, I was the one who took care of you. I've always protected you, Nick. But you've gone too far."

"I paid for this house! I made sure you and the girls had food on the table. And this is how you repay me?"

Jessie stepped to her right. If she could shoot him in the leg, they would be able to subdue him until the police arrived.

"You lied to me," Wendy said. "You lied to all of us. It ends now."

The low growl coming from his throat as he rushed toward his cousin was a sound Jessie would not soon forget.

Another shot rang out.

Nick's body twitched as he fell backward. Flat on his back, his eyes wide-open, he didn't appear to be breathing.

Jessie wanted to get the kids out of the house, but first she needed to make sure Nick was incapable of harming anyone else. Looking down at him, she saw that Wendy had made a clean shot through his chest. She reached for her phone and called 9-1-1. As she talked to the operator, she saw that Wendy had disappeared from the room and Ashley wasn't moving.

Finished with the call, she ran to the kitchen for a towel, anything to stop the bleeding, and then rushed back to Ashley's side. There was blood everywhere. Thick red blood. Oozing and dripping. Puddles of it. She felt dizzy and weak.

Shit.

Her insides did somersaults.

Ashley was her responsibility. She could not die. With no time to waste, Jessie ripped open Ashley's shirt and used the towel to put pressure on the hole in her side.

Just breathe, Jessie told herself. But it was easier said than done. She was so very light-headed. "Hold this," she said, praying Ashley could hear her as she placed Ashley's hand firmly over the towel. She then pushed herself to her feet, relieved to see Wendy reappear. "Make sure she keeps pressure on the wound until help arrives." The last word came out in a rush before she fell backward onto the couch, and the room and everyone in it disappeared completely.

Forty-Eight

Ben didn't bother returning home. Instead he kept an eye on the house set close to the freeway. It was getting dark. There was a light on in the kitchen, and he could see Abigail's coach moving around inside.

He had a missed call from Jessie. He called her back. She didn't pick up.

As he watched the house, he replayed everything that had happened on the soccer field over and over in his head. But he just couldn't see how this was his fault. As far as he was concerned, he had not overreacted.

Why couldn't any of the other parents see what had been right before their eyes for weeks now? The man was too touchy-feely with all their daughters. A quick tap on the shoulder to put a player in a game was one thing, but massaging and kneading while in a huddle was too much.

He'd given the man a warning.

But judging by the look Ben had gotten from the coach after that other parent had helped him to his feet, it was clear that the coach wasn't going to change.

Ben had looked into the eyes of evil. He knew how people like the coach worked. They felt entitled. They felt no remorse. The average child molester would offend two to four hundred times before he was caught, if ever. Many of them began molesting in their teens. Most were sexually abused as children. Kids were told to respect and obey adults, making them easy targets. They sought out shy and naive children and then built them up and made them feel valued.

The thought of the coach's hands on Abigail was too much.

He opened the van door at the same time his phone buzzed. He stayed seated and picked up the call. "Hello."

"Ben, it's Steve Konkoly. The results from the blood sample you brought in just came in. I thought you'd want to know that you were right. It's a match."

"You're sure?"

"Absolutely."

Ben took in a breath.

"Are you there?"

"Yes. Thanks for calling."

"Want me to send the report to you or the police?"

Ben rubbed a hand over his head. "Send it to me. Thanks."

"No problem. Take care."

"Yeah. You, too."

Ben looked back at the coach's house. The kitchen light went out.

Molesters were master manipulators. And they were patient.

And so was Ben.

"I'll be back," Ben said. "You can count on it."

⸻

Jessie stood when she saw the doctor coming her way.

"She'll be here for a while, but she was lucky," the doctor said. "No arteries or major internal organs were affected."

"That's good news. Thank you."

"If you're hoping to see her, you might want to go home and get some rest. Ashley will be in the recovery room for a few hours at least."

Once the doctor left, Jessie plopped back down in the chair to gather her thoughts. She'd been in touch with Ashley's parents. They had been contacted by the nanny and would take care of the boys as long as they needed to.

Wendy Battstel had been taken into custody. Both girls would stay in a temporary shelter run by Social Services while she was away and until they figured everything out.

It was hard to believe she'd found Dakota Bale.

The whole situation was fucked up.

She'd envisioned a completely different outcome. If and when she found Dakota Bale, she'd pictured herself bringing the young girl home to a loving mother and father.

Leaning forward, elbows propped on knees, face resting in the palm of her hands, she was having a difficult time coming to terms with everything that had happened.

How was she supposed to feel about Ashley losing her husband after learning he'd betrayed her in the worst way possible? She took a breath as she sat up. She could only hope that Ashley found a way to pull the pieces together so she could give all her kids a decent life at home.

Nick Bale had manipulated Wendy and Ashley. How had that happened? Was it a form of brainwashing? She almost felt guilty for solving the case. Maybe everyone would have been better off if she'd never found Dakota. Was living lies a better option?

No. It was Ashley's right to know the truth.

It was time to get moving. She needed to go home, take a long, hot shower, and go to sleep and hope everything looked a little different, a little better, in the morning.

She came to her feet just as Colin entered the hospital. The moment he spotted her, he walked over to her. The lines in his forehead told her he was worried. "I got a call that you were hurt." His gaze roamed over her. "Are you okay?"

"I saw blood and I fainted. I'm fine."

Colin took hold of her hand. "All I could think about when I heard you were in Colfax where the shooting took place was I didn't want our last conversation to be our last conversation."

Jessie stepped closer and sank her head into his chest as he wrapped his warm arms around her.

"Nobody at the scene could clarify who had been shot. I couldn't think straight." He took a breath, his emotional pain weighing heavily.

"It's okay," she said, her voice slightly muffled. "I'm okay. We're okay." When she pulled back, she saw another officer standing a few feet away. "Are you here on business, or did you come all this way to see if I was all right?"

"Both."

"Can I give you my statement in the morning?"

"That's fine. And after that, maybe you can find the time to have a cup of coffee with me?"

"I'll take a look at my calendar," she teased.

The corners of his mouth turned upward, and his eyes sparkled.

She smiled back at him. "Coffee sounds great."

On the way home, Jessie's heart was heavy with emotions. At times like now it seemed her job made her rethink the importance of family values. Rickey Talbert's intense love for his daughter, Hannah, had driven him to the edge. Owen Shepard had learned a tough lesson, and yet Jessie wondered if it would change him as a person or if he would simply move on as if nothing had happened.

She thought of her mother then, and that stunned her.

That her mother would pop into her mind at a time like this took her by surprise. Even more bewildering was that Jessie felt suddenly curious as to why she'd left in the first place. Jessie's reasoning had always been that her mother was selfish first and free-spirited second.

But time had a way of making the truth fade. Maybe there was more to it, missed details and unheard explanations for why her mother had left.

Maybe Jessie had never known her mother at all.

Maybe someday she would find the courage to look for answers.

But not today, and certainly not tomorrow.

The last few weeks had merely confirmed that the world could be a fucked-up place at times. Right now Jessie felt the need to spend time with the people she loved and cared most about. Tomorrow night, she decided, she would make dinner: lasagna and garlic bread and a salad with candied pecans and creamy dressing. She would invite Colin, Zee, Arlo, and Ben. It was time she started taking care of her own relationships.

It was midnight when Jessie found a parking spot in the alleyway. She climbed out of her car and saw a familiar van parked in front of her house. She walked up to the window and peered inside.

Ben Morrison was asleep behind the wheel.

She knocked on the window.

His eyes snapped open.

"What are you doing?" she asked.

He leaned over and opened the passenger door, then rubbed his eyes.

Using the handle, she pulled herself into the seat.

"You said you wanted to talk," Ben told her. "Since you weren't home, I thought I'd get some shut-eye."

The sarcasm in his voice was hard to miss. "You got kicked out of the house?"

"I can't get anything past you."

She was too tired to find him humorous. "Do you have a place to go?"

"The van is fine."

He looked like shit. "Come on. You can stay with us."

"I appreciate the offer, but I can't do that to you."

She gestured toward the street. "Then I'll take you to my office instead."

"I'm fine where I am."

"I insist. I won't be able to sleep well knowing you're out here in the cold. Come on. You're going to stay in my office. I keep a cot with blankets and a pillow in the office closet. I even have a spare toothbrush. There's a bathroom with a shower down the hall. It'll be perfect. While we set everything up for you, I'll tell you where I've been because I think it might interest you."

Twenty minutes later the cot was made up and ready. Jessie disappeared for a minute, then brought back two cold beers.

"No, thanks," he said. "I don't drink."

"Well, then. Don't mind if I do." Jessie took a seat at her desk, propped her feet up, opened a bottle, and helped herself. She'd already told him about Nick and Ashley Bale. Now it was time to tell him about her trip to Clarksburg. He was sitting on the edge of the cot. He was such a large man she was surprised the bed didn't teeter to one side.

"Your real name is not Morrison," she said casually. "It's Wheeler."

"I like how you just get right to the good stuff."

She shrugged. "It's late. I'm tired. I saw way too much blood tonight."

"I thought you were going to get help for that."

"I had to cancel my first appointment. It will happen, though."

"Did you find out anything else about my parents?" he asked.

The beer tasted remarkably good. "I did. Your mom died under suspicious circumstances."

"Murdered?"

"Not sure yet."

"What about my father?"

"He's still alive."

"No shit."

She nodded.

"Where's he living?"

"Folsom Prison. Life sentence." Jessie watched him. He hardly flinched. Always cool and calm under fire.

"Do you think Nancy knows?" he asked.

"Definitely. I believe your sister has been doing everything in her power to try to protect you."

"Or maybe she's trying to protect herself."

"Maybe."

"So my father had a dark side."

Jessie exhaled. "It sounds like your mother did, too."

"And what about me?"

The question took her by surprise. "I don't know, Ben. Maybe I'm biased. You saved my life. You've proven yourself over and over to be a good guy. I think you're way too hard on yourself."

His elbows were propped on his knees, his hands resting on the sides of his face. "I don't know. I think I'm seriously losing control."

Their gazes met.

"The blood results came back," he said. "It was a match."

"I already told you if that happened, it means absolutely nothing."

He looked away.

"You helped me find Sophie," she told him. "You gave me closure. I want to do everything I can to give you the same."

Silence.

"We can do it," Jessie went on. "I know we can." She raised her bottle of beer. "Here's to finding out who Ben Morrison really is."

He stared straight ahead. When he failed to respond, she leaned forward and saw that he was fixated on his reflection in the window. His eyes were dark, his jaw tense. She swallowed when he finally looked her way.

Neither of them said a word.

They didn't need to.

They were both afraid—scared to death—of everything. And quite possibly of nothing at all.

Acknowledgments

For me, the stages of writing fiction always seem to go something like this: excitement over all the endless possibilities, torturous madness and what the hell was I thinking, and finally euphoria and extreme gratefulness.

Many thanks to Liz Pearsons, Charlotte Herscher, Amy Tannenbaum, Ashley Vanicek, Robin O'Dell, and all the great people at Thomas & Mercer!

ABOUT THE AUTHOR

Photo © 2014 Morgan Ragan

T.R. Ragan has sold more than two million books since her debut novel appeared in 2011. A former legal secretary for a large corporation, she is now a *New York Times*, *Wall Street Journal*, and *USA Today* bestselling author. T.R. is the author of the Faith McMann Trilogy; six Lizzy Gardner novels (*Abducted*, *Dead Weight*, *A Dark Mind*, *Obsessed*, *Almost Dead*, and *Evil Never Dies*); and *Her Last Day*, the first novel in her Jessie Cole series. In addition to thrillers, she writes medieval time-travel tales, contemporary romance, and romantic suspense as Theresa Ragan. An avid traveler, her wanderings have led her to China, Thailand, and Nepal. Theresa and her husband, Joe, have four children and live in Sacramento, California. To learn more, visit her website at www.theresaragan.com.